CHERYL A. HEAD

WARN ME WHEN It's Time

A CHARLIE MACK MOTOWN MYSTERY

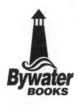

Ann Arbor
2021

Bywater Books

Print ISBN: 978-1-61294-207-0

Bywater Books First Edition: June 2021

Printed in the United States of America on acid-free paper.
Cover design: TreeHouse Studio

Bywater Books
PO Box 3671
Ann Arbor MI 48106-3671
www.bywaterbooks.com

WARN ME WHEN
It's Time

Charlie Mack Motown Mysteries

Bury Me When I'm Dead

Wake Me When It's Over

Catch Me When I'm Falling

Judge Me When I'm Wrong

Find Me When I'm Lost

Warn Me When It's Time

In you I put
All my faith and trust
Right before my eyes
My world has turned to dust.

"Reflections"

Written by Eddie Holland, Lamont Dozier,
Brian Holland
Performed by Diana Ross & the Supremes, 1967

Acknowledgments

Thanks to my Bywater Books family: Marianne K. Martin, Salem West, Ann McMan, Kelly Smith, Nancy Squires, Stefani Deoul—and to editors Fay Jacobs and Elizabeth Andersen for all the heavy lifting. Elizabeth, thanks for keeping me on the queer and narrow. Fay, thanks for all the good questions about character emotions and pacing.

Gratitude to my beta readers: AJ Head; The Writers Writing Group; Lynne Blinkenberg, Teresa Rankin and Veronica Flaggs.

Thanks to Teresa Scott Rankin for love, support, and encouragement. Also, ear rubs to Abby and Frisby Rankin for being part of a writer's life.

Continuous thanks to Detroit for my roots, tenacity, and swagger.

Thank you to E.A. Kafkalas and her dog, Allie, who won the 2020 "What does Hamm Look Like" contest. Allie won out of forty competitors, and is the inspiration for Hamm (short for M.C. Hammer), Charlie and Mandy's dog. I love Allie's face, and could see it as I wrote.

See it here: *www.cherylhead.com/blog/canine-contest-winners/*

Cast of Characters

Charlene "Charlie" Mack
Mack Investigations Principal; former Homeland Security Agent

Don Rutkowski
Mack Investigations Partner; former police officer
and Homeland Security Trainer

Judy Novak
Mack Investigations Associate Partner

Mandy Porter
Grosse Pointe Park police officer; Charlie's girlfriend

Ernestine Mack
Charlie's mother

James Hasani Saleh
Agent, FBI Detroit Field Office

Gabriel Constantine
Ernestine's new boyfriend

Pashia Family
Hassan Pashia, Kamal Pashia, Amina Akhbar Pashia,
Jawaria Pashia

The Turks
Robert Barrett, Frank Wyatt, Walthrop Croft,
Chuck C., Tom Cortez

Hate Crimes Task Force:
Commander Yvonne Coleman (DPD)
Lt. Barry Kerner, Dearborn Police
John Rappon, Oakland County Police Chief

FBI Agents
Agent Kapinski (K)
Agent Riley
Agent Elizabeth Garrow

Prologue
Dearborn, Michigan
2009

"Shit," Robbie said, stumbling on the stairs. "Can't we turn on the goddamn lights?"

"Of course not, you idiot. You want somebody to see us?"

"There's nobody here. The old man left. I told you that."

"Let's just do the job and get the hell out of here. Give me the wire and the detonator."

Frank hated working with the young guys. They asked too many questions, made too much noise, and required too many *atta boys* at the end of the job.

"You do the paint in that room over there," Frank said, pointing. "That's where they pray."

"You sure you know what the hell you're doing with that stuff, Frank?"

"Are we gonna talk about this again? I'm not a newbie like you. I've done this before."

Robbie watched Frank lift the spool of wire in one hand and a canvas bag in the other and trudge up the hall breathing heavily. He could smell Frank's body odor. What he disliked most about this group was they all acted like cowboys. They called themselves "White Turks" but they were mostly a bunch of soft, middle-aged guys with bones to pick about keeping their guns and their stupid flags. *They need more young guys like me who know technology.*

1

That's where the real work is, and it's the key to recruitment. Like those European guys are doing.

Twenty minutes later, the two exited the mosque from the side door, hugging the shadows of the building until they reached the front entrance and stopped. They listened for shouts, alarms, or barking dogs and then split up as planned. Frank headed to his van in the strip mall a block away, and Robbie moved to the bus shelter where his bike was locked to the signpost.

Riding a bike kept him in shape. It was also his opinion that a guy on a bike drew little or no attention. As he pedaled past the mosque he glanced back at the square facade.

A lot of the homes in this community were owned by Asians and even a few Mexicans who made their money working housing construction. Recently, Muslims had overrun the neighborhood. He wondered how the white residents could stand those loud-speakers blaring each day. *Shit. Why can't these towel heads just use bells, and pray on Sunday like everybody else?*

Last week, Robbie had posted in his private online group how happy he was with this initiation assignment. "If we put a scare into these people, maybe they'll think twice before coming to our country to take our jobs. I'm tired of competing with all these browns and blacks just to get an entry-level position. If you come to this country, try and be an American. And if you can't do that, get the hell out."

He'd gotten over a hundred "likes" for that post.

Robbie laughed out loud thinking about tonight's tagging job. *I gave them some good old English words to stare at while they're down on their knees. Fuck them, and their weird-looking language.*

He steered his bike onto Ford Road, staying in the curb lane for his forty-minute ride home. It would be a decent workout—especially if he did some sprints. When he got home, he'd do some online study. *Those soft guys just drink beer and do a whole lot of talking. They don't study. How you gonna beat back the tide of illegals and mongrels if you don't put in the work?*

Hassan Pashia had just reached his freeway exit when the security monitoring company called to report a silent alarm. It was the third time this month.

I bet I forgot to close the inner door again.

It took him thirty-five minutes to get back to the mosque, and he pulled his car up to the side door and left the car running. *It'll only take a moment to secure the double doors and reset the alarm.*

He stopped short at the sight of the side door standing ajar. He stepped inside, flipped on the light, and paused. He heard no noise. He moved along the marble floor, passing the office and several classrooms, including the one he'd been teaching in only ninety minutes ago. He'd noticed a dim glow in the office, but there was a brilliant light coming from the prayer room. The illumination created a triangle on the floor at the end of the hallway. *Something's wrong.* He pulled out his mobile phone and pushed the number that connected him to the alarm company.

"This is Mr. Pashia. I've returned to the building. It looks like maybe there's been a break-in."

"Are you okay?" the female voice at the call center asked.

"Yes. I'm fine."

"Has anything been taken? Is there any damage?" she asked.

"Hold on a minute. I'll see."

"Uh, Mr. Pashia. Do you want to wait until the police arrive?"

"No. I'll be okay. Everything's quiet. I want to take a look."

Hassan stood in the center of the prayer room. Whoever had applied the thick black paint on the walls and *mihrab* wasn't a great speller and may, in fact, have been dyslexic. He had seen this kind of vulgar language painted on the exterior walls, and once on a couple of cars in the lot. This was the first time someone had dared to defile the interior of the *masjid*.

"Yes, there is damage. Please call the police. We've had extensive damage, I'm afraid."

While he waited for the police to arrive, Hassan checked

the other common areas of the mosque. The ablution area was untouched, but the carpet was streaked with the same shiny black paint defacing the walls. He remembered the light in the office and retraced his steps. He peered through the window of the closed door. The glow seemed to come from a washroom in the rear. He knew the police would prefer the room remain undisturbed, but the office was where the mosque's audiovisual equipment was stored. If anything was missing, Hassan wanted to know before calling the imam.

He touched the doorknob, and it turned in his hand. He moved only a single step before he was overwhelmed by a tremendous roar. The force of the explosion propelled Hassan into the hallway. His head smashing against the marble wall was abrupt—only momentarily painful. He saw a flash of white light; then everything went black.

Chapter 1

"Ms. Mack, you have a call holding on line one," Tamela said, sticking her head in the conference room.

Charlie signaled to Judy they'd take a break from compiling the report for the executive office of the governor. She answered the call using the speakerphone.

"This is Charlene Mack. May I help you?"

"Good afternoon, Ms. Mack. I don't know if you'll remember me. This is Kamal Pashia. I met you when you were a teacher at the ACCESS center."

Charlie hesitated. It had been six years since she spent time in Dearborn's Arab Community Center for Economic and Social Services. First as a volunteer, and later as an undercover agent with the Department of Homeland Security. She didn't remember Kamal but that wasn't unusual. She'd taught three self-defense classes each week for almost six months, which meant eighty to a hundred kids.

"I was the short kid who always wore the green Converse sneakers."

"Sure. How are you doing now, Kamal?"

"Not so good really, Ms. Mack. I have my sister on the phone and we want to hire you as a private investigator."

"Oh?" Charlie gestured for Judy to take notes. "What kind of investigation do you need?"

Muffled voices came through the speakerphone. The rapid exchange sounded like a disagreement. There was an insistent voice followed by the noise of the phone being shuffled. Charlie and Judy glanced at each other, then stared at the phone. They waited.

"Uh, this is Amina Pashia Akbar. I'm Kamal's older sister," the clear voice said. "Did you read about the bombing of the Central Mosque last month?"

Charlie paused to remember. There had been a half-dozen newspaper reports of church, temple, and mosque vandalism in the Detroit metropolitan area in the last three months. A series of crimes that had strained the resources of law enforcement and prompted the formation of a multi-jurisdictional task force. Most of the incidents had caused property damage, but one event, a fire inside a mosque, had resulted in a man's death.

"Yes. If I remember correctly, a man was killed," Charlie said. "A teacher."

"That was our father."

"Oh, I'm so sorry," Charlie said looking at Judy. "My condolences."

"Thank you. As my brother said, we need your help. We want you to find my father's murderer."

"The police are already focusing on that, aren't they?"

"Yes, but there's been no progress in almost a month. That's why we're calling you."

"You're taking the case?" Mandy asked, standing at the ironing board. She wore her uniform trousers and a turquoise bra. Under the admiring eye of Charlie, she pressed the wrinkles out of the collar of her khaki shirt.

"I don't know yet. We're going out to Farmington Hills to meet the family this morning. I'm taking Judy and Don."

"You're taking Don?" Mandy asked, with raised eyebrows.

Charlie chuckled. "He'll be okay. Did I ever tell you about Don's change of heart regarding Arab-Americans?"

Mandy squinted. "Something about a young Muslim guy helping Rudy?"

"That's right. I did tell you. Well, he's come a long way since our days at DHS. He's still suspicious. He's suspicious of everyone, but he's not so ..."

"Racist?" Mandy asked.

Charlie flinched. "I was going to say not so reactionary anymore."

Charlie and Don were good friends and confidantes, and she spent a lot of time defending him to others. His Archie Bunker tendencies had been softened by his wife, Rita, and son, Rudy, but he was still evolving on issues of diversity and tolerance.

Charlie and Mandy were in the upstairs laundry room they'd added to their east-side home. It hadn't initially been a planned upgrade to the house, but daily routine had made it a priority. Mandy was a police officer and paid to have her uniform slacks laundered, but she preferred to wash and iron her own shirts, and Charlie's daily workouts meant a wash load of exercise togs every few days. Then there was Hamm. Neither of them had imagined how much laundry comes with having a long-haired pooch. His three doggy beds, assorted towels, and dozen chew ropes always needed laundering. Hamm was sprawled on the floor between the ironing board and Charlie's seat. He looked up as if he could read her mind. She reached down to rub his ears.

"I'm also going to visit Mom this afternoon for a couple of hours," Charlie said.

"Oh? When'd you decide that?"

"I got a text from Gloria while you were in the shower. She looked in on Mom this morning, and had some concerns about the state of her apartment. She said clothes and newspapers were piled up on the floor, and she's never seen it so disorderly."

Mandy stopped ironing and turned to Charlie. "That doesn't sound at all like Ernestine. We were just there two weeks ago, and things were in good order."

"I know," Charlie said, fighting off a twinge of guilt. "I'll go see her after the meeting with the Pashia family."

Mandy wanted to reach out and hold Charlie. She wanted

to insist on going with her to visit Ernestine, but decided not to suggest it. During the first few years of their relationship, the topic of Charlie's mom's care had provided ongoing tension. Ernestine was a proud and independent woman, a retired school principal, with a diagnosis of early-onset Alzheimer's. She wanted to be in charge of her life for as long as she could, and had refused Charlie's offers of help. Mandy had, up to now, sided with Ernestine. This morning's call from Ernestine's independent-living facility might mean it was time to reassess her living arrangements. It would be a hard decision that Charlie and her mom would make together.

"You know there are a lot more of these hate crimes than the papers are reporting," Mandy said, changing the difficult subject. "In the past month our department has investigated three different reports of vandalism at places of worship—graffiti on two African-American churches, and someone breaking windows at a synagogue."

"These crazy incidents seem to be happening more often. It's almost like the backlash we saw after 9/11," Charlie said.

"I think it's exactly like that, but these new hate groups go way beyond a focus on Muslims. They're angry about a lot of things: immigrants, minorities, liberals. And you know the key thing that's triggered the rise of these groups?" Mandy asked.

Charlie did know.

In January, a Black president had moved into the White House, giving every hidden bigot a reason to rise up from underground. Charlie prided herself on her ability to understand human nature—including its darker side. But this resurgence of race and ethnic hatred saddened her. As a Black woman it was extremely frightening. She rubbed Hamm's head again, and he stood for more attention.

"You think we'll *ever* be a post-racial society?" Mandy asked.

"No. At least not any time soon. Mr. Pashia's daughter told me she doesn't think the police are doing enough to solve her father's murder because they're Muslim."

"I hope she's not right," Mandy said, finishing the crease on her shirt and holding it up for inspection.

"James Saleh is on the hate crimes task force," Charlie said. "He called a few weeks ago to discuss who from Homeland Security would be a good representative. You remember James?"

"Of course I do. I make it my business to remember anybody who has ever tried to protect you. I take it he's still with the FBI?"

"Yes, and he's been promoted."

"Good for him."

"The people on this task force know what they're doing. I know a few of them. So, we'll go meet with the family and hear their concerns. I think we'll probably just end up assuring them that the police are doing everything they can."

"That sounds right," Mandy said, donning her shirt.

"But there is one interesting element in this case," Charlie said. "The news reports said Mr. Pashia died in a fire, but the fire was actually the result of an explosion."

"Wow. I didn't realize that," Mandy said. "That's a big step up from graffiti."

"It sure is."

Chapter 2

Don, Charlie, and Judy drove the twenty miles between the Mack Agency's downtown offices and the home of the late Hassan Pashia. Oakland County was Michigan's second-largest district, composed of communities northwest of Detroit where the socioeconomic status was generally higher, and the population whiter. Most of the families in this Farmington Hills neighborhood chose to live here because the schools were better and the streets safer.

The Pashias' large brick home was set well back from the street by an expansive manicured lawn and wide sidewalk. Don parked in the driveway. The young man who answered the door finally triggered Charlie's recognition.

Kamal was five inches taller and more filled in across the chest than when she'd last seen him in her self-defense classes, but he still had the same shy smile. Charlie hugged the boy before making introductions to Don and Judy.

Seventeen-year-old Kamal led them through a rarely used living room into a comfortably furnished family room with overstuffed couches, a mounted 90-inch TV, and tall windows that allowed sunlight to penetrate every corner. There were no visible indications that the home's occupants were of the Islamic faith.

Charlie, Don, and Judy sat on a couch across from the family as Kamal introduced the Mack team to his mother and two sisters. Kamal and his younger sister, Farah, wore Western garb.

Married sister, Amina, and their mother, Jawaria, wore hijabs—the traditional head scarf. Amina spoke for the family.

"Thank you and your partners for coming, Ms. Mack," she said.

"We're all very sorry for your loss," Charlie offered. "We've all familiarized ourselves with the news reports of the police investigation, but we'd like to know more about your father and the unfortunate circumstances of his death."

Amina provided an account of her father's work at the mosque as a lay teacher. He was also an instructor at the local community college—a position he'd held for twelve years. Hassan was often the last person at the mosque because his computer programming classes were held on weeknights. He was usually home by ten o'clock, but twice this month a security alarm had sent him back to the building. The night of his death he'd called his wife to tell her he'd be late because he was returning to the mosque to reset the alarm.

During Amina's account, Charlie twice caught the eye of Mrs. Pashia. She was clearly in mourning, dressed in a high-necked top and a skirt falling to her feet. Her humble, somber presence was dignified and peaceful.

Charlie felt Don begin to fidget. He tired quickly of one-way information, and Charlie knew he was ready to ask questions. She indicated with a subtle nudge of her arm to hold off. On Charlie's other side, Judy listened attentively, jotting notes.

Amina spoke of her father's compassion, saying he was a teacher who took interest in his students' well-being and always offered extra help for someone struggling.

"Some semesters he convened a Saturday tutoring group right here in this room." Amina reached her hand out to her mother who had begun quietly sobbing.

Don cleared his throat and began talking before Charlie could stop him.

"Why have you decided to go around the police in the investigation of your father's murder?"

The abrupt question caught the family off guard. Kamal's

countenance changed. He shifted forward on the sofa and stared at Don with dark, penetrating eyes. He was about to protest when Amina held up her hand to silence him. Kamal slumped back on the sofa, crossing his arms.

"Mr. Rutkowski, is it?" Amina asked.

"That's right. Formerly Detective Rutkowski with the Detroit Metropolitan Police."

"I see. Well, it's not our intent to embarrass the police. The Dearborn detectives have met with us several times, and are coordinating with the FBI. They have, rightly, categorized my father's murder a hate crime. Initially they were very interested and communicative, but for two weeks our contact in the hate crimes unit has not returned our repeated calls."

Amina's response seemed to take the wind out of Don's sails. He clenched his jaw and Charlie picked up the conversation.

"We do know the crime against your mosque is one of several cases in the metropolitan area in the last few months. There's a multi-jurisdictional task force looking into the patterns of these crimes."

"We already read about that in the papers," Kamal blurted.

Amina put her hand on her brother's arm to settle him. The younger sister, maybe twelve years old, sat next to her mother. Farah had been looking up shyly and was now visibly upset. She leaned against her mother's arm and occasionally peeked at her brother.

"Are there some areas of the investigation where you believe the police could do better?" Charlie asked.

"We believe so."

"What in particular?"

"There are videotapes. Security tapes taken from the mosque and nearby street cameras. The police haven't told us what's on those tapes. They also haven't returned my father's laptop."

Judy was already taking that note.

"Anything else?" Don asked with irritation.

"There were things police found at the mosque the night of the break-in. A paint can top, bits of wiring, and a cigarette found in the hedges at the side of the building."

"Okay," Charlie said. "We can probably get your laptop back, and you want to hire us to *supplement* the work of the police. Is that right?"

"Yes, but . . ."

Before Amina could finish, her mother interrupted. "Amina, I would like to speak with her alone, please. I think it is important."

"Of course, Um."

Jawaria Pashia rose to her feet. "Ms. Mack, please follow me."

Charlie stood and, with a look, told Don and Judy to stay seated. She followed the mother into the pristine living room. Jawaria sat on an upholstered bench and pointed to the seat next to her. Now in closer proximity, Charlie could see Mrs. Pashia's natural beauty, which had been cloaked in her heavy, dark clothing. Charlie guessed the woman was probably in her mid-fifties.

"My son likes you very much. He always said you were a kind and competent teacher."

"Thank you."

Jawaria shook her head. "It is a compliment, yes, but you don't understand my full meaning. Many parents at the center felt betrayed when we learned you worked for Homeland Security. Some even called you *khayin*—a traitor. We later learned the reason you left the agency was in protest of the way our community was treated."

Charlie nodded. She didn't want any credit for her decision to leave DHS. The racial profiling of the Muslim community, especially in southeastern Michigan, went way beyond the agency's standard practices, and she had begun to lose sleep over it. She often thought she had stayed longer than she should have but once the decision was made, Charlie convinced her agent/ friend Gil Acosta to depart with her. A month later, Don—who had been a DHS trainer—joined her and Gil to form Mack Private Investigations.

"Even when the others derided you, Kamal was always your defender. He wasn't a popular kid. He was teased at school because he was small and because he was Muslim. He said you made him feel important in class, and encouraged him to be confident. He said you would not have been kind to him if you were a bad person."

Charlie felt embarrassed by the praise. "I know a little bit about what it's like to be treated like an outsider," she responded.

"Let me be frank with you, Ms. Mack. I don't trust the police to find my husband's killer. There have been many incidents at our mosques. The police rarely make any arrests."

Charlie began to argue against Jawaria's concerns, but the woman stopped her.

"The police do not see my husband as someone important enough to spend much time and effort on. We both know the truth of my statement."

As soon as they got to the car Don began to complain. He didn't want to take the case. He also resented being left alone with the children while Charlie met with the mother. Judy had kids of her own and handled the situation well, directing questions to Kamal and Farah about school, sports, and the latest Marvel movie. Don, Judy reported, had sulked on the couch.

"I think we should help this family," Charlie said.

"Why, Mack? The money isn't all that great since you gave them a discount," he said sarcastically. "The police are doing everything we could do."

"You don't know that," Charlie countered.

Judy spoke up only to agree that the case fee was below their standard.

The ride continued with a minute's worth of silence while Charlie thought through her arguments for taking the case. The traffic was light heading back into town, and Don's irritation increased the pressure of his already lead foot.

"You're going to get another camera ticket," Charlie warned, and Don eased off the accelerator. "I promised Jawaria that we'd look into a few things."

"Like what?" Don challenged.

"The husband received a couple of death threats at the community college where he teaches. Anonymous notes. Someone angry about bad grades."

"That doesn't merit an investigation," Don quipped.

"Maybe not. But in the mosque breach, and another incident Jawaria knows about, files were stolen. Student records, and things like that."

"What else was stolen?" Judy asked from the back seat.

"Nothing else. Laptops, valuable artifacts, TVs. All left behind."

"That's odd," Judy said.

"This is about race, isn't it?" Don asked accusingly. "They don't think they'll get a fair shake because they're Muslim."

"They could be right," Judy said.

"That's bullshit. You both know how I feel about bypassing the police."

"We're not going to bypass law enforcement," Charlie said. "You can contact the police and the joint task force and see what they have on the Pashia case. There are a lot more of these incidents than the public knows about. Mandy mentioned investigations her department has had recently."

"It's a waste of time."

"Not to me. You've never been on the hurting side of this kind of racism, Don. Sometimes it's covert, but other times it's right in your face. My mother and father faced it in their day, and their parents before them. I'm sick and tired of it. It's 2009. When is it going to end?"

Don and Judy didn't know what to say. Charlie felt Judy's empathy from the backseat, and she knew Don's silence was his way of giving support. Charlie didn't like displaying her emotions, but the Pashia family's pain had gotten to her.

"Look, you know members of that task force," Charlie said to Don. "They'll trust you."

"Isn't James Saleh part of the task force?" Judy asked.

15

"He is," Charlie said. "He called a couple of months ago, when they were forming the team, to get my advice on who to include from DHS."

"I didn't know that," Judy said. "I haven't spoken to him for five or six months."

Judy's crush on Saleh had begun four years ago when the Mack Agency had collaborated with the FBI on a case that started as a missing person investigation and turned out to involve interstate human trafficking.

"It would be good to be back in touch with Agent Saleh," Judy said quietly.

"You're a married woman with teenage kids," Don shouted to the backseat.

"That's right," Judy responded. "And I still know a good-looking man when I see one."

Chapter 3

Charlie stopped at the front desk of the independent-living facility. The first thing she noticed was the worry on Gloria's face.

"I'm glad you came by Miss Charlene. Your mother was scheduled to go out with her walking group, but she called down to say she was too tired to walk today. Something's going on with Miss Ernestine. I know she resents me keeping an eye on her, but I know that's what you want me to do."

"That's right, and I really do appreciate it, Gloria."

Charlie hadn't called ahead to tell Ernestine she was coming, so she felt like a snoop as she stepped to her mother's door on the fourth floor. Normally she'd just use her key, but today she knocked. Her mother opened the door looking fresh, well-groomed, and happy.

"Oh. Charlene. Uh, I wasn't expecting you."

"I know, Mom. I should have called, but I was in the neighborhood," Charlie lied. "Besides, it's been a couple of weeks since I saw you."

"Is everything all right?" Ernestine asked, waving her inside.

Charlie quickly scanned the apartment. Things were neat. There were no signs of disorder except for the usual collection of newspapers, magazines and books on the dining-room table. Those were the tools of her mother's vigilant watch on the work of local government, and her frequently published newspaper op-eds.

"Everything's fine. Mandy's good and sends her hello."

"I thought you said you just happened to drop by."

"Well, I did," Charlie said. "I was out of the office for a meeting."

She'd continued her assessment of the apartment, peering into the open bathroom door and walking into the kitchen and returning. She and her mother stopped face-to-face in the dining room.

"Gloria called you, didn't she?"

Charlie's face gave her away.

"I knew it," Ernestine said taking a seat in front of her laptop. "Charlie, if you want to know how I'm doing with the Alzheimer's, why don't you just ask me? I'll always tell you the truth. I don't want that woman being your spy."

"She's not, Mom. She cares about you, and I've only asked her to check in on you because I can't always be around."

Ernestine didn't look up from her typing. Charlie sat across the table from her.

"How *are* you doing?"

"There's been some deterioration of my short-term memory. It comes in and out. Some days I'm still very sharp, but other days I can't remember where to find things."

"Will you promise to tell me when you think you need extra help?"

Ernestine looked up at her daughter. Tears sprang to her eyes. She never wanted to be a burden to anyone, but especially not Charlie.

"I'll let you know if I think I can't do this alone. But, mean-while, I have friends here who help me. We help each other."

"That's good to hear. Are they the people in your walking group?"

"Some of them," Ernestine said in a way that made Charlie know she had more to say.

"What *aren't* you telling me, Mom?"

"I, uh," Ernestine stopped talking for a moment, then continued. "I have a gentleman friend. My new neighbor who moved into apartment 410 a few weeks ago."

"Well, that's, uh, good news, I guess," Charlie said. "What's this gentleman's name? When can I meet him?"

"His name is Mr. Constantine. He's coming by this afternoon to show me pictures of his family. Most of them live in California now. I've told him all about you."

Charlie was completely taken aback by the news of a man in Ernestine's life. Especially since after her father's death, her mother had rebuffed the attention of a half-dozen men, choosing instead to put her daughter and her career above male companionship. So it was stunning now, so many years later, that her mother would have a suitor.

"I'm really happy you've found somebody."

"After all these years?" Ernestine offered.

"Well, yes, but it's never too late. I look forward to meeting Mr. Constantine. Does he have a first name?"

Ernestine smiled. "Yes, of course he does. It's just that we're still kind of formal with each other. His name is Gabriel."

Charlie nodded, making a mental note.

"So what investigations are you working on?"

Ernestine was always interested in the Mack Agency's cases. She was a consummate researcher, and had been critically helpful to a couple of their investigations. Charlie also welcomed her questions because it meant her mother was still coping with her slow drag into dementia.

"We got a new client just this morning involving an incident I'm sure you've read about. A man was killed in a recent attack on a mosque, and the man's family has asked us to help the police find whoever's responsible."

Ernestine nodded. "Of course. I've read the accounts."

Civil rights, human rights, and class disparities were Ernestine's chosen areas of advocacy. During college she'd registered voters in the South, and in the last thirty years she'd been a vocal proponent of equal opportunities in education.

"These hate crimes have been popping up all over. Mr.

Constantine and I have discussed them. Are you familiar with the Southern Poverty Law Center?"

"I've heard the name. They're a sixties racial justice organization, aren't they?"

"They're still doing that work. SPLC keeps tabs on these groups committing crimes like vandalizing churches and attacking mosques, and such. Come sit next to me, and I'll show you."

Ernestine opened her search engine and punched in a few keys, and news of a violent right-wing group popped onto the screen. Spun off from the ideologies of the Klan, these members were more sophisticated and tech savvy than the night riders of the fifties and sixties, but just as hateful and deadly. Ernestine had witnessed the proliferation of these groups during her voter registration work in the South, and since her retirement from the Detroit Public Schools, had written two newspaper opinion pieces about the dangers of these so-called alt-righters.

Together, Charlie and her mom perused a series of intelligence reports and white papers detailing the increase in effigy burnings, racist graffiti, beatings, and threats in the past eight years. One article pointed specifically to the anti-immigration sentiments of these groups—especially toward Latinos. Barack Obama's presidency was also listed as a factor in these hate campaigns.

"We can't ignore these groups. They're not going away," Ernestine said.

Judy called a half hour later to say the task force had said "yes" to a meeting and wanted to convene that afternoon.

"Mom, I have to go. Sorry I can't stay to meet Mr. Constantine, but I need to ask you something. When Gloria stopped by earlier, she said she saw clothes strewn around the room. She was worried."

"Oh, so that's it." Ernestine began to laugh. "I was getting some things together for the Goodwill. They're coming to the building tomorrow to do a collection, and I was organizing my donations. I have gobs of clothes I just don't wear anymore; you know that. I wrapped ten pairs of shoes in newspaper because

I don't have the shoeboxes—I had those on the floor—and I was folding sweaters and skirts. Anyway, I have three big boxes of stuff ready to give away. They're in the bedroom. Look for yourself."

Relieved, Charlie pulled her mother into a hug. Before she left, she peeked into the bedroom, then turned and gave Ernestine a wave.

Chapter 4

James Saleh was as handsome as Judy remembered. He shook hands with Charlie and Don, and kissed Judy on the cheek. She blushed for half an hour.

Charlie and Don had first met James in his undercover persona as a young Arab-American shopkeeper in Birmingham, Alabama. He'd called himself Yusef, and worn a full beard and long hair, and had dressed like a savvy street operator. Today he was clean-shaven, with hair cut close to his scalp, and wore a dark suit and tie with a blue shirt.

The Mack team sat together at a small table in an FBI conference room. James had responded quickly to Charlie's call and had organized the impromptu meeting with leaders from the Dearborn and Detroit hate crimes units. While James didn't say much in the meeting, he watched the dynamics in the room play out. The Dearborn police member was clearly offended by the Mack team's involvement.

"So let me get this straight," Lt. Barry Kerner said, using an index finger on the table to punctuate some of his words. "You think you can do a better job at solving this crime than we can?"

Charlie felt Don staring at her, but wouldn't look his way.

"No, that's not what we're saying," Charlie responded. "But the family is understandably troubled by not having more progress in the case. So, with your permission, we'll follow up on a couple of loose ends. It probably won't lead to much, but it'll give the family comfort that they've done everything they can to help find their loved one's murderer."

James had a copy of the evidence roster for the Mack team, along with a list of people who had already been interviewed. Kerner distributed two dozen photos from the crime scene.

The damage to the prayer room was extensive. Dark metallic paint had been sprayed indiscriminately, staining floors, walls, and furnishings. Profanity had been messily scrawled on the walls. The office had received the brunt of the bomb's explosion with little more than rubble left on one side. Desks, bookshelves, and unbroken windows covered in a gray dust were on the other side.

Hassan Pashia had been blown into the hallway. Two photos showed his lifeless body covered in the same gray dust, blood seeping from his lips. His eyes were wide open.

The meeting ended cordially, with an assurance that Pashia's laptop would be returned to the family, but with very little detail on the status of the investigation. There was a round of polite handshakes before the police force reps departed, leaving Charlie, Don and Judy looking at James with grim faces.

"I'll have someone send over a report on the spread of extremist groups in the US," he said to Charlie. "It's not yet available to the public."

"Thanks," Charlie said. "Look, James, we really don't want to step on anyone's toes. Don warned us we'd get that reaction from the Dearborn force."

"Don't lose any sleep over it. The truth is we could use the help. We're stretched thin."

"What about the trace materials left by the explosion?" Don asked. "Nothing's come from that?"

"Nope. Our best leads so far are the latent prints. But a lot of people came in and out of the mosque."

"What about security footage?"

"Nothing definitive."

"Can we see it?" Charlie asked.

"I'll see to it that you get copies of the video files," James said.

"You still have all of our email addresses?" Judy asked.

"Of course I do, and I still have your mobile numbers." James smiled at Judy, then looked at all of them with a more serious look. "I think you'll be surprised at what you'll read in that report. This is not like Timothy McVeigh, the Oklahoma bomber, who was a loner with a grudge against the government. There are organizations with dozens and sometimes hundreds of members. We're keeping an eye on the ones we know about, but new collectives crop up all the time."

"I just saw a list on the Southern Poverty Law Center website," Charlie said. "They include neo-Nazis, white nationalists, neo-Confederates, racist skinheads, and Klansmen. It's disturbing."

"Disturbing and very dangerous," James agreed. "Most are loosely organized gaggles of malcontents, but others are very sophisticated—using encrypted communications to recruit new members, and embedding their messages within apps. It's pretty sophisticated stuff."

"Where do they come from?" Judy asked.

"From all over. We've identified groups in every state."

"I'm sure you must do extensive profiling," Don said.

"We do. But what's interesting isn't what these groups have in common, it's how different they can be. All are disaffected, but for a variety of reasons. Some don't like Blacks or Jews, or Catholics. Others think they lost jobs because of the influx of immigrants, and more than a few of them are former military having grievances with the VA or the government in general. A group calling itself *The Right Flank* has eighty members in Macomb, Oakland and Wayne counties. They're plumbers, telephone company employees, small business owners, teachers, even some EMT personnel."

"I heard these people have also infiltrated law enforcement," Charlie said. "Is that true?"

"I'm afraid it is. Think about it," James said. "A lot of police departments give preferences to veterans, and some of them come back to civilian life with PTSD. Especially the ones who served in Iraq and Afghanistan. They return with issues around trust, disconnected from old friends, and suspicious of people who don't look like them."

"You mean who look like you?" Judy asked.

James nodded.

"How is it for you in the FBI?" Judy asked. "I wondered about it four years ago. How you managed to operate in a culture where your fellow agents might not trust you. It must be a hard way to work."

"It was a challenge for me in the days following 9/11," James said, looking somber. "But I take my job seriously, and I'm a good agent. To tell the truth the hardest part hasn't been the agency. It's been regaining the favor of my own family. That's still an ongoing task."

Don pushed his chair back from the table. "Well, it's getting late. Thanks for the information, Saleh. We really appreciate it."

After another round of handshakes Charlie had one last question.

"Have you met with the Pashia family?"

"No. Should I?"

"It probably wouldn't hurt."

"Well, someone has to return the family's laptop. I guess it might as well be me. It's still downtown with the forensic guys, but when I get it, I'll call you. It would be great if you'd go with me to make the introductions."

Mandy got home late, so Charlie prepared a dinner of sauteed vegetables with shrimp over penne. They were both good cooks, but they also had their go-to meals when the stress or length of a day called for it. Today was one of those days.

By the time Mandy got home Hamm had been walked and fed, the table set for dinner, and a white wine opened and breathing. Charlie followed Mandy upstairs and, as she locked up her gun and changed out of her uniform, told her about Ernestine's boy-friend and her relief that Gloria's concern was a misunderstanding involving clothes and shoes piled up for Goodwill.

They opted for dinner in the family room, watching local and national news. The California Supreme Court was on the verge of upholding a proposition to ban same-sex marriage, and LGBT protestors were taking to the streets. A reporter with PBS NewsHour interviewed a tearful lesbian couple who said they would defy the ban by marrying out-of-state. Charlie and Mandy clasped hands. They had talked about marriage when they bought the house last year but they weren't ready, and even if they took the big step, their union wouldn't be recognized in Michigan. At least for now, they both agreed their domestic bliss didn't require a license.

After the kitchen cleanup Hamm was ready for another walk. There was still an hour of sun, and their neighborhood was showing real signs of spring, but as every Detroiter knew, you didn't put your coat and boots away until after Memorial Day.

As Hamm sniffed his way down the block toward the small park, Mandy eased her arm through Charlie's. "So how's the case going?" she asked.

"The briefing today was helpful, especially the information from James, but honestly I got more background about these hate groups from mom. She's been studying them."

"She's a hell of a researcher," Mandy said. "You know I'm really glad to hear Ernestine's still doing okay, and thrilled at the idea of her having a romantic interest."

"I just wish I'd had time to meet him. He sounds very nice, but you know me. I need to see and talk to the guy before he gets a seal of approval."

"I think Ernestine is a good judge of character."

"Me too, but I still need to lay eyes on this Mr. Constantine."

Chapter 5

Charlie drove her shiny white Corvette with purpose. She was meeting James at the Pashia home, and she wanted to arrive a few minutes before him. Only Jawaria and daughter Amina would be at today's meeting. The two younger kids would be in school. When Charlie knocked on the door, Amina answered. Today she wasn't wearing her hijab, and Charlie remarked on it.

"I don't wear my scarf every day. If I'm not going to be in public, or I'm doing work at home, I don't wear it. Today I'm helping to pack up some of my father's clothes."

"I promise we won't stay long, but I knew you were eager to have his laptop returned, and I also thought it important for you and your mother to meet James Saleh. He's one of the members of the task force, an FBI agent, and also a colleague."

"And a Muslim?" Amina asked.

"Yes."

Charlie had personally seen the effect James had on women. The extra glances, the shy smiles, the outright admiring looks. Mrs. Pashia's eyes were initially stern, but within fifteen minutes she had warmed to the conversation. She asked James a couple of questions in their language. He answered with his hands punctuating his words, and his smile indicating good memories and intentions. Amina stared brashly at James, but Charlie sensed it was more curiosity than admiration.

"We're probably being rude to Ms. Mack," Amina said. "My

mother asked James about his family. He still has family in Iraq. In towns we are familiar with."

Charlie nodded. "We have a few questions about the threats your father received," Charlie said to Amina.

"Yes?"

"Did your father keep copies of the notes? You said they were from a student?" James asked.

"Yes. We showed them to the two detectives who came to the house. We made copies. They looked at the notes but didn't take them."

James and Charlie glanced at each other. Charlie remembered Don had also been totally dismissive of the threats from the student.

"May we see them?" James asked.

"We were just going through my father's things, including files and folders from his desk. I'm sure they're in one of those boxes."

While Amina searched for the notes, Jawaria took the opportunity to ask James more questions. This time in English.

"How long have you been an FBI agent?"

"More than ten years. During the Gulf Wars, the Justice Department began recruiting personnel with Arabic language skills. My father is a Professor of International Law, and one of his colleagues approached me about working for the agency."

"What were you doing at that time?"

"I was a graduate student working on a business degree at Fordham. I grew up in New York City."

"Do you believe you are helping in what you do?"

"I think so, Mrs. Pashia. I can tell you I have been in many rooms where my voice made the difference in the actions of law enforcement," James said.

Amina returned with a folder containing six notes. Two were handwritten. They were amorphous threats complaining of mistreatment by Professor Pashia. Several of the notes claimed he showed favoritism toward foreign students. One note specifically mentioned the hardship of having a *C* on a transcript when competing for jobs with "all these illegal immigrants." Another note warned, "You won't get away with your prejudice." Prejudice was misspelled with a *g* rather than a *j*. Charlie took photos of the notes.

"May we keep these?" James asked.

"Of course. Those are the copies."

"Do you have any ideas who might have written them?"

Mrs. Pashia shook her head. Amina took on a thoughtful demeanor, but said nothing.

"Did something occur to you, Amina?" Charlie asked.

She looked doubtful and shrugged.

"Anything you remember or have thoughts about could be helpful to our investigation."

"Well, it occurred to me that it might be one of the students Baba brought to the house," Amina said, looking at her mother. "There were a lot of different kids, but there were regulars, too. A lot of them were white kids. A couple of them made me feel uncomfortable because of the way they looked at me. They creeped me out."

"Anybody in particular?" Charlie asked.

"There was one. I remember Baba said the boy tried hard in class, but just couldn't seem to grasp some of the concepts. I don't remember his name, but he was thin, really pale with short hair. He had a thing on his face. A mole I guess. It was like the size of a dime."

"Okay, that's good," Charlie said, taking notes. "James, anything else?"

"No. Except to promise to do better at keeping you informed of our progress," James said to Amina and her mother.

Charlie, Don and Judy looked at the six video files the task force had emailed to them. The other tapes, according to the Dearborn Heights PD communications officer, had no significance to the case.

"I want to see the rest of the tapes," Charlie said.

Don agreed. "This isn't much, is it?"

"Don't they know some of these guys will stake out a job weeks or months before? We need to see vehicle traffic, regular comings and goings, and compare the street views between the day of the bombing and other days."

"They probably have it, but didn't think we'd want to see it," Don said, making a lame excuse for his former colleagues.

Charlie gave him a stony look.

"Okay. Okay. I'll go down there tomorrow and see what else they have."

"Meanwhile, can we look at these one more time?" Judy asked.

The first footage was from a camera mounted on the front corner of the mosque. The bombing had been reported just after 10 p.m. The time code on the tapes showed a view of the lawn and street starting at 8 p.m. and continued until the police arrived after the blast. They watched a dozen cars travel up and down the street, but none of them stopped. At 9:15 p.m. a car pulled out from what they thought was the parking lot. The view showed only the driveway. According to mosque leaders, the cameras in the parking lot had been vandalized a week before.

"So that's Mr. Pashia's car," Judy said, jotting notes. "We're sure?"

"It's a Ford Taurus, and that's the make and model of his car," Don said.

They watched another forty-five minutes. There was no activity at the mosque, and only vehicular traffic on the street until one man carrying a large bag was seen across the street heading toward Ford Road.

"Where'd that guy come from?" Judy asked.

"Up the block, I guess," Don said.

"Where's he going on foot?"

"Maybe to the liquor store. There's a strip mall a couple blocks away at Ford Road."

"With a bag?"

"Let's see if we can get hold of the security footage from the strip mall. The liquor store will definitely have cameras," Charlie said.

Judy took the note. "I'll check on that."

A few minutes later a bicyclist came into view. He looked over at the mosque before passing outside the camera's range.

"Hmm," Judy said, looking at Charlie.

"What is it, Judy?"

"Why'd he look over at the mosque?"

"What do you mean?" Don asked.

"Well, did he hear some noise or see a light? Was there some movement over there?"

"Maybe it's just an innocent glance," Don retorted.

"I don't think so," Judy said. "It's not a casual glance. He looks back and stares. It's not just a quick look."

"Reverse the tape. Let's see it again," Charlie said.

The video was being projected to their new whiteboard from Judy's laptop. Judy whizzed it backward, then stopped and hit the play button. They all leaned in, waiting for the person on the bicycle to ride by. When he did, Judy hit pause and inched the tape into reverse.

"Okay, watch what he does," she said.

The rider turned his head deliberately toward the mosque. He was still staring at the building when he rode out of the screen. Judy stopped the tape and reversed it again, this time frame by frame. The cyclist's face could barely be seen. The man, or woman, wore a helmet, and was dressed head to toe in dark garb. They could see just a flash of a white face under the glare of the street light.

"We need to get another view of the street," Don said.

"Maybe some of the houses have security cameras," Judy said. "I'll check on that, too."

"Okay, you work on getting us more security footage from the liquor store and the neighbors, Judy. Don, you and I are going to the mosque."

The mosque was an unassuming brown structure on a mixed-use block, surrounded by homes, small businesses, and low-profile office buildings. The adjacent parking lot was at least as large as the building, and the exterior sign was small and plain. Several cars and trucks were in the lot, and the front exterior was lined with orange cones. Charlie noted the location of the lot's two security cameras before entering through the open side door.

The interior was a work zone. The debris from last month's blast had been cleared away, but the hallway, doors, and portions of the tiled floor were still being repaired. Charlie counted five men, all in hard hats and orange vests, spackling, hammering, sawing, and carrying construction materials to and fro. She counted two more men at the end of the hallway stirring paint and surrounded by drop cloths, brushes, paint rollers and poles. None of the workmen paid any attention to the visitors, but within a minute a man wearing a set of overalls and a *kaffiyeh* atop his head greeted them.

"You are the private investigators?" the man asked.

"Yes," Charlie said. "We're here to see Mr. Rafiq."

"I am Rafiq. Please come in here where we can talk." He led them back toward the side entrance to a door marked *Private*. The deep space contained a storage area, a wall of furniture, and a desk surrounded by five folding chairs. This was the janitor's makeshift office.

"I've been asked to give you every consideration," Rafiq said. "How can I help?" He looked nervously at Don who hadn't said a word or stopped scowling.

"We'd like to know why the security cameras didn't work the night of the break-in?" Charlie asked.

Rafiq's face colored in embarrassment. "Oh, I explained that to the police, and the imam. The cameras had been spray-painted. I think I noticed them five days before the break-in. I was waiting for the replacement lenses I ordered."

"Are the cameras working now?" Don asked, startling the man.

"Why yes. They work fine."

"But not the night of the explosion," Don said sarcastically.

"No. No, I'm afraid not," Rafiq said, feeling Don's intimidation.

Charlie gave Don a stern glance. They wanted this guy to cooperate with them. She lobbed a softball question.

"Mr. Rafiq, I understand the room that had the fire and explosion was an office."

"Yes, that's right."

"Were there explosions in any other rooms?"

"No. I don't think so. There was only damage to the office, the prayer room, and here in the hallway."

"Were there things stolen from the office or any other room?"

"Uh. Some file cabinets were open and papers thrown about that we don't think were a result of the explosion. The fire damaged a lot of our files, so we haven't been able to determine if anything was stolen."

"Had you seen anyone suspicious hanging around before the break-in?" Don asked.

"No. We've had minor property damage before, but nothing… nothing like this," Rafiq said, fighting his emotions.

"Have you ever noticed a guy on a bicycle hanging around?"

Rafiq paused. "I have seen someone on a bike recently, but we get a lot of kids who use our parking lot for skateboarding and those fancy tricks on their bikes. I think they're neighborhood kids."

"Could they be the ones who spray-painted the cameras?" Charlie asked.

"That's what I thought happened. Although they've never done anything like that before."

"Mr. Rafiq, we'd like to see the prayer room."

"Of course."

They paused at the entrance. One of the workmen was stirring paint and cleaning brushes. He nodded at the group. Charlie could see three others painting the walls that had been primed. Rafiq removed his shoes, and Charlie followed suit. She reached for the scarf she'd remembered to bring, tying it under her chin. Rafiq smiled at the gesture. Charlie squinted at Don and pointed to his feet. He didn't move. Then he crossed his arms.

"Yeah. Well, I'll wait out here," Don said. "Maybe I'll walk the perimeter of the building. I'll meet you at the car."

Don retraced his steps through the side door into the parking lot and immediately examined the nearest camera. It was the round-globe type, mounted on a twelve-foot pole. The other camera was the same.

You'd need a ladder to get to those things. Unless you had one of those automatic paint sprayer doohickeys.

From the parking lot he scanned the vicinity. He hadn't spent much time in this area between Dearborn Heights and Garden City. It was a working-class community with a few blocks of expensive homes. He and Rita had considered the area when they were trying to place Rudy in a special-needs school. The lot entrance was on a fairly busy street. It had two lanes in each direction, wide enough for a bus route, and "no parking" signs. Along the front and far side of the mosque were low hedges and the front security camera was perched near the roofline. There were no windows on the prayer room side of the building which faced the adjacent street, and large three-story homes. On the next corner, diagonal to the mosque, was a bus stop. Don crossed the street and checked the view of the mosque from the covered bus shelter, then walked the half block to stand directly in front of the mosque. The sidewalks were wide. Don moved to a tree directly across from the mosque.

"See anything interesting?" Don asked when Charlie got into the Buick.

"Not much. The spray-painter hit every wall and some of the floor. Rafiq said it was automotive paint, the kind used to touch up cars. It took a week to use some kind of degreaser over the paint, and another week to cover it with three coats of primer."

Don grunted. Charlie looked at him.

34

"You didn't want to take off your shoes? You got holes in your socks?"

"I just wasn't in the mood."

"I see. Rafiq also said a couple of prayer caps were missing. They keep spare ones near the shoe racks. They were the knitted kind, not expensive."

Don shrugged. It wasn't that he was uninterested. He was *very* uninterested. Not just because it was a mosque, but because he'd stopped thinking about religion altogether. He'd grown up in a Polish Catholic parish, but quit going to mass years ago. He had a church suit that Rita kept in a storage bag in the front closet. He only used it for funerals, christenings, and weddings.

"How's the outside?" Charlie asked.

"They have pretty cheap security cameras. The mosque has a rear entrance, which looks like it's never used and opens only from the inside. I walked across the street to the bus stop. That would be a good spot to watch the comings and goings at the mosque. I *did* find this."

Don handed Charlie a plastic bag with a chewing gum wrapper and a slender, round piece of aluminum.

"Where'd you find these?"

"Across the street next to the tree."

"What's this?" Charlie flipped the band in her hand, which didn't even weigh an ounce. It had a shimmery yellow coating on the outside.

"I think it's a trouser clip. Bicyclists use them to keep their pants from getting clogged in the chains."

"You think our guy dropped these things? They would have been sitting there for over a month."

"Maybe. The grass in that tree box is high. I only noticed it because I was standing right over it."

Charlie placed the plastic bag in her tote. "Where to next?"

"We have an appointment with the Chief in Oakland County. Then I was thinking about a fish place I know that's nearby."

Police Chief John Rappon was about Don's height, age, and disposition. He had walked a beat in Pontiac, Michigan, at the same time Don had been a patrolman in Detroit. They'd met through a mutual friend at a Fraternal Order of Police fund-raising event. Rappon was a championship bowler, and it was the one recreation, besides working on cars, that allowed Don to relax for a few hours.

As their meeting began, the two men talked about their latest scores and their new bowling balls. Rappon had just won a regional tournament with something called the Brunswick Activator. Charlie learned that Don didn't mind at all shedding his shoes if it was to exchange them for his Strikeforce bowling shoes.

It wasn't that Charlie was uninterested. She was *very* uninterested.

Fifteen minutes into their banter Charlie cleared her throat.

"I think your partner there is ready to get to the matter at hand," Rappon said. "Sorry, my wife says I can bore people to tears with my bowling talk."

"I didn't know a thing about Don's love of bowling," Charlie said, "but it's good to see his enthusiasm."

"You and Don have been doing some good work in your new agency," Rappon said. "It was an impressive accomplishment breaking up that terrorist attack against Cobo Hall. Mighty fine work."

"Thank you, Chief. It was a lot of walking around, asking questions, and no sleep. And as I'm sure you're aware, we were very lucky."

"Luck is always a factor, even with all this new technology. But good police work is all about having the right people on the job. My technology budget has increased by 300 percent, but my staff budget is down thirty."

"Do you have enough personnel on this task force?" Don asked.

"No, not nearly enough. But the cross-jurisdictional cooperation is a good start, and the Feds bring a lot of resources to the work. As you know, Don, a lot of our energy and budget is focused on drugs and gangs. Those are our everyday concerns. These church fires, and such, happen sporadically."

"But they're growing in frequency," Charlie countered.

"That's true, Ms. Mack, and these crimes can so quickly become political. We're taking them very seriously. We have a large Chaldean population in Oakland County—many of them are Catholic—and there have been a few incidents at their places of worship, so the archdiocese has been pressuring us for answers. We also have an affluent Black population in Farmington Hills, Bloomfield Hills, and a few other neighborhoods, and we've heard from *those* pastors. Last week I met with the congregants of Temple Beth El about these crimes. They're the oldest Jewish congregation in Michigan, you know."

"You're right, Chief. It's bound to be political so it makes sense to have a focus on this as a regional problem," Charlie said. "Don and I know from experience that Homeland Security and the FBI can provide some political cover but they also come with baggage. I've heard some of the victims have been resistant to talking to the Feds because they fear being profiled and added to some database or targeted for future surveillance."

"Yes, we've heard that too. Look, I'm not naïve. I have constituents from our minority communities who tell me that even though these crimes are being committed by a bunch of unhinged white guys, they know *they'll* be the ones who get screwed in the long term."

"I didn't know you were such a big bowler," Charlie said as they walked to Don's car. "How could I have missed that?"

"I'm a multifaceted man, Mack. Don't underestimate me."

Charlie scoffed. "Yeah. I'll remember that the next time you won't take off your shoes at a mosque."

Don could usually take a good teasing, but his shoulders

37

sagged and he lowered his head. Charlie shifted gears.

"So where are we getting this fish you promised for lunch?"

At the mention of food Don perked up. "You'll see."

Don's so-called "fish place" turned out to be Lily's Seafood in Royal Oak, one of the most popular dining places in the metro area. The lunchtime crowd was gregarious and hungry. There was a not-too-long wait for a table, but Charlie suggested they eat at the bar. Don ordered fish tacos and fries. Charlie chose the calamari and a side salad. They both passed up the in-house beer selections for soft drinks.

"The last time I was here was when Mandy and I were dating," Charlie said, looking around the restaurant. "I really like this place."

Don nodded and took a long draw on his Coke. Charlie watched him with amusement. The only time she'd ever seen him turn down anything to eat or drink was once when a witness had served them coffee. Once Don discovered it was made with cinnamon, he'd pushed it aside as if it was poison.

When their food arrived, they chatted about microbrewing and the best crab cakes they'd ever tasted. Don recounted the time he'd won a popcorn shrimp-eating competition.

"I could have told the other contestants it was a mistake to go against you in any kind of eating match," Charlie said, laughing.

They hadn't had a meal out together in a long while, and it was nice to eat and relax like two old friends. Charlie picked up the check when it came. "I'll expense it," she said, and they headed to the car.

"Sorry about the mosque thing. Not going into the prayer room, I mean," Don said, looking straight ahead and merging into the line of traffic headed to the freeway.

"Hey, I was teasing you. It's no big deal. I'm just glad I remembered to bring a head scarf."

"I'm still pissed off about 9/11," Don blurted.

"What?"

"I still have a bias when it comes to Muslims. I can't help it."

Charlie didn't say anything right away. She tightened her seatbelt, and they fell into an uneasy silence as they traveled the fast lane on I-96 heading downtown.

Don had law enforcement friends who had perished on 9/11, and Mandy's brother had worked in one of the Trade Center towers. It took four years of therapy to deal with her grief around his loss. So, Charlie understood the painful memories people still carried about that tragic day.

Charlie and former partner Gil had discussed leaving Homeland Security and going independent for six months before suggesting it to Don. He had immediately nixed the idea. "You can't fight terrorism with empathy," he'd said when they pointed out the primary flaw of racial profiling—hurting good people in the zeal to get the bad ones. But a few weeks later Don sought out Charlie to revisit the offer. For very personal reasons, he'd had a change of heart.

He and his wife, Rita, both held full-time jobs so they could pay for the education needs of their autistic son. Rudy was the center of their lives—a great kid with a sunshine smile, his mother's sparkling eyes, and his father's sturdy build. On weekdays, Don's parents picked up Rudy at school and drove him to their house in Hamtramck until Rita got off work. One Wednesday, on the way home from school, his grandfather stopped by a convenience store to buy his weekly lottery ticket and a hotdog for his grandson. Rudy—then three years old—took a huge bite of the sandwich and began to choke. Don's dad, scared into inaction, watched Rudy flail at his throat—his face discolored, and his eyes bulging. That's when Rauf Al-Hamzi took control. The teenage store clerk dropped to one knee and executed several swift blows between Rudy's shoulder blades until the hunk of hot dog and bun dislodged from the boy's throat. Don said his father cried as he described what had happened, saying: "That Arab kid saved Rudy's life." The act of kindness had tempered Don's prejudice toward Muslims, and prompted him to leave Homeland Security to work with Charlie.

"I thought what happened with Rudy at the convenience store had helped you with those feelings," Charlie said after a few minutes.

Don shook his head. "I don't really want to talk about it, Mack."

They were both silent for the rest of the ride to the office. Don pulled into the underground garage and found a spot near the elevator. They didn't speak as they rode up, or when they entered the office where Judy and Tamela were occupied on the phones. They moved to the conference room, checked phone messages, and looked through their notes.

"We can't just ignore what you said." Charlie finally broke the silence.

"I know."

"Does Rita know you're harboring these negative feelings about Muslims?"

Don nodded. "Occasionally something will slip out, and she's warned me about any kind of hate talk around Rudy."

"Don, you're not ever going to be Mr. Liberal, but I know you're *not* a racist."

"Why? Because you and I are friends?"

"No. Not just that. It's because you don't intentionally use your privilege as a white man to keep me at a lower status. You also don't look at the color of my skin and automatically believe I'm less worthy of all the things you want in life."

"So you don't think I'm a bigot? That's what that kid, Kamal, said in my ear when we were leaving his house."

Ahh. So that's what the soul searching is all about.

Charlie shook her head. "You can be sexist, and you're surly and overly suspicious of everyone. I've definitely seen your prejudices—like toward people with substance abuse problems." Charlie paused for a moment to get the words right. "You're also not great at censoring the things you say. But if you dislike somebody, it's *not* because of their race or ethnicity. It's because of their behavior."

When Judy joined them in the conference room they dropped the subject. Charlie passed around copies of the threatening notes Mr. Pashia had received.

"There are six threats from someone who seems to be a former student. Four of the messages appear to be written on pages or pieces torn from a lined notebook. The other two are on small squares of plain paper. Perhaps sticky notes," Charlie said.

Don looked at each one, then slid the notes to Judy. He pulled out his notebook and turned a couple of pages before looking at one note again. He repeated the action with a second note.

"You notice the spelling on these?" Don asked.

"*You* spotted a spelling error?" Judy teased.

Don smirked. "Even I know the *c* comes before the *k* in *fuck you*," Don quipped. "It's in that fourth note, and then in the last note *America* isn't capitalized."

"Why is that important?" Charlie asked.

"Do you remember the photographs of the crime scene? The graffiti had the same misspellings, and the same problems with the writing."

They called James immediately to tell him of their discovery. The student who had threatened Professor Pashia was also responsible for the graffiti in the mosque's prayer hall. It was an early breakthrough in the case. Another avenue of investigation.

"Someone has to reach out to the community college," James said. "Do you have the bandwidth to do that?"

"Yes. We'll take care of that," Charlie said. "We're also trying to get more security footage. The six files we have are very limited. You must know that."

"The Dearborn cops only sent you six tapes? Damn. We have *hundreds* of hours of tape. Okay, I'll take that task off your plate," James said angrily.

"Also, do you know if there's footage from the nearby strip mall?" Charlie asked. "We think that might be useful to have."

"I'm not sure. I'll see if we can get it."

"I think you and Judy should do the college visit," Don announced when they'd disconnected from James.

"Okay, but what will you be doing?"

"I want to sit down with a couple of guys in the hate crimes unit at DPD and find out what else they know. Maybe they'll tell me what other cases they have. If the Dearborn department starts to stonewall us, we'll need another door into the case files."

"Can't the FBI get us anything we want?" Charlie asked.

Don shrugged. "Maybe. Maybe not. I've never seen *any* department welcome the FBI with open arms. James is a good guy, but as long as he wears a dark suit and a lapel pin, he's going to have the suspicion of the uniforms."

"That rings true. Okay, Don, you check in with your contacts at the department."

"I'm calling now. Maybe I can buy a couple of rounds of drinks tonight."

Chapter 6

Notification of the gathering had been posted in a private group page on Facebook. There was to be a special guest, a guy running an operation out of Tennessee called the Knights of the Citadel. The warehouse was located on the outskirts of Detroit. Too far to bike. So Robbie bummed a ride from another recruit. He and the guy had talked a few times between meetings and had compared notes on their initiation assignments. His new friend thought Robbie's mosque tagging was a lot more impressive than his own task, which had been to skim information from a couple of credit cards.

There were already thirty or forty guys mingling around, showing each other their handguns and sharing survival magazines. There was lots of testosterone in the room. The old-man kind. The guest speaker was holding court near the front of the room. He was dressed in a purple robe with two gold crosses. *They don't do this kind of Halloween dress-up stuff in the serious groups like Stormfront.* Stormfront had rules of membership, protocols, training, online discussion forums, and experienced leaders. They had been in touch with Robbie, and had introduced him to their local contact in Lansing.

"I think this is going to be a good talk," the fellow recruit said. "Look at the guy. He must be almost six-four. He looks like John Wayne."

"Yeah, but John Wayne never wore a purple dress," Robbie

said, shaking his head.

Robbie felt somebody staring at him and turned to see Frank. His look wasn't friendly.

"Come on," Robbie said, slapping his friend on the back. "Let's get a beer."

That was another difference between the European and American associations. The European rules were explicit about not drinking, and for those in the upper echelons of the group there were strict health requirements.

The guy in charge of the warehouse had set up a couple of tubs filled with beer on ice—one with long-neck bottles, the other with cans. Every drink was a buck. Robbie paid for two bottles and handed one to his friend. There was also a table set up to purchase books by the speaker. Robbie picked up a book titled *Peril to Democracy*. The cover illustration was a montage of signs, languages, and symbols of America's growing immigrant population. Robbie gave the vendor ten dollars for the book. He was thumbing through the pages when he felt a tap on his shoulder.

"I need to talk to you," Frank said, whispering in Robbie's ear.

"What about?"

"Just follow me, newbie," Frank growled.

Robbie hesitated a moment. His friend had moved over to the group listening to the guest of honor, and Frank was heading to the back of the room near the main door. Robbie reluctantly followed.

"I haven't seen you since the assignment," Frank said.

"No. I've been studying and reading."

"You talk to anybody about what happened?"

"No," Robbie lied.

Frank nodded. He threw back his head, and lifted his can of beer upside down as he finished it off. He gave Robbie a strange look, then crushed the can in his meaty hand.

"You know nobody was supposed to die that night. I must have put the Semtex too close to the door," Frank said, staring

44

into space. "Anyway. Shit happens and sometimes there's collateral damage." Frank didn't wait for a response or any more small talk. "Keep your nose clean, kid. And your mouth shut." He turned and moved back to the beer tubs.

The man from Tennessee, a former prosecuting attorney from California, inspired his audience. He spoke of the courts being overrun with criminals who came over the border and got caught up in gangs and the drug enterprise. He talked of the loss of American values. He blamed the liberals in American politics, the Democrats in Congress, and the university elites. He spoke of the need to take back our institutions and get rid of big government in our lives. He got a standing ovation.

The ice tubs had been replenished, and while the speaker signed books everyone had another beer. Robbie looked for his ride, and spotted his friend waiting in line to shake the speaker's hand. He waited in the last row of seats, pulling up the website for Stormfront and browsing videos on how to construct a pipe bomb. He was startled by the voice behind him.

"You need a ride home, newbie?" Frank asked. His eyes were watery and he wore a goofy smile.

Robbie didn't want Frank to know where he lived. He hadn't thought of it before, but he was afraid of him. Frank had maybe thirty pounds on him and a sidearm affixed to his belt. Frank was also clearly drunk.

"No thanks. I'm waiting for my friend."

"Suit yourself."

Robbie watched Frank move unsteadily to the door and open it, glancing back with a look that sent a shiver up his spine.

Behind the locked door of his attic retreat, Robbie scanned the conversations of a dozen Stormfront members on one of his computers and on the other, he pulled up the Facebook page of the White Turks. Someone had already posted a photo of tonight's guest speaker in his purple satin robe gesturing with one hand, and displaying one of his books in the other. Robbie closed the FB page.

He minimized the Stormfront listserv and typed in the link posted by a member. The photo that popped up was of swarming Guatemalans breaching a fence line in Texas. The accompanying article—from an Arizona blogger—was a list of crimes reported to have been committed by Latinos in the United States. The most heinous was the rape of two young, blond cheerleaders returning home from practice in Bakersfield, California.

Next he viewed a YouTube video about the top ten hybrid bicycles, followed by a thirty-minute tutorial on the safety precautions required to assemble improvised explosive devices. He finally laid across his bed with a pounding headache. *That asswipe Frank! He claimed he knew what the fuck he was doing.*

When Robbie awakened with a start, he'd sweated through his tee. In his dream he'd been running from an explosion that sent shards of tile scattering through the air. He'd been propelled from his bike by the wave of the blast. When he looked back, Professor Pashia was engulfed in flames, beckoning and holding a textbook out to him.

Chapter 7

Judy had made an appointment with the Director of Human Resources at the community college—a woman named Roberta Suttles. She was more than happy to meet with the investigators who were helping the Pashia family. "He was one of my favorite and most effective teachers," she'd told Judy.

Suttles's office was in the administrative building on Fort Street only a half mile from the Mack offices. Charlie and Judy had considered using the People Mover, Detroit's elevated rail system, and then walking the short distance to the college, but finally opted for the quick drive to the downtown campus.

Suttles was an attractive, friendly, middle-aged woman with black curls that bounced around her face as she talked. She reminded Charlie a bit of her mother. It was quickly determined that individual student files were off-limits, but Suttles made a call to the school's dean who gave her permission to make copies of Hassan Pashia's class rosters for the past five years. The forms included student names and their enrollment in particular classes.

"I see several names that repeat over a couple of years," Judy noted.

"That's not unusual for students taking night classes. Professor Pashia taught classes in our Computer Information Systems Program. We offer associate degrees and certifications in that program."

"Is there any way to get more information on the students?" Charlie asked.

"As I said, with a court order *or* if asked by a law enforcement unit. There's a specific protocol they use."

Charlie nodded and thanked Suttles for her help.

"I hope you find the people responsible for the professor's death. He was a very decent man," Suttles said earnestly.

"She's a nice woman," Judy said as they walked to the car.

"Yup."

"What's on your mind?"

"Ernestine has a boyfriend."

"What?" Judy was smiling broadly. "Well, that's great news. Good for her."

"I guess so. It just seems kind of sudden."

"I recall you saying you wish she weren't so alone. She can use the company, right? You won't have to worry about her so much."

"She already has her girlfriends at her building. Plus, she has her walking group."

"And now she's got a man," Judy said enthusiastically. "Go Ernestine!"

Charlie and Judy mapped out the rest of the day's work. Judy would scan social media for the students that showed up multiple times on Pashia's class rosters. It was tedious work but she was good at that sort of research, and she would enlist Tamela, who had already proven herself valuable in online searches. Charlie would focus on scanning security video.

James had delivered on his promise, and this morning a thumb drive had been delivered that included ninety video files. Don was meeting again with his DPD contacts, hoping to gain their fullest cooperation in the Pashia case.

Charlie had no special technique for effectiveness in viewing security footage. In a murder investigation last year, she and Don had pored over hours of footage in a cramped room at police headquarters. Just being able to spread out in her own conference room was already a plus.

She'd organized the files chronologically in each category: street views, mosque cameras, and strip mall. She'd began with the mosque parking lot footage, which had the fewest files, and had been at it for a couple of hours.

"How's it going?" Judy asked, sticking her head in the room.

"Not bad." Charlie's feet were in a chair, and a cup of coffee and notebook by her side.

"Are you ready for a lunch break?"

"Maybe in a half hour. I have one more parking lot tape to look at. How's the Googling going?"

"So far, so good. I've divided the names with Tamela. I started with a general search to see if the students have a social media presence. Most of them have old Facebook pages but many of them post to Twitter, too. One thing we found is a website Mr. Pashia used with his study groups. I'm cross-referencing the class rosters with the study groups."

"Very good, Judy. What were you thinking for lunch?"

"That's the same question I got from Don, who just called. He'll be back by one o'clock. He's grumpy."

"What else is new when he's hungry?"

"I thought maybe I'd have pizza delivered. I know you hate it, but it pacifies Don."

Charlie nodded. "Okay. Will you get me a salad? Extra tomatoes and cucumbers?"

"You got it. Oh, and Don said he'd help you look through the footage."

"That's the least he can do, for us having pizza again."

Charlie looked at her notes. So far there was not much of interest except for the two times she'd watched Pashia's car leave the mosque, only to return a half hour later. This was before the parking lot cameras had been mysteriously disabled.

Don arrived at ten of one. Charlie knew the exact time because the noise level from the reception area and bullpen tripled. Don never entered any room timidly, and a few minutes later he burst into the conference room.

"I'm back."

"I heard."

"Anything from the footage yet?"

"Nope. But I have it organized and you're going to help me I understand."

"Is that the food?" Don responded, heading to the credenza.

They all stopped their tasks for a brief lunch break and to hear Don's report on his meeting with DPD's finest. The night before, he'd bought beers for two members of the hate crimes unit, and today had a conversation with Captain Travers, the officer-in-charge at headquarters.

"Travers sends his love, Mack," Don said, scarfing down a half slice of pizza. "He asked how you were doing."

"I hope you told him I'm fine now that I don't have to see him very often."

"I think he gets that."

"You two really have it in for each other, don't you?" Judy asked.

"He's not my biggest fan," Charlie answered. "And vice versa."

"Travers *did* give me a lot of information to follow up on. I have the names of additional witnesses who aren't on the task force list. He's really pissed off about these white supremacist groups. His own church had an incident. Someone broke into the office and trashed it."

"I didn't know that."

"The church didn't report it. They didn't want the press to get hold of the story but the task force is investigating."

"Judy, do you remember what the FBI report said about

the breakdown of these incidents in the past year? How many churches, mosques, and temples?"

Judy punched a few keys on her newest toy. She was the agency's early adaptor of technology, and she'd been happy so far with her new Windows mobile device. "Thirteen churches, two temples and seven mosques."

"What's on your mind, Mack?"

Charlie shrugged. "Just something I'm noodling on. Let's get back to the security files. I think screening this footage will take the rest of the day and part of tomorrow."

It was almost four o'clock when Don shouted, "I think I found something." He waved Charlie over to his side of the table. "Look here." Don pointed at his laptop screen.

"What is that?" Charlie asked, squinting. "A bicycle?"

"Yep. A guy just stopped it at that tree where I found the gum wrapper and clip, and walked across the street toward the mosque. He hasn't come back into view yet."

"What day is this?"

"A week before the mosque bombing."

They stared at the footage for ten minutes, the time code ticking away the seconds and minutes on the screen. At three minutes after 10 p.m. a figure came in view just below the camera, walked briskly across the lawn and across the street, and retrieved the bike. The face was never in view, and the person's actions at the bike were blocked by the tree. The biker rode out of view, headed north.

"A guy on a bike," Charlie said.

"Or it could be a woman," Don said.

"Good looking out, Don. Let's see if he or she shows up again."

The next two hours were spent with footage from a camera at the bus stop a half block away. That camera caught a glimpse of the biker riding toward the mosque, but lost the image before the tree. Since then the footage had only showed lots and lots of cars and buses, but no bikers.

By six o'clock they were both bored by the task, and Don

scrounged for the last slice of pizza. Judy and Tamela had left an hour ago.

"Where did Judy put it? It's not in the fridge, and I don't see the empty box," Don complained. "How many more tapes are there, Mack?"

"Six or seven. They're from the strip mall."

"Can we tackle them tomorrow morning?" Don asked. "I can barely see straight after staring at that screen, and I promised Rudy I'd play video games with him tonight. I better give my eyeballs a break."

"Yeah. That's okay. I'll finish off the tapes. Tomorrow we can focus on that witness list you got from DPD."

"Sounds like a plan."

Don grabbed the tweed jacket from his desk, then stuck his head in the conference room door. "You parked in the garage?"

"No, I found a space on the street when we got back from the college."

"Okay. See you tomorrow and, uh, thanks for the conversation earlier."

Charlie checked in with Mandy who was already home and starting dinner. A lasagna.

"Oh, that sounds really good but I have to work a couple of extra hours. I have a task to complete for the Pashia case. I'm so sorry."

"It's okay. You can zap some lasagna when you get in, and I'll save you some salad."

The security camera at the strip mall, a couple of blocks from the mosque, had a broad view of the parking lot on the corner of Ford Road. Charlie had two weeks of footage and she watched cars enter and exit, mostly headed to and from the liquor store. Three days before the mosque bombing, Dearborn Heights police had been dispatched, and Charlie watched as they cornered, and arrested, a man who had exited the store. She also saw the unsteady treks of a half dozen people who, even before they made their drink purchases, were too drunk to drive. There was an altercation between two ladies who might not have actually been ladies. Charlie watched as one of the women snatched the wig off the other which led to a brief scuffle just before another police cruiser showed up.

She was up to footage from the last night of Hassan Pashia's life, when she finally saw something that might have a bearing on their case. A biker with a helmet came into view from the direction of the mosque, and turned onto Ford Road heading west. Charlie stopped the tape and watched the biker in slow motion. There was no way to know if this was the same person she and Don had seen in the videotape a week before the bombing, but it could be the one who had looked back at the mosque on the night of the explosion. The timing was close.

Charlie toggled the strip mall footage backwards, and this time spotted the man with the canvas bag. The one they'd seen walking away from the mosque. He got into a small white truck, backed out of the lot, and exited the camera's view. She knew the FBI had the technology to isolate—and zoom in on—the truck's license plate. She jotted several notes into her book and sat back in her chair, pleased with her discovery. She considered calling Don, but remembered his planned time with his family. She did text James to say she'd found something on the strip mall video.

It was almost eight o'clock when Charlie turned off the lights in the three-room office suite. She locked the door and armed the new security system the management company had provided months before. The elevator was at the lobby level, and she adjusted the items in her backpack while she waited for it to chug to the fourth floor. The guard wasn't at his station as she crossed the lobby and exited the front door. Charlie hit the key fob and the Vette's lights came to life. She'd had the car nearly three years now and had thought about trading it in, but it still drove superbly and still had relatively low mileage. Charlie had just opened the driver's door when she heard the voice behind her.

"Give me the bag, lady."

She spun to find a bulky white guy, dressed in camo pants and a dark jacket, his hand near a sidearm in his waist holster. His eyes squinted and his lips tightened into a thin line.

"Don't make me ask again. I don't want to shoot you, but I will."

Charlie always wondered why someone with a gun threatened to shoot a person they confronted. She guessed they thought it sounded menacing. If this man had any notion of shooting her, his gun would already be drawn.

He was a few inches taller than Charlie but he'd made the mistake of getting too close. Charlie reached for the shoulder strap of her backpack, watching the man release the tension in his shoulders and arms. He didn't even see it when she drove her keys into the side of his face, then shoved his head down to meet her rising knee. It was a basic martial arts move for close hand-to-hand combat.

The man's knees crumpled beneath him, and he lay unmoving in the street. Charlie waited a couple of seconds to make sure he wasn't faking unconsciousness, then maneuvered around him to retrieve his revolver—a .34 caliber. She threw her backpack into the Vette and dialed 911. Then sat in the car and opened her glove box where her own weapon was kept.

Charlie insisted that Mandy shouldn't come to help her. "Nope. He's out cold and I have my gun. I'm not pulling it out unless he moves. I don't want the cops to get the wrong idea. I'll call again when I'm done with the police."

The lobby guard, who'd returned to his station, saw the car lights, Charlie's open door, and the man sprawled in the middle of the street. He came running to investigate, standing next to Charlie's car until the police arrived.

Noticing her race, fancy car, and the white man she'd disabled, the police were immediately inclined to find Charlie somehow at fault. It helped to have the security guard on hand to verify her tenancy in the building. While all she wanted to do was go home, they were pushing for her to come to the police station to fill out a report. She reluctantly invoked Captain Travers's name and handed one of the officers his business card. After he phoned the captain, he returned the card and her car keys, and gave a salute as he waved her on her way.

"I'm done, and I'm famished. I also need some wine."

"It's a good thing you called. I was about to come down there," Mandy said.

"Yeah. I know. I had to do a bit of talking to the officers who responded. I even had to use Travers's name."

"Oh. I know you hated that."

"The whole thing was infuriating."

"Come home to me now," Mandy said. "You can eat and then get a hot bath. Hamm and I will take care of you."

"I'm on my way."

Chapter 8

Judy stood, came around her desk and gave Charlie a hug as soon as she walked in the door. Charlie looked over Judy's shoulder at Tamela who had paused in her filing with a worried look. Charlie gave a wave.

"I've called you three times. Johnny at the front desk came by this morning to tell me what happened," Judy said.

"I went to police headquarters this morning to file a formal report. It was an attempted mugging, that's all. I wasn't hurt and the guy didn't get anything."

"You should have called."

"There was nothing you could do, and I know you'd worry yourself the rest of the night. I didn't tell Don either."

"I think he knows though," Judy said. "He called to ask if you were in, then just hung up when I told him I hadn't seen you yet."

It was likely Don *did* know. One of his cronies at the department would have called him once they made the connection between the Mack Agency and the report of an assault. They were pretty well known at headquarters. Last year, they'd worked with the department to amass clues solving a murder case that involved a prominent Michigan family. Two years before that, Charlie had posed as a homeless person to catch the serial murderer of street people, and topple a drug operation involving a rogue police detective.

"What time is Don coming in?"

"He didn't say."

Charlie dumped her backpack and briefcase on her desk in the bullpen. The trip to police headquarters meant little time for exercise. Today they would continue trying to identify Pashia's threatening student, follow up with James on the mysterious biker and the man with the bag, and check out the new witness list Don had procured. Now might be the only time Charlie could fit in a workout, so she grabbed the backpack and returned to the anteroom.

"Judy, I'm going down to the gym for forty-five minutes. Are you back on the students' social media accounts?"

"Yep, and Tamela will be once she's completed filing."

Exercise was a natural part of Charlie's day. It had been a habit since high school when she played softball. As an adult she'd practiced and taught martial arts for a dozen years. Last night's attacker wasn't aware of that until after he'd regained consciousness. She could be obsessive about her physical fitness routine and, more often than not, her food and drink intake. The latter wasn't always easy when surveillances, late-night meetings, and working lunches were the norm.

The building's small gym wasn't fancy. There were two ellipticals, two bikes, and two treadmills. The one weight machine had limited performance. But there were good showers and dressing rooms, and an attendant was always on duty during business hours. Charlie nodded to Deborah, then grabbed a towel and changed into her leotard and top. She listened to the music app Judy had downloaded onto her phone and did a twenty-minute, medium-level program on the bike. Charlie spent the rest of her time with the ten-pound free weights, then showered and changed into slacks and a collared shirt. She ran her fingers through her hair, left a fiver in Deb's tip jar, and, feeling better, took the stairs up to the office.

Tamela was at the reception desk, and looked up with a smile. "We have company," she said, pointing her chin toward the conference room.

Charlie could hear the murmured voices. "Don here?"

"Yep, he's in there with Judy and the gentleman from the FBI."

Charlie bypassed the bullpen. Don, Judy, and James were drinking coffee and looking at last night's security footage on the whiteboard.

"So the gang's all here," Charlie said.

James stood when Charlie entered and offered a handshake. "Sorry about your altercation last night. Are you okay?"

"I'm fine," Charlie said waving off his concern.

"I realize I didn't have an appointment, but I cleared it with Don."

Don grunted and gave Charlie a look she couldn't read. But there was no mistaking Judy's face. It was heavy with worry.

"So did you see the biker?" Charlie asked nodding toward the whiteboard.

"Yep. After I received your text, I separated the footage," James said. "So we have in one file the man leaving his bike and moving toward the mosque, his return to the bike ten minutes later, and then riding off. That was a week before the explosion at the mosque. The other file has the night of the bombing with the biker staring at the mosque as he rides by, and the footage of the man with a bag heading down the street, and later getting into a white truck at the strip mall."

"You know the biker is a man?" Charlie asked.

"Yep. We have technology that tells us that from his gait," James said. "We've also identified the other man, from his license plate, as Frank R. Wyatt Jr."

"That's fast work," Charlie said.

"There's more, Mack," Don said dourly.

Charlie raised an eyebrow toward James.

"Wyatt is the man who tried to mug you last night," James said.

"What?" Charlie said, feeling her heart leap to her throat.

"And the cops found a piece of paper in the guy's pocket with your name on it," Judy said with a pained look.

"Shit!" Charlie said.

Chapter 9

"What do we know about this Wyatt guy?" Charlie asked. She was looking at his photo, and the piece of paper he'd carried with her name printed in neat block letters.

"No record to speak of. A couple of DUIs. A veteran. Fifty-two years old, and lives in a rental house in Garden City. He works as a part-time plumber and owns a website where he bills himself as a handyman. We were able to match his prints to a partial print at the mosque."

"Well, there you have it," Charlie said. "We've found Mr. Pashia's murderer."

"Maybe," James said. "The guy's talking, and he says he didn't plant the bomb. He claims there was some kid with him who did that. He also says another guy is the one who came up with the idea to attack the mosque."

"So you're saying this is a conspiracy?" Judy asked.

"We've tracked almost one thousand incidents by these hate groups, and the members rarely act alone. Even if they do, there's someone who has knowingly, or unknowingly, aided and abetted their criminal activity," James said. "We've labeled them domestic terrorists."

"Let's just call them what they are," Charlie said, stunned by the statistic. "Racists. Angry about the growing influence of nonwhite people."

"... especially a Black president," Don added.

"That too."

"Is Wyatt one of the people in your database?" Judy asked.

"No."

"Can you tie him to any of the other incidents in the last six months?" Charlie asked.

"We're working on it."

"So, what's next?" Don asked.

James loosened his tie and leaned over his arms on the table. "We're going to work the guy to find out how he knew about Charlie."

"Does this mean she's in danger?" Judy asked.

"I think we have to assume that," Don responded. "This guy knows we're investigating the Pashia case. That can only mean there's a leak on the task force."

Charlie gathered her brainstorming tools—multicolored Post-its and dry marker pens—and moved to the whiteboard.

"Let's see what we know, and what we don't," she said.

Charlie's way of making sense of a case involved the tactile exercise of placing the notes on a blank surface, and manipulating them in ways that helped her think differently about the facts, questions, and assumptions of a case. Occasionally an outsider got to see the process. James watched as Don and Judy called out information to be placed on the board. The notes were initially organized by color. As always, there were more questions than answers, more speculation than facts. Sometimes Charlie circled a note or connected two disparate notes that didn't seem to have a connection. Until they did.

"That's impressive," James said. "Do you ever include a time-line or photos?"

"We've used photos," Judy responded.

"But mostly we just let Charlie stare at the board," Don said. "I know it sounds like new-age nonsense, but I've seen it work a lot of times. So now I'm a believer."

"It also helps to hear the big questions that come out of left field. Our former partner, Gil, used to be good at asking those," Judy said. "You met him on the Birmingham case."

"I remember," James said. "He retired, didn't he? That's how you got moved up to investigator status."

"Associate," Judy said.

"That was a smart move."

As Judy and James made small talk, Don got another cup of coffee and munched on a doughnut. Charlie stared at the board and moved Post-its around in no apparent pattern. Then she stepped back and stared some more.

"What if," Charlie began, "these incidents aren't just about spewing hate? What if the vandalism is a cover for the burglaries?"

The three stared at Charlie's display of sticky notes. The greens and reds were spread across the board in pairs and sets of threes.

"Do you have a list of the things missing from these incidents?" Charlie asked James.

"Not with me, but I can have someone email it over."

"Could you please do that?"

James left the room to make a call, and Judy checked on Tamela's progress on the social media searches. Don sat in the chair next to Charlie with something on his mind.

"I don't like it, Mack. A leak on the task force. A man tries to assault you. I don't like it."

"Sorry. What did you say?"

"I said, I'm worried about this case. That guy who assaulted you knew your name."

"He didn't try to assault or kill me. He asked for my bag."

"At gunpoint. So that makes it attempted armed robbery."

"He never actually wielded the gun . . ."

"For heaven's sake, Mack. You're not taking this seriously."

"Okay, you're right. It could have turned out badly. The guy was armed."

"You're unfocused. What is it?"

"Whoever is targeting these places of worship—it's not just because they don't like people different from them. I think these incidents are robberies first, and hate crimes second."

"If that's true, why didn't they take the expensive computers and satellite technology at the mosque?" Don asked. "That stuff must be worth tens of thousands of dollars. Instead, they left the equipment to burn in the fire."

"Maybe they're not after hardware. Maybe they want personal information like addresses, telephone numbers, social security numbers, and bank information. That stuff also has value."

James returned to the conference room with news that the stolen items inventory had been emailed to Judy. "I already asked her to print a set for each of us." He stopped. "What were you two talking about?"

"Charlie has a theory," Don said. "She thinks these hate crimes are really a cover for identity thefts or something like that."

James looked thoughtful. "That's a possibility. But if so, it isn't a very complex operation."

Judy returned with four lists of missing items, and they began to pore over them. In all of the Black church breaches, the offices had been ransacked and files removed. In a few cases, desktop computers had been taken. In at least one synagogue breach, the only things missing were membership records. Things like expensive artwork and valuable artifacts had been bypassed for folders with contribution information and credit card receipts.

"So Charlie's right," Don said.

"At least partially," James agreed. "I'm taking this info to our techs at Quantico to cross-reference these names, accounts, and credit card numbers with our database of flagged transactions."

"Flagged transactions?" Judy asked.

"Purchases of large amounts of ammunition, bomb-making ingredients, airline tickets to countries on our watch list. Those kinds of things."

"Oh, I almost forgot," Charlie said, opening her tote. "Don found these near a tree across from the mosque. It's a gum wrapper and what Don thinks might be a bicycle clip. Maybe it belongs to our guy."

"I'll check it out," James said, standing. "Good work, you guys."

Tamela's initial online search of the list of college students identified six people whose social media posts raised red flags. Judy's task for the rest of the afternoon was to build a dossier on each student.

"Oh, and we all need to finish reading this FBI report," Charlie said. "It's long, but I think it'll help."

"Six hundred pages," Don complained.

"I know, but there might be something in the report that could be pertinent to the mosque attack."

"When are you going to tell Mandy about Wyatt?" Don asked.

Charlie shook her head.

"I know she'll be worried, but you've got to tell her, Charlie," Judy said.

Don picked up the pressure: "You're a target for these guys, so you won't be going anywhere alone. My idea is to put you in your car at night, call to tell Mandy you're on the way, and she can see you into the house."

"I think that's overkill."

"Maybe. Maybe not. And about the leak?" Don asked. "You think Saleh can be trusted?"

Charlie and Judy gave Don hard stares.

"Don't look at me like that. I know you two think the guy is handsome and all that, but we haven't been in touch with James for months. He bleeds FBI. That's all I'm saying."

"I trust James implicitly. I'm following my gut on that," Charlie said.

"Me too," Judy said.

"Okay, okay. I thought you always said there were no bad questions," Don said, pouting.

"Mom called this afternoon. She's invited you and me to her place for Saturday brunch. She wants to introduce us to her new beau."

"You said yes, I hope."

"I did. I know you're as eager to meet Mr. Constantine as I am."

"Is she doing okay? Is she in love?" Mandy asked dragging out the word *love*.

"It's a little fast for that, don't you think? Especially at her age."

"You can't mean that, Charlie. People can fall in love at any age."

"Whatever."

"Are you jealous someone else has sparked your mother's interest?"

"No. Of course not. Mom and I will always be close. We talked a lot today about this hate crimes business. She's really curious about the case."

"I was only teasing. I know Ernestine will always be your biggest fan, and you hers."

Charlie bumped Mandy with her hip. "For the record, I'm *your* number one fan, too."

Hamm yanked his leash to chase a squirrel who dared cross their path, and Charlie pulled him back to the sidewalk. These evening walks were good for all three of them. Now that the weather was milder, they were seeing a lot more neighbors on their porches, and interacting with more dog walkers.

Mandy came from a family of dog lovers. Her parents had presented her and her brother with a puppy when they were very young kids. Since then, she had loved various family dogs. On the other hand, Charlie—raised by a school principal mother and a lawyer father with erratic hours—hadn't grown up with any pets. She was only now learning how much you could love a dog.

"Having a dog is a good way to meet people," Charlie said. "If you own a dog, you can connect to strangers about poop, pet food, grooming, those sort of things. You don't have to talk politics or think about your differences."

"Dogs just want to give and receive love," Mandy said. "We

can learn a lot from them."

Their pooch, MC Hammer Porter-Mack, was a rescue dog, shaggy and gregarious, with big paws and an equally big heart. Hamm had become a bit of a celebrity in their community last fall when he'd been dognapped by bad guys intent on scaring Charlie off a case. Following his rescue, he had gotten more treats and ear rubs than any other dog in the neighborhood.

"Have you Googled this Constantine guy yet?" Mandy asked.

"I haven't had time. It would be a perfect task for Judy but we've all been consumed by the Pashia case."

"How's it going?"

Charlie still hadn't told Mandy the latest about Wyatt. Not about his connection to an organized hate group, or about the deal he'd proposed to avoid prosecution. And not about the note in his pocket.

"Nothing much to report."

Charlie waited until they had eaten ice cream, watched the local news, and locked up for the night before she offered the news about Wyatt. Mandy was angry.

"When were you going to tell me?"

"After we'd had a stress-free evening. I knew you'd be alarmed and ready to defend me."

"Well I am."

"You and Don are on the same wavelength. He says he and I are going to be tied at the hip during this case. He walked me to my car before we left the office today."

"Charlie, promise me you'll be careful. Don't take any unnecessary chances, and don't try to protect me by withholding information. Please."

"I won't. I'm sorry."

Charlie nudged Hamm off the human bed to sleep in his own, and pulled Mandy into her arms.

Chapter 10

Robbie's appointment with the local recruiter of Stormfront was in a few hours. The man was in Lansing, but they'd agreed to meet in Ann Arbor when Robbie admitted he didn't have a car.

There was a bike trail that would get him to the appointment in two hours, and the ride would give him an exceptional workout. The round trip and the meeting would take most of his Saturday.

He'd slept well last night even after staying up late to watch an online training on the effects of tear gas. This morning, he'd showered and dressed for his trip and now he was having cereal. His mother had started nagging him about not helping around the house, so when he got back home this afternoon he had to clean the gutters and mow the lawn.

"*When* will you be back?" his mother asked.

"I told you. Before five. I'll have plenty of time to do the outside work then."

"Biking is not your job. I depend on you to help around the house."

"I know. But I have a business meeting today. I'm not just fooling around."

"Robbie, don't let me down."

"Get off my back, Mom. How many times do I have to tell you, I'll do the damn yard work."

Robbie couldn't wait to get his own place and get away

from his pain-in-the-ass mother and his juvenile delinquent kid brother. In the meantime, he was glad to have his own space in the attic. He kept it orderly, with his books and videotapes organized on shelves. He had two computers and a laptop. His handgun and a rifle purchased from a big-box store were stored in his closet. One time Robbie had found his brother in his space taking selfies with the rifle. He gave the kid a beating just like the kind his loser father had given him before he left for good five years ago. Since then he'd padlocked the attic door to keep his nosy brother out.

Robbie methodically ticked through his bike safety checklist. Air in tires. Check. Cables not cracked. Check. Handle grips tight. Chain lubed. Pedals tight. Make sure the saddlebag has a spare tube, tire levers, hand pump, Allen wrench, bike clips, goggles, gloves. Check.

The day was bright, dry, and mild—great for a bike ride. By the time he hit the Ann Arbor bike trail he was in a peaceful, focused state. He'd agreed to meet his contact, Arthur Spader, at an outdoor market area. Robbie spotted the guy sitting at a picnic bench near the man-made lake, and secured his bike to a rack. Spader said he'd wear a red cap, which he'd done. It stood out among the blue and maize scarves, hats, and jackets worn by the University of Michigan fans. Spader was clean shaven, lean, and from the tug of his jacket at his shoulders, he looked fit. He was in his mid-thirties or early forties. Not handsome, but probably considered so because of his aqua blue eyes.

They shook hands.

"So, you're a serious biker from the looks of you. What was your trip, maybe two hours?"

"A little over two, and with the hills it was a great workout. I try to do a two to three-hour ride a couple of times a week."

"That's impressive. Tell me about yourself," Spader dived in. "Wait, I'm sorry. You want to get a chowder or hot dog or something? All the food in the cul-de-sac is good. You could get something more substantial if you like. I'm buying."

"I could eat a fish sandwich. Maybe some onion rings."

"Beer?"

"Make it a Coke."

"Okay. You wait here to save the bench. Everybody wants to sit near the water. I'll be right back."

Robbie watched Spader walk away. His leather jacket had an eagle painted on the back. His jeans and boots made him look like a motorcycle guy. Robbie took off his jersey and spread it on the table to discourage anyone from trying to sit with him. He looked around. This was a typical Ann Arbor crowd. A lot of mixed-race families with kids ranging from peach-colored to caramel. A bunch of minorities, liberals wearing Obama tees, and college kids who thought they were better than him.

Spader returned with two trays of food. "I got you a bowl of chili, too, in case you were hungry after your bike ride."

Robbie shook his head. "Naw. I don't eat red meat."

They sat for a while, looking at the goings-on at the market. At the gazebo a bearded, long-haired guy with a guitar played old-fashioned folk tunes. A few college students were throwing a Frisbee, and a guy at a booth was registering people to vote.

"So what do you do besides bike?" Spader asked.

"I work in the IT department of an insurance company. It's a new job. Before that I was doing deliveries on my bike. I took night classes to get my associates degree."

"You a Christian?"

"Uh, I mean, I used to go to church when I was a kid, but I haven't had much time for that lately."

"Jesus is the light and the way," Spader said. "The Christian right is part of the solution to the flood of foreign ideologies to this country. The country might be going down a cesspool, voting for a man from Kenya for President, but in my county we put four new independent candidates in office. They believe in the second amendment, the white man's role as leader, and the right to life."

Robbie knew Spader was associated with the European groups and they talked a lot about the cleansing of society, and returning it to its original status where it was run by free white men. They were suspicious of national governments, corporations, and the liberal media.

"I haven't really thought about most of that, but I do believe a man should be able to buy and keep a gun, and have a job. There are too many people trying to keep *both* those rights away from us."

Spader nodded and smiled. "I understand you're affiliated with the White Turks. I know some of those guys. What do you think of them?"

Robbie wondered if this might be part of a test of his allegiance to the cause. "I, uh, they're all right. I guess. They don't seem like they're doing a lot of preparation for what has to come."

"What do you mean?" Spader asked, scooping a spoonful of chowder.

"Well. Most of these guys are soft and old. They have guns and talk about defending their way of life, but they couldn't run a half mile if they had to, and they aren't learning the modern skills they need to fight a war. They watch army movies and fight wars in their imaginations."

"I see what you mean."

They talked for almost two hours, then Robbie watched Spader amble to a new Jeep Cherokee and glance back before he drove away. He had said Robbie was just the kind of young guy with computer skills the group leaders were looking for. He promised to be in touch.

Robbie used the Porta-John, filled his water bottle at the fountain, and got back on his bike. The return ride was into the wind, and on the hills he had to downshift more than usual. He began to feel his legs getting tighter. Pulling over to take a break, he drank half the bottle of water. *I probably shouldn't have had the onion rings. Empty calories.*

It was four-thirty when he locked his bike in the garage. Glancing up at the sagging gutters before he went into the house, he heard his mother yell his name repeatedly as he climbed the stairs to his attic room. With his legs burning he locked the door behind him.

69

Chapter 11

Charlie brought Danishes, orange juice, and a small tray of fruit into the conference room and set it up on the table. Sometimes she liked getting into the office before the others. She looked around the bullpen desks where she, Don, and Judy did the bulk of their work and silently thanked God for their good fortune. Many small businesses didn't last past three years, but the Mack Agency was now in its fifth year of operation.

Charlie heard the front door open. "Judy?"

"Yep. It's me."

Charlie joined Judy in the reception area and watched her unload files, her tote, and a couple of bags from McDonald's.

"Great minds think alike," Charlie said, pointing at the bags. "Did you bring in food too?"

"Pastry, OJ, and some fruit."

"I bought ten hash browns."

"I guess we both know we're getting to that point in the investigation where eating and brainstorming is everything."

"Yep. You're in early. Did you sleep okay?"

"Not really. I wanted to come in and look at the board for a while. Sometimes you have to look at just one thing, and get that right. After that the rest of the picture becomes clearer. Like 'Finishing the Hat.'"

Judy put her scarf on the clothes tree. She and Charlie stared at each other. They both knew another game of "name that Broadway show tune" was afoot. It was their ongoing fun to invoke a musical that fit their immediate problem. Judy smiled.

"You know it, don't you?" Charlie asked.

"*Sunday in the Park with George*," Judy said.

"You see. *That* is why you and I will always be together. I can't do that with any other human being in the world."

"We're certainly two nerds of a kind," Judy agreed.

"Okay, I better get to it. Don will be here soon and I won't have the quiet I need. Come in and get some fruit and a Danish if you want."

Charlie had put the Post-its back into their categories: questions, facts, what-ifs. She lifted a note from the board. Hassan Pashia was killed in a mosque attack. Charlie placed the note in the middle of the table. She was doing a reset. She grabbed a strawberry, took a bite, and stared at the board.

Why was he killed? That was the question that kept them involved in this case. Did an aggrieved student plan his death? If so, the student would have to know Pashia's schedule, his routine. Was his murder an accident? A robbery or hate crime gone wrong? Charlie scrolled through the task force report on her computer. Ten cases in six months. Five churches, two mosques, one temple, two funeral homes. All connected, but how? The attacks happened at night. One man, a caretaker at a funeral home, had seen someone running away from the facility. He described the person as a white man in a baseball cap. The witness also heard a truck or SUV squeal away from the location. Besides Mr. Pashia, no one else had been killed in this string of crimes. Why had the mosque attack become personal? Why did Mr. Pashia have to die alone at the end of a normal workday?

Charlie stood back from the board taking in all the questions. After a few minutes she moved to Judy's desk in the bullpen.

"How's it going?" Judy asked.

"Nothing, so far. Did you find anything interesting in the student profiles?"

"There's one guy . . ." Judy said.

Robert Christopher Barrett was twenty-one years old, a graduate of Garden City High School. He'd applied for, and was accepted into, the Computer Information Systems Program at Wayne County Community College. He'd taken night classes and online classes at the college—four of them taught by Hassan Pashia. His known address, in Garden City, was a home owned by Susan Barrett. He'd worked as a sales clerk at a Walmart, as a computer assistant at FedEx, and was now employed at Guardpost Insurance Company in Southfield.

Judy had included several photos of the boy pulled from his social media accounts. In one he posed in camo pants, holding a long gun and wearing a baseball cap labeled *Security*. Charlie thought he was the kind of kid who might have been bullied in school for being too skinny, too pale, too geeky.

"He certainly doesn't look like a domestic terrorist," Judy said.

"Maybe not," Don said chomping on a Danish. "But he does look like a kid on the path to self-radicalization."

"I think we all have a prejudgment about what these people will look like. Barrett's pretty close to the profile actually," Charlie said. "But these guys come in all shapes, sizes, and backgrounds."

"Look at the next page," Judy said. "These are posts from his Facebook page. Look at his writing. Remember the weird spellings in the mosque graffiti?"

Barrett liked to write a lot, and his posts were about a range of topics. What he didn't like about Detroit seemed to be a favorite topic, and he had a definite anti-immigration bent. Sometimes he recommended books and websites to prove his points. Other times his posts were personal rants about how he had been mistreated. Each post had misspellings, letters gone astray and placed in the wrong part of a word or sentence. The most obvious one was in the last post on the page. *Fukc these mongrels!* he had written with the *c* and *k* transposed.

"That's got to be our guy," Don announced.

"Yep," Charlie said, looking at the whiteboard. "Judy, were there any photos of him with a bike?"

"No."

"Let's have Tamela create a list of the bike stores in the metro area. Maybe James can get a team to contact the shops and see if Barrett has an account. The more we have connecting him to the mosque bombing the better to make a prosecution stick."

"We better call Mr. FBI, don't you think, Mack?"

"I'll text James now, and set up a Skype call."

Their new SMART Board had come as a bonus from building management for signing a multiyear lease at the beginning of the year. The board could be used for simple note taking, as a projector screen, and as both a TV and online monitor. Judy was enthralled with the whiteboard and, so far, only she knew how to operate all its functions. They mostly used it for the low-tech tasks, but today they were doing a video conference with James and one of the Detroit police members of the task force.

Charlie, Don and Judy sat side by side at the conference table, lined up across from the electronic board. On the other end, James and Commander Yvonne Coleman sat across the table from each other. Charlie knew of Coleman. She had worked her way up the ranks during eighteen years on the police force, but they'd never met.

"We've identified the student who likely sent the threats to Mr. Pashia," Charlie began. "We think he's also the person who wrote the graffiti at the mosque."

"Who is it?" Coleman asked.

"His name is Robert Christopher Barrett."

James and Coleman looked at each other. "That's the name Wyatt gave us. He's called Robbie, and Wyatt says the kid was the bomber at the mosque."

"Do you believe Wyatt?" Don asked.

"Some on the task force are ready to make a deal with Mr. Wyatt, but I'm not so sure," James said. "He's definitely involved with an extremist group. They call themselves the White Turks. We've been able to make that connection through his computer and phone, but I think he's railroading the Barrett kid."

"What do you think, Commander?" Charlie asked.

"Whether he's railroading the boy or not may be irrelevant. Wyatt's given us what we think is credible information about another attack. I'm more concerned with that right now."

"What's he saying?" Charlie asked.

"He says there's to be an attack on a Black church and a temple," Coleman said. "A planned simultaneous action involving incendiaries."

"Doesn't that seem like a quick escalation?" Don asked. "I mean the first casualty in these incidents was at the mosque, and it looks like that might have been something personal. All the other events were just property damage."

"Wyatt says some of the members want to make a dramatic statement about their disdain for President Obama," James said. "That's been the game changer for some of these dudes."

"We're pretty sure Barrett is your guy for the mosque. At least for the graffiti," Don said. "And we think there's enough evidence that you could pick him up for questioning."

"What kind of evidence?" Coleman asked.

"Copies of the threat notes sent to Pashia with the same misspellings that are on the mosque walls. Plus a direct connection with Professor Pashia—Barrett was one of his students. There are also his social media rants about immigrants, and guns, and taking back America."

"That's circumstantial," Coleman responded.

"We also think Robbie might be the biker who shows up on the security tapes," Charlie added.

"What biker?" Coleman asked James.

"The Mack team spotted a bicyclist on the security tapes the day of the bombing, and in an earlier tape stopping across the street from the mosque," James said.

"Why hadn't I heard about that?"

James began an explanation, but Charlie interrupted.

"You can't see the biker's face, but if we can prove Robbie owns a bike, that adds to the case against him. We're compiling a list of the bicycle shops in the area, and hoping the task force might have the personnel to call and ask if they've sold Barrett a bike."

"I'll find someone to make the calls," James said, writing a note. He looked up at the Commander. "Sorry about not passing on the info about the biker. It just came up."

"What else do you have?" Coleman asked.

"There's the bicycle clip Don found at the tree near the mosque," Charlie said. "Did you find any prints?"

James flashed another *I'm sorry* look at Coleman. "We found a few partial prints on the clip, and the discarded gum wrapper."

"Once you have Barrett in custody, you can compare the prints," Don said.

"Yep."

"What about Wyatt's attack tip?" Charlie asked. "What are you doing about that?"

"He claims he's a player in the upcoming attacks. He'll give us names and more details if he gets a deal."

"How is he involved. What's his role?" Don asked.

"Securing materials for the improvised explosive devices," the Commander answered.

"But then he claims he wasn't the demolition guy at the mosque?" Don asked incredulously.

"That's why we have our doubts about him," James said.

"You're not letting him go back into the group, are you?" Don asked.

"We're considering the deal proposal. I don't see how we can put one of our guys in, so late in the game," the Commander said. "We'd have people nearby to watch Wyatt."

Charlie, Don, and Judy folded their arms.

"I can see from your postures you don't agree," James said. "But the clock is ticking. If Wyatt's people don't hear from him soon, they'll suspect something's gone wrong."

"Did he tell you why he was sent to attack Charlie?" Don asked.

"He said higher-ups were aware she was asking questions about them, and they wanted to know what she knew."

"What if we made Robbie our informer?" Charlie asked out of left field.

"What?" the Commander said leaning toward the camera.

"He's young, maybe on the path to being self-radicalized, but as far as we know all he's done is write some badly spelled threats to his teacher, and spray-painted dirty words in a place of worship. He's pissed off that he doesn't have a better lot in life and he's blaming Black and Brown and Muslim people for his lack of success. But I'm guessing he's relatively new to all this domestic terrorism stuff. If he knows we're aware of what he's done, and that Wyatt is blaming him for the bomb that killed his teacher, it'll shake him. And if he understands these guys plan to really hurt some people in their next attack, maybe he'll think twice about what he's doing," Charlie said.

"Yeah. Plus, we can tell this Barrett guy his skinny white ass will go to prison if he doesn't help us," Don added.

James and the Commander locked eyes. Coleman shrugged.

"We'll give it some thought," James said. "Meanwhile, we'll work on getting a warrant for his arrest."

"Since we think we've got our man, that takes us off the case," Don announced.

"I'll set up a time to visit with the Pashias and let them know we've turned over our leads to you," Charlie said to James.

"We'd appreciate it if you didn't ID this guy to the family yet. We'd hate to have his name get out before we've had a chance to detain him."

"Of course," Charlie said. "By the way, any idea who's responsible for the task force leak?"

"That's something else we wanted to speak with you about," Coleman said glancing at James. "We're not so sure the leak is coming from inside."

"Where else would it be?" Don said.

"Have you spoken to anyone else about working on the case?" the Commander asked.

"Only the Pashia family," Charlie said. "Don also talked to a couple of guys he knows at DPD."

"We also met with the HR person at the college," Judy reminded Charlie.

"Right. I forgot about her."

"What's her name?" James asked.

"Roberta Suttles," Judy answered.

James and Coleman made notes on the pads in front of them.

"We only started our supplemental interviews yesterday," Charlie said. "We haven't discussed the case with many others."

"What about family members?" Coleman asked. "Did any of you speak to them about the mosque bombing?"

"What are you implying?" Charlie asked angrily.

"It's just a question."

"Why? Because you think the leak couldn't come from inside?"

"Ms. Mack, we know your, uh, domestic partner works at a suburban force. Someone suggested that maybe information was shared during bedroom talk. You know. It happens," Coleman said.

Don and Judy leaned toward Charlie in a show of support. Judy quickly wrote something on her notepad and pushed it in front of Charlie.

"Commander," Judy said in an icy tone. "There are people at DPD who don't care for Charlie. They believe she's made them look bad in the past."

". . . and people on your damn task force who resent that we've been asked to investigate this case," Don added.

"As I said, it's a question, not an accusation. Any of us might casually talk about a high-profile case. Sometimes people repeat things they've heard. It's not done to harm the investigation, but . . ."

James quickly insinuated himself into the conversation.

"We're not in a position to make any accusations, but we've handpicked the people on this task force. They're seasoned professionals and influential in their individual organizations. It would be very disappointing if the leak had come from any one of them. That being said, we're following a line of inquiry that we can't talk about right now."

They said good-byes with faked politeness, and Judy disconnected the Skype call. She got up to pour a cup of coffee.

"I'll take one, Novak," Don said.

Judy poured for Don and jiggled the carafe toward Charlie who shook her head.

"Better not. I'm wired enough."

"You were good, Mack. You kept your cool. We don't need to further alienate the DPD," Don said.

"Whatever."

Charlie looked down at Judy's note. *Who does that bitch think she is?* It had really helped. Charlie shifted into manager mode.

"Judy, please call Amina Pashia and set up a time for me to see her on Monday. I'm going to start the final case report today. Don, I know you don't want me out of sight during this case, but I need a serious workout tonight, and you don't have to babysit me."

"Okay, Mack. But just let one of us know when you get home."

Charlie spent a couple of days each month working to maintain her fourth-degree black belt skills in Taekwondo. She enjoyed both the physical and mental aspects of the practice and the discipline it required. She'd had her own martial arts school for several years, but now she enjoyed occasional teaching and mastering the techniques of other disciplines, like Aikido, which helped with balance, flexibility, and how to fall. Both disciplines made her a lethal threat in a physical fight.

Tonight, she'd taught a class of black belts striving to become instructors. In the last hour at the *dojang* she'd practiced one-step sparring with another black belt, executing attack and defense foot drills.

By the time she looked at her phone, she saw she'd missed a call from her mother's facility, and three from Mandy.

"What's wrong?" Charlie asked before Mandy could say anything.

"It's Ernestine. She's had a fall. She's in Henry Ford Hospital. I'm here now. Are you finished with your training?"

"I just finished. I can be there in twenty minutes. What happened?"

"I don't know exactly. Mr. Constantine called our home number. He's here with me in the waiting room. Ernestine apparently climbed a step stool and lost her balance. The good news is she was alert by the time the ambulance came."

"Did she break anything?"

"Mr. Constantine said the lady EMT didn't seem to think so. He rode in the ambulance with your mom. He said she asked for you all the way to the hospital."

Charlie had spent time in Henry Ford Hospital's emergency room not long ago, when her ex-husband had been shot by unknown assailants in one of the most uncomfortable cases of her PI career. Today she rushed through the sliding doors, anxious and out of breath. She spotted Mandy at a row of chairs against the wall. Next to her a gray-haired white man with a thin mustache and tortoise-shell glasses slumped in his seat. They both looked worried, and Mandy pointed in Charlie's direction when she saw her.

"How is she?" Charlie asked, walking into Mandy's embrace.

"We don't have any word yet. This is Mr. Constantine," Mandy said, introducing the man, who was now on his feet. He wore a white collared shirt and khaki pants. He and Charlie were about the same height.

"Gabriel. Gabe," he said extending his hand. "Charlene. I'm sorry to meet under these circumstances."

"Same here, and you can call me Charlie." She stared into his gray eyes. "Can you tell me what happened? How she fell?"

"It happened so fast. I ordered food for our brunch tomorrow. Salads, sandwiches, and chips. Some sausage and cheese. Ernie and I went shopping yesterday to get chorizo. She says that's one of your favorites."

Charlie nodded and tightened her squeeze on Mandy's hand.

"Anyway, Ernie wanted a platter for the sandwiches, and it's in that cupboard over the refrigerator." He spoke with his hands gesturing, and now they dropped. He picked up the story again but more slowly. "I told her I'd get the platter, but she insisted she could do it. She said she didn't want to be treated like an old lady." Again, his hands fell to his sides and his chin to his chest.

"She tells me that all the time," Charlie said.

"Well, she pulled out the stool she keeps in the corner and put it in front of the refrigerator, ready to climb. So I stood next to her to make sure she was steady. I think what she did was to grip the freezer door as she got to the top shelf, because the door swung open and she fell away from me. I was kind of able to catch hold of her, but she got her foot caught on the stool." Gabe took off his glasses and wiped at his eyes. "If I'd been standing on the other side, I might have caught her, I think."

"The good thing is she didn't hit her head," Mandy added.

"That's right," he said. "If she'd fallen all the way, she'd have hit her head on the counter. She was in pain, and she twisted her left ankle, so I didn't try to move her. I just called the EMTs. They were there in fifteen minutes. Gloria from the front desk came up with them and she said she was going to call you, Charlie, but I thought somebody should ride to the hospital with her."

"I'm grateful you did."

The emergency room was on full Friday-evening boogie. Those bleeding were given top priority and were whisked through the inner doors to examining rooms. Police officers came in and out, sometimes with handcuffed prisoners. The front desk nurses were both intake and triage experts. There was a medium-level din of noise in the room, which, once you adjusted to the decibels, you could just ignore.

Charlie and Gabe took the time together to talk a bit about themselves, and a lot about Ernestine. He was a widower of almost six years, with two adult children living on the West Coast. He'd worked in corporate communications in the Upper Peninsula for twenty years before retiring earlier in the year.

"I love the U.P.," Charlie said. "I don't get to visit very often. I also ran a PR firm for many years here in Detroit."

"Yes, your mother told me. I'm sure we were at some of the same conferences over the years."

When the inner doors opened, all eyes turned toward the swooshing sound. This time it was an ER doctor pushing Ernestine in a wheelchair. Charlie, Mandy and Gabe ran to her.

"Are you all right, Mom?"

"Yes. Yes. Fine. I have a sprained ankle. Dr. Markle wrapped it nice and tight. It doesn't even hurt anymore."

"I also gave her a painkiller," the doctor said, handing Charlie the discharge papers. "When it wears off, she'll have some discomfort, but there's a prescription there." The doctor put both hands on Ernestine's shoulders. "And Mrs. Mack is to stay off that ankle for a week."

The front desk had several wheelchairs, and Charlie signed one out for the rest of the week. Then a hospital attendant helped lift Ernestine into the front seat of Mandy's sedan. Gabe got into the backseat. Charlie followed behind in her Corvette. When they got Ernestine into the apartment, Charlie and Gabe stayed with her while Mandy went off to get the prescription filled.

After Ernestine had a cup of tea and two cookies in front of her, Gabriel announced he was leaving. "I hope we can still do brunch tomorrow. I can take care of all the preparations. If Ernie is feeling up to it."

"Oh, I'll feel just fine," Ernestine said cheerily. "I'm sorry to put everybody to so much trouble."

"It was no trouble at all." Gabe patted Ernestine's shoulder.

"I'll call you first thing in the morning to see if you need anything." He waved his good-bye.

Charlie turned to her mother. She decided she wouldn't fuss at her about climbing on the footstool. They'd already argued about that before. Ernestine looked at Charlie over the rim of her cup. She looked tired, but pretty, wearing small gold earrings and a dark turtleneck.

"I think it's better to postpone tomorrow's brunch. You should rest that ankle like the doctor said."

"All right, Charlene. I'll call Gabe to let him know. Maybe we can do next weekend."

Charlie nodded. "It's a good thing he was here."

"He's nice, isn't he?"

"Yes, he seems to be," Charlie responded. "Oh, and what's this Ernie business?"

Chapter 12

For what Charlie knew would be the last time, she parked in the Pashias' driveway. Amina opened the door, and escorted her to the family room where her mother was already waiting.

"You have news for us, Ms. Mack?" Jawaria asked.

"I do. We've found the young man responsible for the threatening notes sent to your husband. We also have evidence that he was at the mosque the night your husband died."

Amina held her mother's hand, and they sat quietly for nearly a minute. Mrs. Pashia kept her eyes closed. When she opened them, they were wet, but she remained stoic.

"You have evidence?"

"We've provided the evidence to the hate crimes task force . . ."

"And to Mr. James Saleh?" Jawaria asked.

"Yes. Directly to him. Amina, we believe it's one of the students who attended your father's study sessions."

"Do you have a photo?"

"Yes. I can show you a photo, though I can't provide you his name. The FBI plans to arrest him soon."

"What is the delay?" Amina asked.

"They must get a properly signed warrant and organize a plan to arrest him. He didn't act alone and is probably not the man who actually planted the bombs. But he was there with the bomber and was the person who defaced the prayer room."

"May I see the photo?"

Charlie handed Amina copies of the two photos Judy had retrieved from Barrett's social media. She looked carefully at the pictures, and her mother leaned over to see them.

Amina nodded. "Yes, he is one of the students who came often to our home."

"He's only a boy," Jawaria said. "Not yet able to grow a beard."

Charlie placed her report on the table in front of Jawaria. Amina stood, and Charlie began to extend her hand, but lowered it when she remembered it wasn't the proper thing to do. Amina offered a handshake. "Thank you very much, Ms. Mack."

"How was the family?" Judy asked.

"They were sad, but grateful. I met with Amina and her mother. I showed them Barrett's picture. Amina recognized him from her father's study group. Mrs. Pashia was surprised at how young he looked."

"Yeah. He's just a kid," Judy said. "Don called. I told him you were still with the Pashias. He was in James's office and they're both coming over."

"Fine."

"You want me to get the invoice together to send to Amina?"

"Yes. She's expecting it. But have Tamela do it. That's not your job anymore," Charlie said taking a seat in Judy's side chair.

Judy had gotten to understand Charlie's body language, and knew she was unsettled. "What's the matter? We identified the people responsible for Mr. Pashia's death. That's what the family wanted."

"I know. But it's a matter of now I know too much," Charlie said leaning back in the chair. "There's an evil energy fueling these acts, and frankly it frightens me."

"Do you still believe these are a cover-up for identity thefts?"

"Stealing personal information has something to do with it. I'm sure of that, but there's something else going on that's more sinister. Did you finish the FBI report?"

"Uh huh. It's scary. The most startling part to me is how these groups operate in the open," Judy said. "I guess I thought they would all be secret, you know? But they have websites and membership dues like they're the Boy Scouts or something."

Charlie nodded. "That's what makes it so insidious. They parade around relying on their constitutional rights to organize, carry guns, and spew their hate speech."

Don and James arrived with lunch—fish sandwiches and cole slaw from Scotty Simpson's. Charlie dug out soft drinks from the mini-fridge, and Judy retrieved paper plates and napkins as Don and James passed around fries, fish sandwiches and tartar sauces. Tamela came in for her meal and returned to her desk.

"I've been told this is the way the Mack team rolls when a case gets intense," James said.

"Yes. But our case just got closed," Charlie said, opening a packet of ketchup. "I talked to Mrs. Pashia and her daughter this morning and told them we'd handed everything over to you."

"Well, I want to discuss that, but let's eat and talk."

After a couple of bites of the deep-fried cod sandwich, Charlie spoke up. "What do you want to talk about?" she asked, wiping at runaway tartar sauce.

"We declined Wyatt's request for a deal," James said.

"As you should."

"We think he's blowing smoke up our butts about being an insider with the Turks, but the internet chatter confirms there's a plan for another attack on a mosque or church. Something big. We also arrested Robbie Barrett early this morning. We raided his mother's house. He lived in the attic behind a padlocked door. We took two desktop computers, a series of notebooks, two weapons, and a huge stash of videotapes."

"Drugs?" Don asked.

"Nope. The kid doesn't even smoke cigarettes, although we confiscated a drawerful of chewing gum with the kind of wrapper you found near the mosque."

"Did he resist arrest?" Charlie asked.

"He was too scared for that. His mother was screaming and crying, and after we put Robbie in handcuffs, I thought he was going to bawl, too. His little brother was the tough guy. He told my agents where to go when they tried to ask him questions."

"I feel sorry for Robbie," Judy said.

"You would, Novak. The kid's a damn menace to society. Already involved in one murder, and probably on the road to being a neo-Nazi," Don said.

"What happens to him now?" Charlie asked.

"He's being interrogated. My guys have been at it for six hours. We'll see how much he knows about the leaders of this group. See if he'll confess to the mosque bombing, and if he'll roll over on Frank Wyatt. So far, all he's confessed to is writing the threats to Mr. Pashia, but the lab techs have already confirmed the bike clip you found near the mosque belongs to him."

"He'll be charged with conspiracy, breaking and entering, and criminal harassment for the threatening notes, right?" Charlie asked.

"Second-degree murder, too. Possibly first-degree since Pashia's death occurred as a result of arson."

"That'll be a stretch," Charlie said, using her lawyer's knowledge.

"Look, Charlie. I want you and Don and Judy to stay on this case. We want you on the task force."

"We? I'm sure Commander Coleman didn't vote for that."

"She did, actually. She read your writeup on the evidence against Robbie. She was impressed with the Mack team's work and analysis."

Charlie wanted to roll her eyes as a dismissal of what Coleman said or thought. Instead, she squinted her skepticism.

"Coleman realizes she could have done a better job with the

question about the leak," James said. "Speaking of which, we have a plan to reveal the leaker."

"Great," Charlie said. "But I'm not sure about us joining the task force. We could just continue our informal relationship. What's the benefit?"

"Nimbleness. We still have a lot of bureaucracy. It's to be expected in an interagency operation. There will be tasks that a PI firm can do easier and faster. Plus, we're working with communities that have an ingrained distrust of law enforcement, not to mention federal law enforcement." James opened his folder and put a sheet on top. "I'm prepared to give you a persuasive argument about how important it is to sniff out these guys, and put metro residents at ease about our efforts to stop these attacks."

"That's not necessary. We know the importance of the work. We've all read your report now. It's alarming to say the least."

Charlie looked at her two partners. "Let's see where we stand about joining the task force. Don? What's your vote?"

"I vote yes if it's not for more than a couple of weeks, because we ain't getting paid."

"I vote yes, too," Judy said. "We can't let these people infiltrate our communities and recruit our sons. They're no better than these violent Islamic groups—like Al Qaeda."

"That's three yesses, James," Charlie said. "So I guess you have us for the next two weeks."

"Well, that's great. Fine," James said, smiling. "Thank you."

"We'll want to sit in on all the major meetings," Don said. "And have access to the case files."

"Of course."

"We have other cases," Charlie said. "There may be times when all three of us can't be at every meeting, but I want Judy to get as much exposure to strategy sessions as possible. She's already very good at technology, but I'd also want her to have a chance to see what your lab guys do."

"That's not a problem."

"What's next?" Charlie asked.

"The leak. We've already seen internet discussion about Wyatt's arrest, which further a firms an inside leak. Commander Coleman and I have been authorized to monitor the email of every single member of the task force, and we're going to push some disinformation into our next meeting to see where it leads."

"Maybe you should wait to announce that we're coming onto the task force until after you determine the leak," Charlie said. "In fact, why not announce that we're officially *off* the Pashia case? Instead of disinformation, give them a small piece of truth."

"Not a bad idea," Don agreed.

"Okay, we'll go with that right away. Charlie, I was wondering if you would sit in on the interrogation with Barrett. The guys downtown have texted that they're getting nowhere. I thought a woman might bring a different response from him."

"From the posts I've seen on his Facebook page, I don't think a Black woman asking him questions is going to loosen his lips. What about Judy? She's got kids almost his age, and she already feels some empathy toward him."

James looked skeptical. "No offense, Judy, but I think this requires someone with a lot more experience . . ."

Charlie interrupted. "I've seen Judy get people to open up over the phone. In person, she's hard to resist. Look at her. She looks like somebody's mom—trusting, kind, someone ready to bring you warm milk."

"Uh, thank you, I think," Judy said.

"Those were definitely compliments," Charlie said. "We all bring different perspectives and personal skill sets to this work. That's what makes us strong."

"Are you up for it, Judy?" James asked.

"I'm up for it."

Robbie had been in police custody for fifteen hours. He was exhausted, hungry, scared as hell, and his legs were cramping. He'd refused any food or drink and was determined to fight back against what he believed to be government oppression. Officers had been moving in and out of the interrogation room every hour or two, so he barely moved when he heard the door open again.

"FBI agent James Saleh and investigator Judy Novak initiating interrogation of Robert Christopher Barrett at fourteen hundred hours on May 19, 2009."

Robbie lifted his head from his outstretched arm. He smelled warm cocoa and the faint scent of Judy's citrusy cologne. He opened his eyes to look at the woman in front of him and the dark-skinned FBI agent.

"I brought you some hot chocolate," Judy said, pushing a cup toward him. "I bought myself a cup, too."

Robbie squinted at Judy. He looked at her small gold earrings, the light blue blouse under her black jacket, and her short hair. She wore a light pinkish lipstick. His brother's social worker wore lipstick like that. He stared at the cup of chocolate, desperately wanting it although he didn't want to give the Feds an edge on him. Robbie turned his attention to James. *How could he be an FBI agent? This guy looks like one of those towel heads.*

Judy sipped her hot chocolate slowly. She picked up her napkin and dabbed at the thin line of brown foam on her lip. She knew Robbie was watching. They all sat quietly for a few minutes, with James writing notes on his legal pad and Judy savoring the cocoa. After Robbie picked up the hot chocolate, James waited another thirty seconds to begin the interrogation.

"Barrett, we know you're not responsible for the explosion at the mosque on February 12th when Mr. Hassan Pashia was killed."

James and Judy both noticed Robbie's shoulders relax a bit. He took another sip of hot chocolate, then resumed his defiant stare.

"But we can also prove you were in and around the mosque on more than one occasion. Robbie, do you own a Riverside Decathlon bike?"

"What about it?" His voice was surly.

"We have security film of you on your bike at the mosque the night of the bombing."

"I didn't bomb anything."

"We know," Judy said.

He turned again to Judy. She noticed his soft hands with long fingers. A start of peach fuzz had gathered at his chin, but was absent from his lip or jawline. His stringy hair hung in clumps around his ears. *What a babyface with those close-set, intelligent eyes.* She could tell he was curious about her. She would use his curiosity to get him to drop his defiance.

"My son has a touring bike," Judy said nonchalantly. "He takes it on road trips where he camps overnight. I think he saved for over a year to buy that bike."

"I couldn't afford one until I got my new job," Robbie said, looking down at the table.

"Robbie, did you know Frank Wyatt said *you* planted the bomb at the mosque?" Judy asked.

"Frank's a fucking alcoholic liar."

Judy winced at the profanity. Robbie saw it and dipped his head, but his anger spewed again.

"Sorry, but he's an asshole. He armed that bomb, and he didn't know shit about what he was doing."

"You had nothing to do with buying components or building the bomb?" James asked.

Robbie glared at James. "I'm not talking to you, mongrel. The FBI must be getting desperate if they hired someone like you."

James smiled. "You don't have to talk to me. I can send the white guys back in here, but believe me, they really want to nail your ass for this bombing. They *believe* Wyatt, and want to put you in a prison cell for the rest of your life."

Robbie pushed back in his chair, folded his arms, and glared at James and Judy. He wasn't sure if he should scream, curse, or cry so he bit down on his lip and looked away.

"I don't think you killed anyone, Robbie," Judy said. "I think you're mad about not knowing what your future looks like. My kids are going through the same things. College is expensive, and jobs are hard to find. They want to get their own places but can't afford it. Navigating work and life and relationships is really confusing."

Robbie peeked up at Judy, then dropped his head again. Judy signaled to James that they should wait. They did. Almost three minutes in silence. Judy finished her hot chocolate. James made notes and checked his phone.

"Are you done with me?" Robbie finally asked.

James looked at him and smiled. "Oh, we've only just begun. If it were up to the FBI, you'd be on your way to Gitmo. This lady here thinks we need to give you a second chance."

Robbie shifted his glance between the two, finally landing on Judy. "What kind of investigator are you? Like for social services? Child Protective Services?"

"No. I'm with a private investigation firm. I'm here because I want to try to understand why you're involved with Stormfront, and the White Turks." Robbie's eyes grew wide at the mention of the names.

"Yes, we know about those groups," James explained. "We've confiscated your computers. We know all about you, and your communications with these groups."

"Fascists." Robbie spit out the word.

"No. Just smarter than these homegrown terrorist guys. What they're doing is not the way to show dissatisfaction with the government. That's not how you make things better," James said.

"America would be a whole lot better without people like you," Robbie snarled.

"Help me to understand, Robbie," Judy said. "What makes these people and their philosophy so appealing to you? What has made you go this far?"

Judy and James arrived back at the Mack agency after more than four hours of questioning Robbie. He had, finally, admitted to his role in the mosque attack.

"It's what we expected. He's new to the White Turks, and the mosque attack was his initiation. He did the spray-painting, but Frank Wyatt placed the bomb. He says he's also being seriously courted by other groups."

Charlie and Don waited for more information.

"Judy was magnificent," James said. "We'd worked out a couple of techniques like just sitting quietly, and me being the bad cop, but the rest was Judy's improvisation. She insisted we stop for hot chocolate, for instance. The boy started to loosen up the moment he smelled the cocoa."

"It always worked when I had tough talks with my boys," Judy said, smiling.

"I told you," Charlie said to James. "Did he agree to help in the investigation?"

"I think he will. It took some talking to convince him that these groups he's so fond of are hell-bent on starting a global race war that could cause the deaths of thousands of innocent people."

"That can't be news to him," Don said. "He must know that based on the stuff he's posted on social media."

"He knows. He's even said worse in his personal correspondence. We're still going through his videos, notebooks, and computer files. He's had hundreds of interactions with these groups, but there's a difference in talking about removing people, and finally realizing that means *murdering* people. Judy sensed right away he's not so far gone that he's lost his humanity."

"I told him about something I read in the FBI report," Judy said, "that one of these fringe groups in Europe had planned an attack that killed more than a hundred students. I reminded him that's probably more students than were in his high school graduating class. That seemed to get to him."

"You also reminded him of the many kindnesses Hassan Pashia had shown him. Robbie was only focused on the grades he received, not the fact that Pashia had spent dozens of hours with him one-on-one and in the study group."

"He tried not to let on, but he's really shook up about Pashia's death," Judy said.

"The long and the short of it is, after a good meal, he'll be tucked away for the night under special security, and we'll talk to him again in the morning," James said. "He did ask for an attorney before we left, and we've asked the district court to appoint one for him."

"How has Commander Coleman reacted to us coming onto the task force?" Charlie asked.

"Honestly? She has mixed feelings. She knows our investigation has been stuck for weeks and it's only been since your involvement that we've had a breakthrough. At the same time, professional pride keeps her from wholeheartedly endorsing the need for help."

"Like every cop I've ever known," Charlie said, and then pointed to Don. "Including that one."

"It doesn't help that we've now discovered the leak came from DPD," James said.

"You don't say," Charlie said gleefully.

"It was one of Coleman's officers. Someone who helps with her correspondence and schedule, and has access to the Commander's email. As soon as we'd announced that you guys were now backing off the Pashia case, this woman emailed someone with that information."

"Who did she contact? And why?"

"We're still trying to figure that out. She told a guy who hasn't left much of a footprint. He hasn't been on our radar, but he is now."

"What's happened to the officer?" Judy asked.

"Furloughed with pay, pending investigation."

"That's the police union process kicking in," Don announced.

"So now we're officially on the task force?" Charlie asked.

"You are, and I hope you'll like this bit of news. I've gotten an okay to pay each of you a per diem as consultants. It's not a lot, but at least it'll take care of your expenses, and some of your time."

"That's really appreciated," Judy said.

"It's the least I can do," James said, standing. "I'm out of here. It's been a long day. I have people talking to Robbie and his lawyer in the morning, and there's a task force meeting tomorrow at noon. I'll see you all there."

Charlie, Don, and Judy spent fifteen minutes with Tamela, giving her assignments for the rest of the week, and for the first time she received a key to the door and the passcode for the alarm. She was delighted.

They all departed the office together. Tamela exited the elevator at the lobby level, and the Mack partners continued to the P1 parking level. They said their good-byes and headed to their cars. Charlie was almost at the Corvette when she heard a shot, then a second one. She instinctively ducked behind a column.

The sound of the shots ricocheted through the garage together until they were joined by a third noise. A scream. Judy's scream. Charlie swiveled her head from side to side in search of the sound, then, giving up, grabbed her handgun from the glove box.

She started out in a running crouch in the direction of Judy's car, and within seconds Don was beside her.

"That sounded like a .38."

"Judy," Charlie hollered. "Judy!!"

Don and Charlie bolted upright when they heard tires screeching near the exit ramp. "Get to Judy," Don ordered and took off running. Charlie wasn't exactly sure where Judy had parked, and there were still dozens of cars in the garage. She finally heard a whimpering sound and as she creeped past a van, she saw Judy cowering on the ground at her driver's side tire. She was holding her bag tightly against her chest. Her eyes were closed. Charlie squatted in front of her, fearing the worst.

"Have you been shot?"

Judy's eyes opened slowly. Her stare was filled with terror. She didn't answer or move.

"Have you been shot? Are you hurt?"

Finally Judy blinked and her eyes shifted.

"Oh Charlie. Oh Charlie."

Charlie yanked at Judy's purse. First she resisted, then finally let go. Charlie checked Judy's chest and arms and neck. She felt behind her back, and when she pulled her hand out, she was relieved not to see blood.

"I think you're okay."

"Somebody shot at me. I felt the bullet zip past my cheek. I dropped to the ground, and I think another one just missed my head. I think I hurt my knee," Judy's words poured out, mixed with tears, and Charlie held her friend in a tight embrace.

"Mack, where are you?" Don's concerned voice rang out.

"I don't want him to see me this way," Judy said, wiping at her eyes." I'm all right. Please help me up," Judy said, grasping Charlie's shoulders.

"Okay, but let me look at your knee."

"Charlie, where are you?" Don shouted.

"Over here, Don, near the column marked seven."

Judy was on her feet, shaking a bit but not crying when Don emerged from between cars. He looked at both of them and put his gun in the shoulder holster.

"What happened?"

"Somebody took a couple of shots at Judy."

"That somebody tore away in a green Jeep. I saw it turning the corner at Griswold, but it was too far away to see the license plate. The asshole did lose a wheel cap, though, when he drove over the curb," Don said, waving the metal cover. He stopped talking to take a good look at Judy. "Are you all right, Novak? You didn't get nicked, did you?"

"Nope. I just skinned my knee when I dived to the cement."

"Good girl."

Charlie and Judy shared a look. He started picking up Judy's things from the ground. Two bags, her scarf, and car keys.

"Did you call the police, Mack? Or James?"

"Not yet. Why don't you do that. I'll help Judy get her stuff in the car."

"Judy, which way were the bullets fired?"

Judy pointed over her shoulder.

"Shit. Novak, you could have been hit. I've had it with these assholes," Don said. "They want a war, they got a war." Don lumbered away cursing under his breath.

Charlie sat Judy in the passenger seat. She had understated her injury. It was more than a little skin off the knee. It was a nasty abrasion.

"I think you're going to need antiseptic and a bandage."

"I have both of those in the back," Judy said.

"You do?"

"I still have two teenagers at home, and I'm always prepared," Judy said, sounding like her old self.

"Judy, I feel awful about this," Charlie said. "I thought with the leak discovered we'd no longer be a target. I guess I was wrong."

Law enforcement arrived at the parking garage with noise and fury. Seven police cars, plus an ambulance, a forensics team, and three FBI units. Based on Judy's details—and with Don's assistance—they found two bullets. Shell casings were found not far from the elevator. The medical technicians examined Judy's knees, but agreed her bandage job was as good as they could have done. They did say she might have some pain in her wrist where she caught her fall. DPD interviewed Charlie, Don, and Judy. FBI agents interviewed them again. When the late-arriving task force members showed up with the same questions, Don had had it.

"I'm going home, Mack. It's damn near nine o'clock."

"I know, Don. Judy, you should go home too. You want me to drive you?"

"No. I'll be fine. I know Mandy's called twice."

"I'll have a car escort Judy home," James said from behind them. He'd been conversing with the various teams and generally keeping the work moving. He'd made eye contact with Charlie several times, and now they stood together and watched Don, Judy, and her escort exit the parking garage.

"What the hell happened here, James?" Charlie asked. "I thought the leak was plugged."

"It is. But the Turks already knew about the Mack team. Maybe this is retaliation for Wyatt's arrest."

"Why go after Judy? Is it possible this rogue communications officer saw her today during the Robbie interrogation?"

James paused to think. "It's possible. The officer was still around this morning for a few hours. Maybe she hadn't left the precinct before Judy arrived. Damn, I'm horrified this happened."

"We are too, and now you're going to have to pry Don away from this case. He's worked up. I've never seen him move so fast as when he pursued that car up the ramp on foot. He pretends to give Judy a hard time, and the two of them irritate the hell out of each other, but he'd kill anyone who hurt her."

"He'd kill anybody who hurt you, too. I've seen that for myself," James reminded Charlie.

It wasn't anything she'd ever forget. When her missing person case collided with the Bureau's human trafficking investigation, the leader's henchman had attacked Charlie. When Don caught up with the guy, he made the man pay for it.

"Yeah. I think we all do as much as we can to protect each other."

"That's why you're a great team," James said. "Come on. I'll walk you to your car."

Charlie was famished, but opted to join Mandy for Hamm's late walk before heating up her dinner.

"Another long day for you," Mandy said as they walked Hamm down the driveway and out to their street.

"And they won't get much shorter. We officially joined the task force today. By the way, that information is no longer embargoed. They found the leak."

"Within the task force?"

"On the Commander's staff."

"Ouch. That must have felt like vindication."

"Yes and no. James believes the cop responsible for the leak might have seen Judy arrive for the kid's interrogation, and that's what made her a target today."

"How *is* she?"

"In shock. She got bumped around. I told her to take the day off tomorrow, but she won't. She doesn't want to miss the task force meeting."

"Poor Judy. She's always said she didn't want to be involved in any of the violence that comes with being a PI."

"None of us had any idea we'd be dodging bullets on this case."

"You're dealing with people who think they're divinely empowered to keep the world the way they want it to be. These guys are crazy, honey," Mandy said.

"I know. Until we finish this case, keep up your guard around the house and at work."

"I will. And you, too. Maybe we should only walk Hamm when we can do it together."

Charlie nodded. "Sorry, buddy," she said, rubbing Hamm's whiskers. "For a while you'll have to do most of your business in the backyard."

Chapter 13

They'd already been at it for an hour and Don was starting to fidget. He sat across the FBI conference table from Charlie and Judy. Oakland Chief of Police John Rappon was reminding task force members of the funds spent to date on their efforts. Apparently his coffers, along with the FBI's and DPD's, were footing the bulk of the costs.

Don rose to get more doughnuts and refill his coffee cup. Every person in the meeting watched his trek, and his move inspired a few others to line up behind him for the spread of pastries. Rappon paused for a minute to count the defectors, then continued.

Charlie was used to long meetings—some with PI clients, and before that with the clients in her public relations business. But the bulk of her experience with managing meeting fatigue came from being the daughter of a single mom who was also a high school principal. She'd sat through hours of evening school assemblies, PTA meetings, and school board convenings. Charlie's technique was to doodle, which to all but those sitting near her looked like note taking.

Commander Coleman had begun the meeting, announcing the attack the night before against the Mack team in the garage of their office building. Those who hadn't already heard gasped in outrage and anger. The questions that followed took up twenty minutes before Coleman could finally announce that Wayne

County prosecutors had cut a deal with Robbie Barrett and his attorney.

James took the lead in reporting the other new business. He described efforts underway to identify the Stormfront group operating in southeastern Michigan, the case being built around Frank Wyatt in the death of Hassan Pashia, and their strategy to use Robbie as an informer against the White Turks. Barrett would be released from custody tomorrow, and FBI agents would be his handlers. Gaining Robbie's cooperation was a win for the task force, and Coleman graciously named the Mack team as pivotal to the effort. The announcement sparked a brief smattering of applause. Don raised his coffee in acknowledgment, with chocolate from his last doughnut clinging to his lip. Judy pointed to the corner of her mouth. Ignoring the napkin in front of him, Don dabbed his mouth with his hand.

Not everyone thought the Stormfront organization merited its own investigation, believing the focus of the task force should remain on the credible threat of an attack on another place of worship.

"Based on our threat assessment, Stormfront is a high priority. They're a much more violent group, and much better funded and organized," one of the FBI agents said. "They're based in Norway, but they have chapters in dozens of countries and across the United States. The Turks are primarily a loosely-knit group of disgruntled weekend warriors. They should be easy to infiltrate."

"Plus, this Stormfront group is interested in Robbie," Charlie said. "If he's reinstated in the Turks, it will make him more appealing to the larger group, and that can only help the task force in the long run."

James put the issue to rest when he noted that the FBI could walk and chew gum at the same time, and agreed the Bureau would pay for the Stormfront elements of the investigation. The most spirited debate occurred around Robbie's efficacy as an informer.

"I've read his dossier and the statements he's made," Rappon said. "I don't think the kid has enough stature within the group to be helpful."

Several members agreed and suggested reconsidering a deal with Wyatt.

"Wyatt can't be trusted," Coleman said. "He's already given us several false statements. He'd turn on us or run as soon as he saw the opportunity."

"And Barrett won't?" Captain Kerner of the Dearborn police asked.

James allowed everyone time to express their views, then made his own case for Robbie's involvement. He surprised Judy by asking her to present her views.

"Well," Judy began tentatively, "on the question of whether Robbie would run, he might want to, but he doesn't really have any place to go. He lives at home with his mother and brother. He doesn't own a car, and he's still on probation on a new job. He's very smart, and really not a bad kid. He just wants to belong to something to build up his ego, and it's easy for him to be a member of these groups that lurk on the internet. If he knew how, he'd probably just join a gang."

Judy looked down at Charlie's doodling. She'd written *go, Judy, go*.

"Anyway," Judy continued. "It doesn't take much to see that Robbie is broken up over his teacher's death."

"Even though he wrote the teacher those death threats?" Kerner challenged.

"Yes. It was a passive-aggressive reaction, in my opinion," Judy responded. "He doesn't really want to hurt anybody although he talks like he could. With enough exposure to these groups and the hate and violence they promote, he might be able to be a terrorist. Right now, he's merely a nerdy boy who's a whiz at computer technology and doesn't know what to do to make his life better."

"In other words, we hope we can turn him around and make him part of *our* gang," James said.

They took a stretch break before reconvening into working

teams. One would focus on the plans for thwarting another church or mosque attack; the other would map out a strategy to effectively re-embed Robbie within the Turks. Don would sit in on the tactical group, and Judy and James would discuss Robbie's assignments. Coleman and Charlie would float between the two rooms.

"I was so proud of you in there," Charlie said to Judy.

"Yeah, Novak, good job, and you didn't even whine about being shot at."

"I got my tough-guy pointers from you, Don."

Don gave a thumbs-up, and moved toward the food table to grab another doughnut and an apple. He began a chat with John Rappon. Charlie pulled Judy aside.

"How are you doing after last night?"

"Okay, I guess. Still shaken up a bit. I have bruises on my legs, and my wrists are sore. I didn't realize it last night, but I must have bumped my head on the car because I have a knot," she said, touching the back of her head.

Charlie was flanked by Judy and Coleman as Captain Kerner, leading the discussion on embedding Robbie, went on and on about the obstacles. He spoke about Robbie's youth and inexperience and, in contrast, what he considered the sophistication of the White Turks. He waxed on about his department's efforts to infiltrate the hate groups in Dearborn. That's why he thought an older, more seasoned man was needed for the job.

Charlie had finished a salad and, while waiting for Kerner to run out of steam on the defense of his department, she began to doodle. She'd written stream-of-consciousness words and phrases and geometric shapes for several minutes when she felt Coleman nudge her. Charlie looked up to see Coleman smiling and pointing to Charlie's note pad where she'd written the word *mansplaining* and circled it several times.

"With all due respect," Coleman said, speaking up. "You're

overstating the sophistication of the Turks. In our interrogations of Robbie and Frank Wyatt, they both admitted the mosque explosion was simply to have enough combustion to start a fire in the office. Clearly someone, and we believe it was Wyatt, didn't have the demolition skills necessary for that job."

Kerner didn't have much more to say after that, and the ideas started flowing.

Robbie would be reintroduced to the Turks as having been arrested and released by the Feds after Frank tried to implicate him in the mosque bombing. The cover story would be that Robbie didn't talk, the Feds had no proof of his involvement, and they let him walk. He would pretend the arrest had further hardened him against big government and recommitted him to the cause of the group. The Feds would let it leak that Wyatt had been shipped off to Guantanamo detention center.

It seemed a good plan, and Judy would help James prepare the boy for the ruse. Robbie would have a team of four FBI handlers keeping an eye on him. His phone, email, and internet searches would be monitored in the unlikely event Robbie might go rogue.

In the other meeting, six members of the task force were building scenarios for the dramatic terror event Frank Wyatt had warned about.

"You said he wasn't truthful," Rappon said to James. "Why do you trust that *this* information is credible?"

"Because we've confirmed it through internet chatter, and we're monitoring both Wyatt's and Robbie's phones. There's something big afoot, and now that Wyatt is out of the picture, the Turks are looking for another explosives man."

"Maybe that provides an opening for us," Don said. "Can you bring another guy inside the group? In addition to Robbie? Somebody who has experience with explosives?"

"I think they'd be suspicious of an outsider. With a big job coming up they'd want to keep it in the family."

"Can we bring Robbie up to speed on explosives?" Rappon asked.

"No," Don said not waiting for James.

"He knows technology."

"Not *that* kind of technology. I don't care how many 'how to make a bomb' videos he's watched, you also have to have the nerve. Just seeing Robbie's rants on social media tells me he doesn't have the temperament for explosives work."

"I agree with Don," James said. "We need to put someone in who has the right personality and look. Someone who can fit in quickly. We can build a profile and create the documents and background. So, I think it's got to be one of my guys."

"I can do it," Agent Riley said, raising his hand.

Every eye turned to him. He was six-foot-three, broad-shouldered with a square jaw and penetrating dark eyes. No one responded for ten seconds. Don couldn't stand it.

"Are you kidding? You look like Dick Tracy," Don bellowed. "There's no way you could pull it off."

There was a collective exhale after Don, in his own way, said what everyone around the table was thinking. The agent stared at Don, then at James, and finally, defeated, sat back in his chair.

They were still debating the infiltration strategy when the other group joined the room's discussion.

"We're still hashing out a plausible plan to get Robbie some backup in the Turks," James said, "and we're running with the idea of finding someone with demolition know-how who can pose as a replacement for Wyatt."

"That's a good idea," Kerner said. "I've been telling this group that Robbie's not going to cut it as an informer."

"It's a good idea for him to have some backup," James said.

"What's the plan so far?" Kerner asked.

"I want an agent to take the role. We don't think Agent Riley, here, could pass for the kind of person the group would welcome with open arms," James said diplomatically. "He doesn't look the part."

Charlie had noted Riley's good looks and physique earlier in the day. The other agent in the room was a woman, Agent Samuelson, and that left her out.

"So, no women, no Jews, or any other, uh, people of color," Kerner said. "Nobody who looks like a fed. Where does that leave us? I can think of a couple of guys in my department who fit the bill, but they might be recognized if the Turks have targeted a mosque in Dearborn or Dearborn Heights."

"What about me?" Don asked.

"What?" Charlie said, loudly, staring across the room at Don.

The room was quiet again, and everyone stared at Don. Just before it became really awkward, Don began making his case.

"I look the part. A middle-aged white guy with a bit of weight around the middle. I don't look like I work out every day. I did explosives in the Marines."

"But, people always take you for the police, Don," Judy said. "It happens all the time."

"Well, I'll say I'm an ex-cop which is true. I understand there are a lot of ex-military and ex-cops in these groups."

"That's what the data says," James agreed.

Commander Coleman spoke up next. "You and Ms. Mack have been involved in a few high-profile cases," she said. "You might be recognized."

Don shook his head. "I doubt it. Mack is always the spokesperson. I'm very rarely within camera view or make the newspapers."

"Well, I don't like it," John Rappon said. "A civilian taking this kind of risk just doesn't sit well with me."

"Oh, come on, John. You know me. Ex-marine, former Detroit police officer, former Homeland Security agent. I'm not exactly anybody's civilian."

Charlie stared at Don while the conversation continued. He was as courageous a man as she'd ever met, but she was surprised he'd volunteer for work like this. This assignment would take him away from home for a week, maybe two. Undercover work was hard and perilous. She'd done it a few times, and you could never let down your guard. One mistake with these self-made, far-right militia groups could cost Don his life. Sophisticated or not, these guys were serious about disrupting society, and now they wanted to make themselves known with a single act of terrorism.

Half the task force was against using Don. The arguments included objections to using non-law enforcement personnel, and Don's lack of bomb-making experience. Those in favor of the idea—and Charlie, oddly, was being persuaded—had solid reasons for recommending Don. First, he was well known and trusted by the law enforcement community in the region. His Homeland Security background would be useful in the job. He'd had some experience with explosives while in the Marines. And, finally, he really did look the part.

"What do you think, James?" Charlie asked.

"I'm not sure."

"What would this kind of assignment entail?" Judy wanted to know.

"Well, let's think it through," James said. "We'd need to set up a new identity for Don that keeps as many factual things as possible—like his military background and police experience. We'd give him a new surname, new driver's license, identity cards, credit cards. All of that is easy to do."

"Mr. Rutkowski would have to live away from home while he was undercover," Commander Coleman said.

"Yes, that's right. We can put him in one of our safe houses."

"I'd need a refresher on explosives, detonation techniques, and chemicals, I guess," Don said.

James nodded. "Explosives have changed a lot since your Marine training. Technology has seen to that. We'll show you enough that you can fake it. People don't really want to be around explosives, so I don't think you'll have to assemble a bomb in front of these guys. We can make it look like you know what you're doing."

"Good," Don said.

"We'll get you another car, some guns. These guys really love guns, and we'll set up a social media presence for you. You might also want to do some cosmetic changes. Nothing big, maybe dye your hair a bit darker, grow a beard. You have a tattoo?"

"Semper Fi, and the eagle, globe and anchor."

"That'll do."

The task force meeting ended with a consensus to use their collective resources and know-how to help Robbie Barrett return triumphantly to the White Turks, and to introduce Don—using an alias—to the group as a replacement for their arrested demo man.

Don shook hands all around before the conference room began to empty. He sat next to James and Charlie. Judy sat across from them with Commander Coleman.

"Well," Coleman said to Charlie, "It looks as if your agency's involvement with the task force has, uh, intensified."

Charlie wasn't in the mood to mince words, neither was Judy. Judy was angry, and spoke up first.

"Don, what the hell are you thinking? You can't endanger your life like this. You have to think about Rita, Rudy, and the new baby."

"Wait a minute—" Don started. Judy cut him off.

"And you can't even master your mobile phone, let alone a detonator. You're going to get yourself killed, and then what are we supposed to do? What the hell are you thinking?"

"Are you done, Novak?" Don deadpanned.

"I agree with Judy," Charlie said. "I get that you have the background and skills for the job, but I sure wish you'd reconsider."

"It's done, Mack. I know what I'm in for."

They spent the next two hours working out an aggressive timeline for Don's identity transformation, relocation to the safe house, and training. Charlie and Judy were reluctant participants. The undercover assignment would basically happen overnight. Agents were already hard at work on the back-end duties: new last name, identity cards, and credit background. Anyone searching for Don's new persona on the internet, or paying for a background check, would find the new information.

"You shouldn't go near your office for the next couple of weeks, and stay away from your wife and kid. I'll bring you your new documents and everything else you'll need. You should leave your personal car at home. I can come pick you up if you like," James said.

"I'll pick him up," Charlie said.

"I'm going home now," Don announced. "I need to talk to Rita."

"I'll call you tonight," Charlie said.

Don shook his head. "No. Not tonight, Mack. I'll see you tomorrow. Pick me up at ten thirty. I want to drive Rudy to school and pack a suitcase."

They all watched Don exit the conference room. Judy had tears forming in her eyes, and Charlie was trying to control her emotions. Except for weekends, holidays, and vacations, Charlie, Don, and Judy were always together. Charlie hadn't felt this low since Gil left the Mack agency six months ago.

Charlie cooked dinner but wasn't much in the mood to talk, so she and Mandy had a quiet meal with WDET-FM in the background. They'd walked Hamm, and watched a bit of TV. Now they were upstairs. Hamm was settling into his bed, and Mandy was reading Barack Obama's *The Audacity of Hope*.

"I feel horny," Charlie said.

Mandy turned to look at her, and slipped a bookmark between the pages.

"What you really are is worried and scared, and it comes out as horny because you don't know how to face being scared."

Charlie leaned to kiss Mandy's hand. Mandy stroked Charlie's hair. They lay entwined together for a few minutes.

"I don't know what I'd do without Don."

"I understand that. He kind of grows on you. Like roasted Brussels sprouts," Mandy teased.

Charlie smiled at the thought. "That may be the one thing he'd never eat. Brussels sprouts."

"Don knows what he's doing," Mandy said. "He has a lot of experience, and he'll be alright. I know you'd try to replace him if you could."

"I would."

"That would be a good one, a Black woman trying to be inconspicuous in a right-wing hate group."

Charlie didn't laugh.

"I guess there's no cheering you up, huh?"

"I can think of something."

"You're shameless."

"No I'm not. I just have the audacity of hope."

Chapter 14

Robbie felt silly wearing a hooded yellow satin tunic over his shirt and jeans for this so-called induction ceremony. A cheap plastic medallion had been placed around his neck and the man he knew only as "the Angel" said some words over him and the others wearing yellow satin. Finally, they'd taken a pledge of allegiance.

Two dozen men patted Robbie on the back as they walked around the rental hall moving to or from the food table, or in search of a beer. It was the first time Robbie had seen women at these gatherings. Three of them served the men from steaming platters lined up in the catering pans. Macaroni and cheese, beef stroganoff, northern beans, mashed potatoes, and sliced ham. He got in line behind the last man, but several members stepped back to move him up the line.

"Get up there, boy, you're one of us now," one man said.

Robbie sat at a front table with the other inductees. He noticed the Angel staring his way, and a few minutes later the man approached him.

"Talk to you a minute? Come on, let's go over here. Bring your plate."

He and the man stood at a bar top table against the wall. Robbie looked down at his plate. He didn't think he should eat while the man stared at him.

"Your chapter leaders have told me some good things about

you. I hear the police held you as long as they could before they let you go."

"They don't scare me. If it hadn't been for that asshole, Frank, they wouldn't have picked me up at all."

"Yes. Brother Wyatt has disappointed many of us. He had a valuable skill, but he couldn't beat his alcoholism demon. We all have them, you know, demons. For some it's drugs, or pornography. Some of these men will tell you they like little boys."

"That's sick," Robbie said.

"Is it?" The man stared at Robbie. "You should eat your food. A few of the wives prepared this feast especially for the new members."

Robbie scooped a forkful of macaroni into his mouth as the man watched. Someone had told him the guy's real name, but he couldn't remember it. He ran a media company or something like that.

"What's your demon, Robbie?"

"What?"

"Is it shoplifting, smoking weed? Maybe you're like some of these guys who get off on shooting guns or blowing up stuff."

"No. That's not me. I guess I'm a bit addicted to being fit. Exercise and biking."

Robbie felt uncomfortable as the man's gray eyes scanned him. "You're not a big man but, yes, I can see you are quite fit. Apparently mentally fit too."

"Uh. Thank you. You know it's not just that Frank drank too much. I don't think he knew what he was doing, uh, you know, as a demo guy. I'm on a lot of chat boards, and I'm aware of guys who have a lot more experience with explosives than that loser, Frank."

The Angel's countenance changed. He was suddenly bored with the conversation, looking around the room.

"Uh, yes, that's good, Robbie. Let your chapter leader know how to get in touch with those people. We're looking for somebody to replace Brother Wyatt. I'm going to get another plate of food. It was good to speak with you."

Robbie watched the man turn and walk away. He quickly finished his food and downed his beer. He entered the alcove and took off the clown outfit, dropping it into the cardboard box to be used for the next ceremony. He tucked the medallion into his pocket, and slipped out the door into the parking lot.

He didn't think anyone saw him leave, and if they did, he didn't think they would care one way or the other. Robbie unlocked the chain on his bike, clipped his pants, and gracefully lifted his leg over the seat. He wouldn't need his helmet for the ride home. It was a short distance away. His mother had been cool since his return, and glad that the FBI hadn't found a reason to arrest him. His younger brother had shaken his hand, and there was a brief glimmer of the admiring look he used to get when they were kids.

Robbie thought about the ceremony. The White Turks were an embarrassing bunch of losers, and that Angel guy had creeped Robbie out big time, licking his lips as he hovered over him. Robbie shook with the memory, then let the whirr of the wheels and hum of rubber on the pavement soothe him. He glided into the night air and away from the darkness behind him.

Chapter 15

Charlie was parked in front of Don's house five minutes early. The Rutkowskis lived in a well-maintained, attractive bungalow with a half story and a sloped roof. The house was nestled between two similar homes on a narrow street in Hamtramck.

At 10:35 the front door opened and Don and Rita stepped out onto the small porch. Don put down his suitcase and held his wife a long time before he kissed her and held her again. When he pulled away to grab his luggage and start down the steps, Rita waved and Charlie waved back. Rita stayed on the porch while Don stuffed the case in the back and wedged himself into the passenger seat of the Corvette.

"Damn, Mack. Why don't you buy a real car. Let's get out of here."

Don turned to wave again to Rita, and Charlie gunned the Vette up the street. It was only a fifteen-minute drive to the office.

"I brought you a coffee."

"Thanks," Don said, swooping up the cup.

Charlie remained quiet, letting Don sit with his thoughts. After Charlie merged onto I-75, he spoke up.

"It was tough dropping Rudy off at school. He's not going to understand why I won't be home for two weeks."

"He knows you have to travel for work sometimes."

"Yeah, but this will be the longest it's ever been."

Charlie glanced at Don. "Help me understand why you've decided to do this."

"That's exactly what Rita asked."

"I'm sure."

"The last five years have had an effect on me. You know I can't stand whiners and people who feel life owes them something. Like this Robbie guy. I was raised that you stand on your own two feet. You want something, you work for it. After Rudy was born, I had to think differently about that. Sometimes people get a raw deal. They grow up with circumstances they can't control. Not only like Rudy's autism, but you know, someone who grows up in poverty or is hated because they look different from everybody else."

Charlie didn't respond.

"Aren't you going to make some kind of wisecrack?"

"No."

"Well, I know you and Judy have made fun of my views. I just speak my mind and tell it like I see it." Don stopped to take several sips of coffee, then continued. "Some of the cases we've had lately have gotten to me. You'll think I'm crazy for saying this, but I get it now that as a straight white man I have privileges I never had to work for."

Charlie was having a hard time keeping the car in her lane.

"You had an epiphany about that?"

"I know you've called me out on it before, but I really understand now. It started with our work on the homeless killings case, and then the Fairchild investigation."

Charlie nodded. The serial murders of the homeless had shaken the entire Mack team. The Fairchild case was a powerful example of extreme privilege leading to the murder of three people. Charlie, Don, and Judy still expected to be called as witnesses in the case.

"It pisses me off, Mack, when I see these guys who think they have a God-given right to be in charge of the world. It has to be some kind of crazy—mixed with arrogance and ignorance—to blow up a church or mosque because you think nonwhite people, or poor people, or folks looking for safety in this country are keeping you down. It makes me embarrassed for my own kind."

"And what about your feelings about Muslims and 9/11?" Charlie asked.

"Well, I admit I still have some work to do."

"Your new name is Don Curtis, Jr.," James said. "You live in Dearborn Heights and work at Donovan Construction in the city. That'll be your explanation for having access to explosives."

Don nodded, looking through the folder of documents in front of him. Judy sat next to him, and Charlie was across the table. Coleman sat at the head with James.

"You're a veteran and a former police officer. You were fired for too many excessive force complaints. You're divorced, with two sons, and you live alone. You're angry about the rotten deal you've gotten from DPD, and the social services people who took away visitation rights with your kids. You have an arrest record for DUIs, and owing back child support. You drive a 2004 Ford Ranger."

"God, I sound like a real loser."

"That's the point," James said. "You'll be one of the guys."

"We already have your fake Facebook page up, and we've added posts adding credibility to your story," Coleman said. "We've set up utility accounts in your name, and opened a banking account for you. You have a couple of credit cards set up for your use."

"You'll report to work tomorrow at the construction company," James continued. "That's where you'll receive your demolition refresher from a couple of agents. When you leave this afternoon, you should pick up some groceries and anything else you need and drive to your new digs. An agent will be there to show you the security measures we've put into place. Then you can have your night. Go get a beer, watch TV. We *do* want you to spend some time on social media, and in the chat rooms of the Turks and some of these other groups. We also want you to talk about your experience with explosives, and your military background. We want people to be curious about you and look at your profile."

"I may need some help with the social media stuff," Don said.

"He'll definitely need help," Judy agreed.

"There will be one of my people in the apartment building. They can do the online stuff and make sure Don has a presence on the message boards."

"How will I stay in touch?" Don asked. "Will I have a point person?"

"We still need to figure that out," Coleman said. She pushed a phone in a plastic bag to Don. "That's your new phone. I'll need your current one."

Don reached in his pocket. He cradled his phone for a moment before sliding it down the table to Coleman.

"Don't worry. You'll get it back. This new one has a tracker and an emergency code that will bring your security guys running."

"I'll have security guys?"

"Yes. But if you see them, they're not doing a good job," James said.

"I won't be able to contact my wife?"

"No. We can't guarantee your communications won't be traced. We won't be the only ones watching you."

"I thought you said these guys weren't that sophisticated," Judy said.

"Their communications systems are actually pretty good," James said. In fact, Robbie is partly responsible for that. Now *we'll* be able to use his expertise."

Don looked worried.

"What's wrong?" Charlie asked.

"What if Rita needs to reach me. What if there's an emergency?"

"She can call me," Judy said. "Day or night. I'll call her today and let her know."

"Thanks, Novak. I really appreciate that."

"So if Don needs help, I assume you don't think he can just pick up his phone and call."

James responded to Charlie with a headshake. "Phone messages can be intercepted, and as a new member he'll be under scrutiny."

"You can set up some communications back channels, right?" Judy asked. "Maybe use the direct messaging function of Facebook?"

"I'm not sure how secure that is. I'll talk to my tech guys."

"We can always go low-tech," Don offered.

"You mean leave a note in a flower pot?" Charlie asked.

"Something like that. A signal that lets you guys know I have information or I want to meet. We can set up a couple of predetermined locations."

"I have some ideas about that," Charlie said.

"Let's hear them," Don said.

Before they split up, they had a viable plan to keep in touch with Don, which included a twice-a-week rendezvous with Charlie, rotating between a city park near the White Castle restaurant on Michigan Avenue and the MGM casino. If he were being watched, it would raise suspicions to be seen with an African-American woman, so Charlie had an idea for a disguise she'd used before. In case of an emergency, or if he needed to speak to James between the Charlie meetings, they'd come up with a signal.

Judy hugged Don when he left with Coleman to pick up his truck, and he and Charlie shook hands.

"I'll see you day after tomorrow," Charlie said. "Don't eat too much pizza."

"I think that's the least I'll have to worry about, Mack.

Tomorrow I'll have my hands on some explosives."

"You'll do fine, my friend," Charlie said, trying to believe her own words.

The ride back to the Mack offices was quiet. Charlie looked at Judy's dour face in the elevator and reached out to put a steadying hand on her shoulder.

"He's gonna be okay. Don has shrewd street instincts, and he's suspicious of everybody so he won't let his guard down."

Tamela spotted their mood the second they walked in the door. She brought phone messages and coffee to their desks even before they'd settled in.

"Is Mr. Rutkowski gonna be okay?"

"Yes, but he'll be away for a while. He's on an assignment. If anyone calls for him you should just say he's out of the office. It's a confidential matter."

"You mean I can't even tell my brother?"

Charlie and Judy looked at each other. Judy was about to call Rita, but put her phone down.

"Do you tell your brother about our cases?" Judy asked.

"Well, he asks me all the time if I did anything interesting. I told him we were trying to find out who killed that Muslim man who died in the fire last month."

"What kind of work does your brother do?"

"He's a security guard at the union. But he wants to be a police detective."

"What union?"

"United Auto Workers."

Charlie asked Tamela to pull up a chair to sit between her desk and Judy's. Tamela looked between their stern faces and knew she was in trouble.

"This is my fault, Tamela," Charlie said. "I should have told you that a lot of our work is highly confidential. Not all of it, but most of it, and we shouldn't talk about it outside of the office."

"Are you going to fire me, Ms. Mack?"

"Of course not. These things can happen. We probably all talk about our cases at home. My partner is a police officer and we talk about our cases all the time. The difference is she understands the confidential nature of our work. Most of the time our clients are hiring us to do private work. Do you understand?"

"Yes. It's just that my brother is so impressed when he finds out I'm doing real detective work and not just filing and typing."

"We understand that," Judy said. "However, now that you're getting more and more responsibilities, you'll have to keep your work to yourself."

"Okay."

Charlie and Judy's faces said everything as Tamela returned to her desk. Commander Coleman might be right about them being a source of leaks after all.

Judy got on the phone with Rita. Charlie thought about her first rendezvous with Don, and planned her disguise.

"How do I look?"

Hamm sniffed at Charlie's leg then backed up and barked.

"Apparently Hamm and I share the same opinion," Mandy said. "Where'd you have those socks and sneakers stashed?"

"They were in an old duffle in the car trunk. I'd forgotten they were there. Good thing I kept them. Most people don't look very hard at homeless people. I think it'll work."

"When are you meeting Don?"

"Tomorrow at noon."

Chapter 16

Robbie signed his message to Spader with the closing he'd heard in a recruitment video: "Yours in Solidarity." He'd had two messages asking him to complete the online membership form, and inviting him for a live chat next week. He filled in the form as his FBI handler had advised. Ninety percent of the information was true, and the rest made him a better fit for the group.

Next he wrote a note to the chapter president of the Turks recommending Don for the demo work they needed for the upcoming church attack. The wording came from his handler. He'd always had trouble with spelling. Sometimes the letters got mixed up, so he copied the note word for word.

Robbie spent the next few hours doing what he always did when he was home. He trolled the internet. He'd helped the FBI set Don up with a registration on the Turks website and had given him a handle: SemperDon. He paused to monitor the Turks social media. The chatter about the upcoming attack had intensified. It was described as a "major event that will make everyone take notice," and members posted their comments on the group's Facebook page, listserv, and the chat rooms.

Most of the back-and-forth was in veiled terms and coded language, but occasionally members—even Turks leaders, who didn't give a damn about hiding—spoke in plain terms. Robbie noticed Don was also in the chat rooms tonight.

Posted by: CRAZYASAFOX
Are we talking about experience with medium loads or large loads?

TURK#2 In Reply to: CRAZYASAFOX
Large load event. Need CR4 or equivalent experience. Munitions.

Posted by: LOCKEDNLOADEDSC
Sounds like you're gonna have a grand old time up there in Motown.

Posted by: TURK#2
These Nigs are in for a big surprise. Stay Tuned.

Posted by: SEMPERDON
Still looking for your powder man?

TURK#2 In Reply to: SEMPERDON
What are your credentials???

SEPMERDON In Reply to: TURK#2
Check out my FB profile. www.fb/semperdon/1293920

Posted by EASTSIDEGUY
I hope this sends a wake-up call to the Governor. He's a traitor to his race.

Posted by LOCKEDNLOADEDSC
First we need to get rid of that monkey in Washington, DC!

TURK#2 In Reply to SEMPERDON
Impressive, man! I'll DM you.

"What does DM mean?" Don asked Agent Elizabeth Garrow.

"Direct Message. You can have a private conversation on Facebook through the instant messaging function. Look here. The guy has already sent you something."

Don leaned over the agent's shoulder to read the note from Turk#2.

Chuck C. here. We're looking for someone with your experience in explosives. Would you be willing to meet?

"How do I answer him?"

"You just type here in the chat box. I can leave chat open so you always know where it is and set up the notifications so that each time you get a message you'll hear a ding."

"Do I really want that?"

Garrow looked at Don. He reminded her of her father who didn't want anything to do with the internet. The only thing he'd learned to use with some dexterity was the TV remote.

"In real life, no. But for the purposes of this case, I'll leave notifications on. Come on, sit and answer the guy," she said, trading places. "I'll watch you."

"What do I say?"

"Just type in: *Yes. When and where?*"

Don did as she said. "What now?"

"We wait for his response."

There was no immediate reply. While they waited, Garrow showed Don how to use emoticons and to "like" other people's pages.

"Remember to stay in role. Don't hit 'like' if someone says something liberal. Write a post or two on your homepage that lets folks know who you are. Obama bashing is good. Also, you can post links to right-wing websites. I'll put a list together for you. I can monitor all your online activity from my own computer."

"Okay. Can I practice posting something now?"

"Sure. Let's find a link to some conspiracy theory. Or a meme."

"Meme?"

"We'll save that for another time. Here's one website I look at pretty regularly. The people who run the site claim crazy things like 9/11 never happened. They say Hillary Clinton killed a guy. They're the ones who started the rumor that President Obama wasn't born in the U.S."

"So how do we post a link?"

"You just copy the link up here in the link bar, like this." Garrow showed Don. "Then go to where you want to put the link and paste it like this."

"Let me try one," Don said.

"Okay, here's a good story to post. It's about a group of Israelis being involved in 9/11. From what I've seen the Turks love to Jew bash."

Garrow patiently walked Don through the process of copying the URL bar and pasting it onto his Facebook home page.

"Wow. This is my home page? Where'd the photos come from? I like the ones of the bed full of guns. Who are the two boys?" Don asked excitedly.

"Probably photoshopped by one of our techs. Those boys are supposed to be your two sons."

"And this one with me showing my tattoo? I never took a picture like that."

"We're the FBI. We can fake a photo of you meeting with the Queen of England if we want to."

Don's computer dinged loudly. "What was that?"

"It means you have another instant message. See? The guy wants to meet tomorrow night after he gets off from work."

"I'm supposed to meet Mack tomorrow after work."

"What time?"

"Six."

"Okay, well, tell him you can meet at six thirty. He suggests getting a beer, and says you should name the place."

"I know a bar we can go to."

"It shouldn't be any place where you'll be recognized," Garrow reminded Don.

"Oh yeah. That's right."

"Where are you meeting Ms. Mack?"

"Near Corktown."

"Okay, let's pull up a few places in that area," Garrow said, her fingers flying along the keyboard. "What about this Irish pub? Let's suggest that. That sounds like a good place for a couple of white guys to meet."

Don put his laptop aside. He'd been scrolling through Facebook pages and chat rooms for hours. This apartment was well furnished and comfortable, nothing like the one-bedroom space he'd lived in when he worked as a beat cop. That was before he made the wise decision to marry Rita. He missed her already. He knew she'd be in bed reading a magazine or one of those romance books she liked. When he had hours to kill, he polished his bowling shoes or cleaned his gun.

He tore a paper bag and spread it on the desk, setting his cleaning tools and oil to one side. He released his Ruger from his shoulder holster, removed the magazine, and racked the slide to eject the cartridge. He planned to keep the gun on him at all times during this assignment. He deftly disassembled the gun, then rubbed the exterior and interior surfaces with a soft, dry cloth. He sprayed a solvent on the small interior elements and rubbed them dry. Finally, brushing inside and out with a toothbrush, he pushed a small piece of cloth through the barrel with a tool that looked like a knitting needle. He reassembled the Ruger and hung it in the holster on the bedpost. As it most often did, the ritual relaxed him.

He peed, drank a full glass of water, brushed his teeth, and lay on the bed. He let his head sink into the soft pillow. His prayer for Rita, Rudy and his baby girl ended with the sign of the cross. Within minutes Don slept for the first night as Donald Curtis Jr.

Chapter 17

Donovan Construction was a full-service quarry yard. Don arrived at the locked entrance at 8 a.m. He announced his business, and the automatic gate slowly opened. He spotted cameras on both sides of the gate. Don drove a half mile to the employee lot past giant excavators and mountains of slag, sand, and rock. He counted twenty men in hard hats and safety vests operating machinery and walking around the work site. He presented his badge at the door of the main building, and a man wearing a security guard uniform pointed him in the direction of a double-wide office trailer. The Dick Tracy look-alike, Agent Riley, and an older man were waiting for him.

"Sleep okay, Rutkowski?" Agent Riley asked.

"That's Curtis if you don't mind."

Riley offered a two-fingered salute. "Absolutely right. This is agent Kapinski. We just call him Agent K."

Don offered a nod. "I slept fine. Did a lot of social media. Grew a beard," Don said rubbing at his whiskers.

"Ready to delve into the world of explosives?"

"Yep. Just enough to fake it and not get blown up, of course."

"Well, you at least need to be able to talk the talk in case somebody in the Turks has a passing acquaintance with bomb-making. They probably don't if they're looking for someone to replace Wyatt," Agent K said. "By the way, Wyatt really botched the job. He used enough Semtex to blow a hole through a weight-bearing wall. He could have used a third of the plastic to start a fire if that was the goal."

Don, Riley, and Agent K started with a glossary of terms on a chart on an easel. Then K pulled out a bag and laid a shitload of explosives and a half-dozen bombs on the table. He gave a tutorial on each bomb and the most practical use for each. They went straight through to 1 p.m. until Don complained about needing lunch.

"I already ordered lunch," Riley said. "It should be here any minute."

"Well, let's take a break until the food gets here. I'm supposed to check my social media and show that I'm engaging during my lunch break."

Don was fairly sure the trailer was for the exclusive use of the Bureau because no one from Donovan Construction ever disturbed them. He replied to a racist rant on the Turks message board with a thumbs-up emoticon, then shared an image on Facebook of a guy and his two dogs wearing Confederate flags. His last phone task was to confirm drinks with Chuck at 6:30 p.m. Gratefully, lunch arrived before he could do another Facebook post.

"I don't see how people can sit around all day doing this social media shit. I'd rather do a stakeout in an ice storm," Don said, getting the two agents to laugh.

His mood was better after eating spaghetti smothered in cheese from the aluminum containers delivered by a nearby deli. It wasn't very good, but it was hot and there was a lot of it. Riley had also sprung for Cokes and chocolate chip cookies.

"Okay, Don," Agent K said. "Let's spend the next few hours doing a review. Are you done eating?"

"I can eat, think, and talk at the same time, K."

Don was on a roll, quickly identifying four different IEDs, the difficulty in their assembly, their effectiveness, and the most recent times they'd been used in terrorist attacks. He identified the plastic explosives easily, and could describe the properties of Semtex and C4.

"The orange brick is Semtex, and C4 is white; they're both considered putty explosives because they're moldable," Don explained. "Both require detonators. They're often used for construction and demolition. Semtex was used at the mosque."

"Yes. But way too much of it. If it had been detonated two hours before there would have been great loss of life," K said. "Okay, let's look at the IEDs."

The explosives tutorial went on until five o'clock when they stopped for the day. The training would pick up tomorrow. Don would watch videos of explosives being constructed, and practice putting a few bombs together himself.

Rush hour in Detroit was always serious business. But driving was a habit in this city and while volume was clearly a factor, the dance of cars on the freeways and streets was as smooth as Isiah Thomas, in his prime, moving from a rebound on one side of the hardwood to a finger roll layup on the other.

Don arrived at the neighborhood park a few minutes early. He eyed the White Castle, and for appearances, he bought four cheeseburgers. He moved to a bench at the edge of the park and scanned the block, but didn't see Charlie or her car. He waited. Out of the corner of his eye he saw a homeless man shuffling up the block. The guy stopped and leaned over the trash receptacle at the corner, then wiped at his face with the back of his glove. Don knew he'd been spotted when the man continued his shuffle heading Don's way.

Geesh. Just what I need.

"I don't have any money," Don shouted.

The man stopped and peeled off one glove. He held out his hand. Don waved him away.

"What about some food? You got enough to buy a sister a couple of burgers?"

"Charlie?" Don growled. "Dammit, why didn't you tell me about the dress-up?"

"Shake your head like you're telling me *no*," Charlie said.

Don executed the pantomime.

"You okay?"

"So far. I have a meeting in a little while with someone from the Turks. They responded to me in the chat room."

"I know. The FBI will have someone near the bar in case it's not what it appears to be. Okay, now wave your hand like you're shooing me away," Charlie said.

"I've got a better idea," Don said. He began searching his pockets for change. "Let everybody know I'm okay, will you? Tell Rita I miss her like the dickens."

"Judy spoke with her this afternoon. They're gonna talk every day."

"Tell Novak I really appreciate it," Don said dropping a handful of coins in Charlie's hand. "And make sure she tells Rita I send my love."

Don turned away.

"See you in a couple of days," Charlie said to his back.

Happy hour at the pub was not what Don remembered from ten years ago. A lot of young people were milling around the bar, and the place had been redecorated, perhaps to appeal to the new clientele. Don sat at a side table as far away from the noisy bar as possible. A waitress came to the table right away, and Don ordered a beer.

"Are you here to meet Chuck?" she asked.

"Uh, yeah I am."

"He's waiting for you at the back bar where it's a bit quieter. You can still order your beer there," she said.

Don unbuttoned his jacket to make access to his gun easier and walked to the back room. Half a dozen people were sitting at the tables, and a bartender and waitress were hovering at the bar. Don looked over the tables, then spotted the man sitting solo against the wall. He gave Don a wave.

"Chuck?" Don asked.

"That's me. Sit down, Don. Nice to see you," he said, shaking Don's hand. "You look pretty much like you do on Facebook. Maybe a little older."

"I'm definitely getting older. By the minute. I need a beer. Can I get you another one?" Don asked.

"No, no, I'm good. I've been here since about six. I don't think I've ever been to this place."

"It's changed. More fancy than it used to be."

"You used to frequent it often?"

"No, just a beer now and then back when the stadium was open," Don said.

"Those were the days," Chuck said. "After I messaged you, I found out that our chapter president already has his eye on you."

"How's that?"

"One of our members had seen your posts on some of the other sites and noticed your background in explosives."

"Oh, I see. I hear your other guy didn't do such a great job for you. It's all over the chat rooms," Don said lowering his voice. "Overkill at the mosque job."

"You stay on the message boards a lot?"

"Where else am I going to get accurate news? The media is too liberal to tell the truth about what's going on in America."

"I sure do agree with you there, Don. So, tell me about yourself. Where'd you get your demo experience?"

Don told a lengthy story about his military service. All true except for the actual work he'd done. "When I got out, I was fucked up, but I got some counseling and after a few years I was able to get on the force. By that time I had a kid and one on the way," Don said, now digging into his false background.

"I have a couple of kids myself. A boy and a girl. The boy will be graduating from high school soon, and I don't know if I can afford college tuition. My plant is downsizing."

"Tell me about it," Don said.

The two men spoke for another half hour and another beer each. The noise from the front was beginning to thin out, and in the back room a few neighborhood old-timers had arrived for a quick bar-food dinner.

"I think I'm going to order some corned beef and cabbage. I don't get to have that very often at home," Chuck said. "My wife tends to cook a lot of casseroles."

"I'll order the same," Don said.

By eight fifteen, the two men had gone their separate ways. Don had to remind himself that he shouldn't like Chuck Caserta, but he did. Although Caserta wasn't a card-carrying racist, he had expressed his resentment about illegal immigrants coming to this country to work for lower wages, at a time when the bad economy was forcing some plants to shutter their doors. While still at the table, Chuck got a call from another Turks member—a man in charge of the strike force for the upcoming action. From the one-sided conversation Don could overhear they were planning an attack on a Catholic church with a predominantly Hispanic congregation.

"The chat room members were talking about a Black church," Don said when Chuck hung up.

"That's a red herring. Most of the members aren't privy to the details of this attack. We're not trying to kill people," Chuck said. "We're just trying to make a statement everyone will pay attention to. This country belongs to the people who have fought for it, like me and you."

Don had impressed Chuck enough to be invited to their meeting tomorrow at a warehouse in Garden City. He had to get word to James.

He resisted the instinct to drive by his house in Hamtramck to look at the lights in his living room, and imagine Rita and Rudy in front of the TV. They'd be watching a rerun of *Andy Griffith* or a movie on the Disney Channel. The baby would already be asleep. At nine o'clock Rita would put Rudy to bed.

Instead, he turned north on Trumbull headed to I-96. For a few blocks he thought he noticed the headlights of a car following him, but by the time he got to the freeway there were no other vehicles behind him. He pushed the sluggish truck into fourth gear, resigned to the idea of another night of website surfing and sleeping alone.

Charlie was on her way home. She knew Mandy was growing tired of keeping dinner warm, and she'd borrowed Mandy's car, but Charlie couldn't just leave Don after he mentioned the meeting with a Turks leader. She'd discreetly followed him to the Irish pub and loitered across the street for two hours waiting for him to leave. When he did, he exited with a man who looked a lot like him. Same height and build, wearing the same slouchy pants and black shoes. They shook hands and walked in opposite directions to their trucks.

Charlie darted to her car parked on a side street and caught sight of Don's truck turning up Trumbull. She followed for a few blocks, then worried he might spot her headlights. He was good at that sort of thing so she eased up and turned.

Her phone rang, and she was sure it was Mandy.

"Sorry, honey, I'm heading home now."

"That's great Charlie," James said.

"Oh. Sorry. I thought . . ."

"Charlie. Listen. You can't follow Don. That wasn't part of the deal. You're only to briefly make contact with him to receive or pass on messages."

"How did you know? Oh, I guess your guys saw me, huh?"

"They did. And if anybody else is trailing Don, they saw you too."

"I thought maybe I could get away with it. I'm worried about him," Charlie said. "I didn't want him walking into a trap tonight."

"You didn't have to worry. The bartender in the pub is one of our guys."

"Oh."

"Look, come to DPD tomorrow morning to meet with me and Coleman. Don's meeting with the guys planning the church attack tomorrow night."

"How do you know that? Did he already get word to you?"

"Our guy put a bug at their table. The Turks are planning an attack on a Catholic congregation, not a Black church."

Chapter 18

Robbie was at his desk on the ground floor of Guardpost Insurance. The job wasn't difficult. He didn't do the customer service work and didn't have to deal with the assholes on the upper floors. And, since he started work at seven, he got off early enough to do a training ride before the peak of rush hour.

The Turks had invited him to a meeting tonight with the team planning the church attack. He'd already informed his FBI handler, but it meant he had to cut his evening ride short to change and grab a bite before the warehouse meeting at six. Robbie would get to meet the guy he'd introduced to the Turks' inner circle. The bomb guy using the handle "SEMPERDON." Robbie had helped build the profile and posting history that had impressed the Turks.

His FBI handler called on his lunch hour warning him, again, not to give away his knowledge of Don when he attended the meeting.

"You have to be professional about this, Robbie. Don knows you'll be there and he'll be playing it cool. You have to as well. Just follow his lead. He's got the experience."

Yeah, but I'm the one who put in the good word for him that got him the job.

Robbie was enjoying the work with the FBI. It was exciting. He was in regular communication with FBI techs who had already penetrated the Turks' membership database and were monitoring their private chats using some of the programs he'd originated. He was particularly proud of his work in developing a chat space for the Turks within an online gaming platform. It was the latest tactic in keeping the Feds eyes off the organizing work of private groups. The good ones and the bad ones.

At two o'clock Robbie's desk phone began to blow up. The actuary database was down, and every agent in the office and in the field was unable to write policies. That meant he would have to skip the bike ride and hunt for the cause of the crash to that part of the network.

I bet some idiot on the executive level clicked on a link from the outside. How many times do I have to tell those jerks not to do that?

At four thirty Robbie was still working at getting the database back up. He was smart enough to have a copy of the actuary program on a hard drive, and that allowed him to set up a temporary clone site that the agents could access for the policy estimates. But he still had to find the point of the breach and clean up any other virus that might have been introduced to the network.

Damn. I'll be late for the meeting. I hope this doesn't mean I can't be on the team. That's where the action is, and I want to be part of the action.

For two hours straight Don watched videos on the assembly of a variety of improvised explosive devices.

"I can't believe you can just find this shit on YouTube."

"You feel my pain," Agent K said.

"The most sophisticated of the terrorist groups make their own videos and embed them on their websites, sometimes behind password-protected portals. It makes it very difficult to find and delete them," Agent Riley said.

"Are you ready to practice building your own, Don?"

"Sure. I'll give it a go. We're not using real explosives, are we?"

"How else will we know you're doing it right unless we have something we can take out back and blow up?" Riley answered.

Don stared at the two men, not knowing what to say. He had no intention of building a real bomb. Finally, Agent Riley started to snicker.

"You should have seen your face, Rutkowski, I mean, you know, Curtis," Agent K said, folding over in laughter. "We had you going. Believe me, as your trainer let me formally say I don't want you building bombs. But you do need to *look* like you can build one. Let's get started, and we promise you a good lunch in a couple of hours."

"How about pizza?" Riley asked.

"God yes. It's been three days since I've had any."

By five o'clock, Don had built eight IED models. It was meticulous work. He was sweating and had an ache in his back.

"This is hard work. Especially the wiring on the detonators. You'd need special equipment, steady hands, and . . ."

"A death wish?" Agent K said.

"How'd I do?" Don asked.

"Not bad at all. You can certainly fake it if anybody asks you for a demonstration."

"That's good because I'm on my way to a meeting with the guys who might ask."

"We heard. Don't let them see you sweat."

When Don walked in the warehouse door, he didn't recognize anyone in the meeting. He'd certainly know Robbie from his social media photo, but as far as he could tell, Robbie wasn't there. Don strode to the center of the room where three six-foot tables had been set up. A few men were in conversation, but the guy at the head of the table stood and extended his hand.

"Don Curtis?"

"Yes," Don answered, grasping the man's hand.

"We're really glad you could join us. I'm the Chapter President, Tom Cortez. You come highly recommended by Chuck and Robbie Barrett."

"Well, I'm glad. I haven't actually met Robbie in person. Is he here tonight?"

"No. He had an emergency at work. He hopes to join us later."

"I don't see Chuck either."

"He's not a member of this strike force. He doesn't have the stomach for the work. Have a seat."

"I really don't like sitting with my back to the door."

"Oh, well of course. Then sit there," Cortez said pointing to a side chair.

Don took off his jacket and put it over the back of his chair. He watched Cortez's eyes register the sight of his Ruger.

"Before you settle in, there's pizza on the side table and cold beer in the barrel. Please, help yourself."

"I'm always ready to eat pizza," Don said.

There were six strike force members, and they were all serious men. They rarely smiled even while eating the pizza and drinking beer. They spoke earnestly about the work that had to be done. There was still some difference of opinion about the attack location. One church had been designated a sanctuary for immigrants. Most of the team thought it should be the target, but one man held out.

"It's a small church in a small parish, of no particular significance to the community, the archdiocese, or city hall. If we really want to make a statement, we need a bigger target."

The man looked vaguely familiar, though Don couldn't place him. He had well-cut hair, nice glasses, and appeared to be in his late fifties or early sixties. He wore a suit but had discarded his tie, which was stuffed in his pocket. The burgundy tip hung out. He had a bit of the air of an aristocrat unlike the rest of the good old boys around the table. The Chapter President had called him Walt, and he didn't eat or drink.

Don didn't say a word as the men debated the location of the attack, and he recognized the name of every church they mentioned. He'd attended Catholic school from grade school

136

through high school. So had Charlie. He didn't want any emotion to register in his eyes so he let them wander across the document in front of him—a one-page manifesto.

"Mr. Curtis, what do you think?"

Don looked up from his third read of the document. Walt had asked the question.

"What do I think?"

"Do you have an opinion on which church we should target?"

"The only input I can give you is from a technical point of view. Some Catholic churches are large buildings with stone and steel foundations, lots of corridors and columns. Marble floors, large windows—many of them leaded. The kinds of cathedrals you see on television. These buildings symbolize the power, history, and stability of the church, and they're not easy to destroy. It would take a tremendous payload to cause impressive damage to that kind of building, and it would be very expensive. A smaller building, even one with brick walls and foundations, will be easier to impact with an explosion, or set of explosions. Because many of those churches have wood pews, altars and even paneling, an explosion would cause significant damage."

"I think that's very well thought out," Tom Cortez said. "Don't you think so, Walt?"

"Yes. But his analysis doesn't solve our problem. If our goal is a serious wake-up call to those in power about the issues facing our city, region, and country, we'll need a significant demon-stration," he said passionately. "Our immigration policies affect every man at this table. We want to focus on a church with a substantial congregation of Hispanics, and one that isn't so small that the whole affair will be forgotten in a few months."

"I think that leaves us with three churches to consider," another strike force member said rising from the table. "These three."

He wrote the names of the churches on an easel pad. Don's heart sank. He had been married in one of those churches. When they heard a whoosh and felt a gust of air, everyone turned toward the door. Robbie stepped in out of breath and still wearing his bike helmet.

"I'm, I'm sorry I'm late. We had a network crash at work, and I had to stay to get the system up again."

"It's okay, Robbie," Cortez said with obvious irritation at the disruption. "You're here now, so take a seat. We were just discussing the possible church locations. Don here has provided a very helpful analysis of the costs and challenges of each job."

"Oh, of course, yes, Don," Robbie said, ripping off his helmet and taking a seat.

Robbie looked at Don wide-eyed, then his face reddened and he quickly looked away. Don was pretty sure Walt had seen the whole thing.

"Don, how soon could you get an estimate on the cost of the explosives you'll need?" Cortez asked.

"I can give you a rough estimate now. I used to be a patrolman with the Detroit Police Department, and I'm familiar with the three churches," Don said, standing. "I'll rank them from highest to lowest in terms of expenses." He marked a *1* next to St. Anne's, a *2* next to Holy Redeemer, and a *3* next to Juan Diego.

"We're talking about twenty grand for number one, five for the second, and probably three to five for the smallest church," Don said. When he turned to the group, he saw Walt staring at Robbie.

"That's fine," Walt said slowly, switching his gaze to Don. "Now we have just one more piece of business. No offense to you, Curtis, but we have only your word for your experience with explosives ..."

"And you want a demonstration of my skills," Don said. "I'm happy to answer any questions you have now. I could even return another time with the materials I need to assemble a simple explosive device for you."

"Oh, no. We don't think that would be a good idea," Cortez said. "No, no, we don't want you to bring explosives here."

"We had something else in mind," Walt said.

They met for another hour. Don grew anxious as the men outlined a plan to use a Memorial Day event as the opportunity to inflict violence and destruction against an area Black community. It was as much a test of Don's commitment to the cause, as it was proof of his bomb-making experience. He needed to get a message to James.

When the meeting finally adjourned, Robbie rushed over to Don to shake hands.

"Hi, kid, glad to meet you in person," Don said loudly.

Walt walked up behind Robbie and Don, and then stepped closer. "I though perhaps you two already knew each other."

"No, no," Robbie began in a flustered state.

"It only feels like we know each other," Don said, interrupting. "We've had many online conversations. We have a couple of groups in common."

"Oh? Which ones?"

"Besides this one, a group called Stormfront," Don said, remembering the name.

"They're based in Europe," Robbie added.

"Yes. I've heard of them."

"Well, it's been good to meet you both," Don said, trying to get away before Robbie said something stupid. "I've had a long day and I'm heading home. I look forward to our chat tomorrow, Walt. Will it just be the two of us?"

"No, of course not. Our treasurer will be there. We'll want to give you the funds you need for our little test project and get your ideas on the best way to implement it."

"I'll do some thinking about the task," Don said. "Will we meet here?"

"No. We'll meet in my office. Tom has your contact information?"

"Yes."

"He'll get you the address and time. Good to meet you." Walt turned away from them.

"You okay, kid?" Don asked in a low voice.

"Yes. Sorry to be late."

"That's okay. Just be cool. Listen more than talk. Oh, and watch out for that Walt guy."

Don needed an immediate conversation with James. He turned on the lights and the TV of his fourth-floor apartment, then walked to the window. He looked out and flashed the blinds once before closing them. In five minutes there was a knock at the door.

"There's a call for you," the tall man said.

Don followed him down the hall. The agent was barefoot and wore suit pants and a T-shirt. They arrived at an apartment, and the man unlocked the door and held it open for Don. It was a studio but with no bed. There were four sleeping bags on the floor, one chair, a TV, and three desks—all with computers blinking from various web pages.

"I'm agent Schlitz. The phones are over there," he said, pointing to one of the desks.

Don found a landline phone plugged into the wall, the receiver resting on the desktop.

"Hello," Don said.

"Hi, Don. You called?" James's voice rang out.

"I need to talk to you, Saleh. They threw a monkey wrench into the works tonight."

"What happened?"

"They want a demonstration to show I know what I'm doing with the explosives."

"We expected that. We'll set up something. How soon does it need to happen?"

"It's already scheduled."

"What do you mean?"

"It means they already have a test job planned for me on Monday. They want me to set off a bomb at the Memorial Day parade in Inkster.

"Shit."

"Exactly. What do I do?"

"Come to the construction trailer at nine. I'll be there, and I'll bring Charlie with me."

Chapter 19

"I've got nothing but bad news to report," Don said when James and Charlie had taken seats in the Donovan Construction trailer. Agents Riley and K were also on hand, and Commander Coleman was expected. "First, the Turks are targeting a Catholic church with a large Mexican congregation for their big event. They've asked me to do the estimates on materials and other expenses. Charlie, one of the churches is Holy Redeemer."

"Oh my god," Charlie said. James looked between them quizzically. "Don was married at Redeemer."

James nodded. "When are they planning the church attack?"

"They're talking a week from Sunday."

"What about this parade bombing you mentioned?" James asked.

"That's supposed to be a test of my abilities and nerves, I guess. The city of Inkster has one of the oldest Memorial Day parades in the state. They want me to plant bombs along the route."

"They want you to blow up a bunch of kids at a parade?" Charlie asked incredulously.

"They specifically want to blow up Black people at a parade."

"Who's blowing up Black people?" Coleman asked, entering the makeshift conference room. She was dressed in plainclothes.

"The Turks," James explained. "They want Don to disrupt the Inkster Memorial Day parade."

"There were five guys at the meeting, and they debated for a while about which parade they wanted me to do," Don said. "In the end it came down to the one that would do the most damage to a Black community."

"I really hate these guys," Charlie said.

"Me too," Coleman agreed.

"I'm meeting with one of the bigwigs in the group, and his money man, at three o'clock. I'm supposed to bring them the final plan."

"Who's this bigwig?" James asked.

"I'm not sure, but he's got some juice. Here's his address. We're meeting at his office."

James jotted the information from Don's phone and passed it to Agent Riley who moved over to a laptop.

"I am not doing this test if it'll hurt anybody," Don announced.

"No, of course not," James agreed. "We'll brainstorm something plausible to fake an attack."

They talked and planned for almost three hours, looking at maps, calling trusted contacts at the Inkster Police and Fire Departments, pulling up diagrams of IEDs and identifying personnel for the day of the staged incident. The Turks would have observers at the parade, so the bombing would have to appear real. The execution of this plan would require a lot of coordination, money, and manpower.

"I can build a few small-load bombs that will make a lot of noise, and flames, but won't do much damage," Agent K announced. "We can place two or three of these devices, maybe in waste containers, tree boxes, or Porta-Johns, and have each guarded by an officer."

"Good thinking," James said.

"How do we convince the Turks of injuries—bodies, blood?" Charlie asked.

James answered, "We can have our people use dye pellets. We should make sure we have five or so people near each device posing as parade viewers."

143

"We should have EMTs standing by, and fire personnel too," Coleman added.

"Don, what you'll tell them is this is the kind of job better suited to IEDs," Agent K advised. "You'll only need about five hundred dollars for materials and supplies."

"Okay," Don said, jotting notes.

"The city website says the parade starts at noon and travels up Michigan Avenue toward City Hall," Agent Riley said, handing James a diagram of the parade route and a note. "Maybe Don and I can go out tomorrow and scout the route."

"They may be watching me, Riley, and you still look like a G-man."

"I'll go," Agent K said.

"I thought you didn't like field assignments?" Don asked.

"I don't. But it'll help me figure out the best way to construct the bombs if I can see the location."

"I think the Turks will suggest you plant the bomb at Inkster City Hall," Charlie said. "If they want loss of life, that's where the crowds will gather at the end of the parade."

"You have a point, Mack," Don said, running a hand across his growing whiskers. "I think I'll tell them if you really want to incite terror, you put a bomb where people go all the time. Some people have never set foot in City Hall, but everybody in Inkster has been on Michigan Avenue at one time or another. They drive it every day. The school buses take that road. People ride their bikes and walk their dogs on Michigan Avenue."

The truth of Don's statement held the people in the trailer momentarily transfixed. Charlie felt a shiver pulse up her spine.

"You should say it just like that, Don."

"Okay, so we have a game plan," James said. "Go to your meeting, Don. I don't think we should get together again today. I'm still worried about you being watched. We know you were followed to the warehouse last night. Instead of coming here tomorrow, stay in your apartment until late morning, spend a little time on social media playing the role, and then meet Agent K."

"This test might be a godsend," Charlie said.

"How do you figure that, Mack?"

"Maybe with this event we can identify all the leaders, key members, and funders of the Turks. Draw them out into the open now so we don't have to worry about an even bigger attack."

"I hope you're right," Commander Coleman said.

Coleman and the agents left the trailer to get the operation rolling. Don asked Charlie and James to hang around.

"I'm worried about Barrett."

"What's the worry?" James asked.

"He got to last night's meeting late. He was flustered. Talked too much. Looked at me like he was waiting for me to give him orders. That Walt guy noticed."

"Oh, by the way, that Walt *is* a bigwig. The address you gave us is for the law offices of Walthrop J. Croft. He's a commissioner for the Airport Authority, and on the governor's Economic Development Committee," James said.

"He's no fool," Don said, "and I can tell he's on the fence about me. I think this whole test is his idea to see if I am who I say I am."

"We're already running a check on him," James said. "I'll also reach out to Robbie. Maybe give him another hacker assignment. Keep him busy. The guy's really good at that stuff."

"Whatever you say, but the kid's already acting like he's FBI. You might have to release some of the helium in his head. Oh, and the other night after meeting that Chuck guy, I *did* have the feeling a car was following me. You think it's the same one who followed me last night?"

James and Charlie looked at each other. Charlie examined her nails. After her homeless performance, she'd gotten a manicure.

"Uh, that was me," Charlie finally said. "I was worried you were walking into a trap at the pub. I won't be doing that anymore as you already have enough protection. I'll just stick to our rendezvous schedule."

Don shrugged. "I thought I taught you better, Mack. You know you're supposed to stay at least three car lengths behind."

Chapter 20

Robbie was excited about his second face-to-face with Spader. This time it was during his lunch break at a McDonald's close to his job. The restaurant was a short bike ride from his office building, and he spotted the green Cherokee in the parking lot as soon as he arrived. He put his lock on his bike, tucked his helmet under his arm, and was about to enter the restaurant when he heard his name called. He turned to find Spader leaning against the Jeep.

"Hi. Sorry to be a few minutes late. You ready to go in?" Robbie asked.

"No. Look, I'm going to have to skip lunch. I just got called to a meeting downtown, but I wanted to check in with you. See how you're doing. See if you're still interested in Stormfront because we sure are interested in you."

"Yes," Robbie hesitated. "I'm still interested."

"You don't sound so sure. I've looked for you on the message boards, and you haven't been around."

"I just been kinda busy. Our network went down the other day, and I'm still trying to weed out all the malware and Trojans."

"See, that's what I mean. You have impressive knowledge and skills. We need a guy like you."

Robbie felt the blood rushing to his face. He liked the attention. Everybody wanted him now. The White Turks, the FBI, Stormfront. He shifted his shoulders back and shrugged nonchalantly.

"Yeah, thanks, I try to keep up with stuff."

Robbie and Spader traded a smile and a nod.

"I see from the rooms the Turks have a big job coming up. Anything you can talk about?"

Robbie thought about what Don had said: *listen more than talk.*

"Well, I, uh, can't really say." Robbie shifted his helmet to the other hand.

"Aww. Come on. I bet you're on the inside. For a big job they'd be fools not to pull you in."

"I *am* on the inside."

"So?"

"We want to make a dramatic statement about these immigrants coming over the border."

"Outstanding. How long do we have to wait?"

"Not much longer. We're going to end the month with a bang."

"June is busting out all over, huh?"

Robbie's face went blank, then cracked open with a smile. "Hey. I like that. I'm gonna use that."

"Well, I gotta go," Spader said, reaching out his hand. "Your application is still working its way up the ladder."

"Thank you," Robbie said, shaking hands.

"How's the kid doing?"

"He's okay," Spader said, staring through the windshield at the restaurant. "I buttered him up. He's feeling pretty good about himself."

"You still think we can use him?"

"He's got mad computer skills. I don't think he has any idea how much he could make working in the private sector. He's being underpaid at some insurance company right now. I put a virus into their network with an email, and I've watched him systematically trace the bug. He's really good."

"So you think we can bring him in?"

"I do, but I want to check him out a little more. I put a tracer on his bike. I don't think he'll find it, at least not for a couple of days."

"Okay. Let me know."

"Will do. Now I'm off to a meeting with Croft."

Don's instructions were to park in the rear of the building and use the service entrance. He casually noted the six vehicles tucked into the narrow lot and looked disdainfully at his borrowed truck. He poked the doorbell at the iron door and pushed it again after thirty seconds.

"Can I help you?" the male voice asked from the combined camera/speaker.

"I'm here to see Walt," Don said. He heard a buzzer.

"Take the stairs. Fifth floor."

On the second-floor landing, Don passed a tall guy with short-cropped hair and wearing sun glasses. He was moving quickly down the stairs. *Damn, don't they have elevators in these old buildings?* He was panting a bit by the time he got to the door marked 5. He paused to slow his breathing before stepping through. A young man with wavy hair and round glasses sat at a desk a few yards from the door. He was looking Don's way. He rose slowly, gathering a notebook and a handful of pink message slips before approaching Don.

His eyes flicked to Don's and then away. "This way," he said, leading him along the carpeted hallway. The man swished as he walked, which Don hoped wasn't meant for him.

Walt's office was impressive. He sat at a large walnut desk with a phone in his hand. He swiveled his chair toward the windows when Don came in the door. The built-in bookcases on the side walls held neatly shelved, thick-bound books. There were two pieces of art that looked like they belonged in the DIA and facing the desk was a long contemporary sofa. The male secretary gestured Don to a round table near the door, then swished to Walt's desk to deposit the phone messages.

"Mr. Croft and Mr. Grady will be right with you," the secretary said passing the table and exiting.

Croft spoke in low tones with his back to the room, so Don took the opportunity to check out his surroundings. The books at the front of the office seemed to be law journals, but behind Don's seat were political biographies and history books. On the opposite side, a bookcase held a series of photographs. Men in dark suits posed in pairs, and threes, and in small groups. Don squinted to better see a photograph of Croft with the governor of Michigan and another of a much younger Croft with President George H. W. Bush.

Don sat upright when the door opened and a man who had been in the strike force meeting entered. He shook Don's hand. "Bernard Grady. Thanks for coming in, Mr. Curtis."

"Sure."

"Let's get started, shall we? Mr. Croft will be off the phone soon. Did you bring some estimates for the work?"

Don reached into his inside jacket pocket to retrieve the folded sheet of paper Agent K had prepared for him. It listed materials and supplies with costs.

"I don't know anything about the cost of explosives or the associated components, but these numbers seem reasonable enough."

"Those are liberal estimates. I may need to go to two or three places to purchase the items. The sale of a lot of these items trigger alerts. So it's better to buy these things in small quantities so as not to raise suspicion."

"I understand," Grady said.

When Croft joined them at the table, he'd discarded his suit jacket. His shirt was monogrammed and he wore expensive gemmed cufflinks. He looked older in the fluorescent light, and Don noticed a wedding band.

"Everything in order, Bernie?"

"Yessir. It looks good. A modest budget actually. Should we make the usual arrangements?"

"That's right."

Bernie left to do whatever the usual arrangements meant. Croft poured water from a carafe into a glass.

"Water, Don?"

"No thanks."

"None of us drinks enough water."

"My wife says that. Or, she used to," Don said, catching himself.

"You have kids?"

"Two boys. One's nineteen. The other is sixteen."

Walt nodded. "I have three girls. That Robbie kid seems to like you."

"Hmm. I don't really know him. Just from the chat boards. He seems like a good enough kid. A little green maybe. He reminds me of my oldest boy. He likes bikes, too. Motorcycles. I helped him buy his first one. That's why I'm driving my piece of junk truck."

"Well, our kids . . . that's what it's all about, isn't it? Keeping the country safe and secure for our kids. We've had the good days. You and I. When America was great for the white race. I'm committed to making sure we keep our way of life. Like it was when we were growing up. All our institutions have let us down. The church, the government, our corporations, even the military," Walt said.

Don was relieved when he heard the door open and Croft ended his tirade. Bernie stepped in with a white envelope and a piece of paper.

"We're giving you cash, Don. That's the way we like to do things. If you'll just sign this receipt."

Don scanned the paper. It was succinct, and a big fat lie. "For landscaping services rendered" it read. Below the signature line was "Curtis Landscaping Company." He signed the paper and accepted the open envelope. It was filled with one-hundred-dollar bills.

"If you don't spend the full amount, you can keep the difference," Bernie said.

The door opened again, and the secretary poked his head in.

"I'll see you out," he said.

Don slipped the envelope into his inside pocket and the three gawked at his gun.

Back in the parking lot, Don squeezed into his truck. The BMW next to him had parked too close. Don noticed the Jeep was gone, but all the other cars were the same. Since the meeting with Croft and his treasurer was straightforward, Don didn't need to contact James.

What does a guy do with a wad of cash and the whole evening ahead of him? He felt, briefly, cheerful. Then he remembered Croft's chilling diatribe. He exited the lot and turned the Ford in the direction of home. *Home,* he thought dolefully.

Man, what a fool you are, Rutkowski.

Chapter 21

Charlie had switched cars with Mandy again so she could return the wheelchair, and drive Ernestine to her follow-up doctor appointment. The swelling on the ankle was completely gone, and only a hint of bruising remained. The doctor had said Ernestine could return to her normal activities, including rejoining her walking group. They decided to celebrate with lunch at Cyprus Taverna in Greektown.

"I haven't been here in years," Ernestine said looking at the wall of photos and Detroit memorabilia.

"Greektown has really changed since the casino was built. Hellas restaurant closed last year. I hope this one can hold on," Charlie said.

"Your father and I used to come here quite often. It was one of our date night spots."

Charlie smiled. "You and Daddy made a striking young couple. I carry around this picture of the two of you," Charlie said pulling out her wallet and handing Ernestine a small photograph. "I think you said it was taken at Belle Isle."

"Oh my goodness, yes. It was at Belle Isle. Your dad and I had only been married a year, and he'd just gotten his first job as a lawyer. We used to go to Belle Isle as often as we could for picnics, the beach, and skating in the winter."

"I remember your stories about that. You both look so happy in that photo; that's why I keep it in my wallet."

The owner stopped at their table to take their orders. They both ordered a glass of red wine, and Charlie got *horiatiki*. Ernestine ordered the lemon chicken soup. For appetizers they got olives and hummus. The food came quickly and, as always, was delicious.

"How is Mr. Constantine? You haven't mentioned him."

"Oh, Gabe's fine. He's been very busy lately. But he calls every evening, and he's checked on me twice since I sprained my ankle."

"Good. He seems nice. Maybe we can do brunch now that your ankle is better."

"He'll be away this weekend. He's visiting some of his grandchildren on the West Coast."

"I see."

"Isn't it about time that you and Mandy had your first cook-out? There's a long weekend coming up."

Charlie laughed. "It'll have to wait. Mandy and I are both working over Memorial Day. Let's plan something for the Fourth."

"Everyone's so busy these days," Ernestine said wistfully. She took a sip of wine.

"Well, now that the weather's getting nice, we'll bring you over to the house. Watching Hamm is pure entertainment, and I'd love to get your advice on a flower garden."

"That sounds good, Charlene. I really think I need to get out more. Do some new things. Now tell me, how is your hate crimes case going? Gabe asked me about it when he called last night. He's very taken with the idea of a lady private investigator."

"I can't tell you much about the case, Mom, except to say the task force is working around the clock on these crimes."

Ernestine seemed disappointed. "Well, I just hope you can get justice for that poor Muslim family. Your father used to say it all the time. Justice isn't really blind. You know that already, don't you Charlene?"

"I know it, Mom. Say, how about we split some of that homemade pineapple cake this place serves."

Chapter 22

Don met Agent K at a Home Depot near Telegraph Road. They pushed two shopping carts through the store gathering nails, nuts, duct tape, rags, PVC tubes, galvanized pipes, battery-operated power outlets with remotes, and various pipe caps. Don also bought contractor's towels, trash bags, and gloves.

K purchased his items with cash. Don used his FBI-provided credit card. They walked out with ten of the store's brown bags stuffed with their purchases, then drove to Lowe's and repeated the process. In the Lowe's parking lot they stuffed all the bags in K's car trunk and rode together in Don's truck toward Inkster City Hall.

"This place is awfully close to the Police Department," Don said. "As a matter of fact, the Dearborn Heights police are only five minutes away."

"That should help us. After the first explosion we want a quick response from the police, which will keep the Turks observers at a distance, especially from the three areas where our fake injury victims will be down."

"Okay. Let's drive the route in reverse, and then loop back," Don suggested.

The route wound through a sparsely populated commercial street before turning onto the four-lane Michigan Avenue headed eastbound. They parked in a strip mall, walked the route, then crossed the street and walked back.

Late May was one of the most beautiful times in Metro Detroit. Some years winter resisted leaving and a late storm could dump snow or ice, but around the Memorial Day weekend spring took a ferocious foothold on the area. The grass on the Michigan Avenue median was green and mowed, and a few flower beds were blazing yellow, purple, and red.

"This will be easier than I thought. Lots of trees on either side of the avenue, even on the median. It's a good path for a parade. Wide road with lots of open spaces for people to stand, and lots of places to park cars. I do think the porta-johns might be a good idea. We can stack six of them side-by-side and lock two with out-of-order signs. Our agents can use those for surveillance. The Turks will be observing, too, but we'll be watching for them," Agent K said.

They returned to the truck where the agent made a few sketches. He took some photos with a camera that had both a long lens and a wide lens. Don suggested they drive to a Dairy Queen they'd passed, where he bought two chicken strip baskets, chocolate and vanilla milk shakes, and an Orange Julius. Charlie's voice sounded in his ear, so he ordered one side salad.

"I got chicken, shakes and one salad," Don announced proudly as he stepped into the truck. "Plus an Orange Julius for me."

"Great, I'll take the salad if you don't mind. My wife has been on me about too much junk food," K said.

"I have a real wife and a work wife who say the same thing," Don said.

K put down his notebook, opened the salad, and stuck a plastic fork in it. "Ms. Mack seems quite competent. You guys have a good reputation around town. That was extraordinary work in the trafficking case."

"Yeah, well, we sort of fell into that one. We met Agent Saleh on that case."

"He's a good man, a supervisory agent now. He should continue to move up the ranks quickly if he stays with us."

"Is he considering leaving?"

"You wouldn't believe how competitive the Bureau is, and how cutthroat. There are more than a few men, and some women, who try to better themselves at others' expense. He's an easy target for that kind of self-interest. I know he prefers the casework to the politics. He's told me so." K pointed with his salad fork. "Uh, is one of those chicken baskets for me?"

When Don dropped K off in the Lowe's parking lot, they had a plan and a timetable. The agent would lead a team of techs in producing a half-dozen modified pipe bombs that would be more showy than lethal. Two of the bombs would be elaborate noise-makers, while the others would have enough punch to topple trees and send earth flying. They'd plant the devices early the morning of the parade, day after tomorrow, dressed as public works staff hauling porta-Johns. They'd have a crew of six, and another ten agents would be on the scene a half hour before the start of the parade. All the devices would be detonated remotely.

With any luck the charade would convince the Turks that Don was the real deal, and the incident would get enough media attention to keep this group of domestic terrorists eager to execute the big event they'd been promising for weeks. With more luck, the Turks would reveal the full extent of their reach, resources, and numbers. Then the Feds could scoop them up, like fish in a barrel, before there was any more loss of life.

Don was to meet Robbie Barrett at the MGM casino. He'd picked that location so he could later rendezvous with Charlie near the quarter slot machines. It was James who suggested the dinner.

"He doesn't have many friends outside of the knuckleheads in these right-wing communities. My agents say he's eager to belong, and I want to keep him close," James said.

"Why me? He and Novak hit it off."

"He needs a male role model. He's monitoring some dark

net activity for us, and I want to keep him curious and interested in working for the good guys. I talk to him a couple of times a day, but I'm the wrong color. He's asked me about you a couple of times."

"You don't think he's trying to sell me out to the Turks, do you?" Don asked.

"No. We're monitoring everything he does. So far, he's been on the up and up. We're interested in this Walthrop Croft, and Robbie's already managed to attach a monitoring program to the guy's office computer. I think the kid just admires you."

Don decided to dress up for the dinner. Instead of his tweed sports coat and khaki pants, he wore a collared shirt under a long-sleeved gray sweater and a pair of gray Dockers. Without a jacket he secured his gun to a belt holster covered by his sweater. He'd called in a reservation to the steak house but didn't need it because the place was half empty. When Robbie showed up, he'd also dressed for the occasion, wearing a pair of clean jeans and a polo-style shirt. Don had been nursing a scotch at the bar and greeted Robbie at the door.

"You ever been here before?" Don asked.

"No. I can't afford a place like this on my salary. Not even for a special occasion."

"Well, you're going to get a sample of the good life tonight."

Don ordered a steak. Robbie opted for swordfish.

"Don't you eat red meat?"

"Not anymore. It clogs your arteries."

"You're one of those health nuts? Ride a bike, carry around a water bottle, and only eat chicken and fish?"

Robbie's face stiffened. Don realized he was getting off to a bad start. He was being Don Rutkowski, not Don Curtis.

"Listen kid. I'm just messing with you. I don't care what kind of food a man puts into his body. What's important are his ideas. What's in here." Don pointed to his head.

Robbie dropped his shoulders and leaned back into the soft

leather of the booth seat. He'd ordered a beer, and a gorgeous server with short red hair and a pierced nose placed it on the table in front of him.

"Can I get you anything else for now?" she asked, showing beautiful teeth and crimson lips. She looked from Robbie to Don and back again.

Robbie couldn't manage to say anything. "No. I think we're good for now," Don replied.

Don watched as the boy's eyes followed the woman's exit. When he finally looked back, his face was flushed.

"She's pretty good looking."

Robbie nodded and took a drink of his beer, licking the froth from his lip.

"How long have you been with the Turks?" Don asked.

"Only five months. First, I paid the associate fees, twenty-five dollars, to get access to the membership benefits. You know, streaming videos, tees, and an online newsletter. After a couple of months, I started attending the meetings."

"You like these guys?" Don asked.

"Some of them are okay. I hated Frank Wyatt. What an asshole," Robbie said.

"Yeah. He's pretty much a loser," Don agreed.

"You like working for the FBI?" Robbie blurted out the question.

Don swiveled his head to take in the room. No one was within earshot. "You have to be careful with what you say. You never know who's listening."

"Yeah. I'm sorry. I was just curious, you know. You don't look like all the other guys I saw at police headquarters."

"I'm not with the police. I'm a private investigator. But I've been a cop. I also worked with Homeland Security."

"No way," Robbie said. "That's serious, man. What's it like being a private investigator? You think it's better than being an FBI agent?"

"I don't know that it's better, but you have more control of your life."

"That's cool."

"So the Turks like you and your work?" Don asked.

"I think so. They steal credit card and bank information so they can fund their activities. The membership and associate fees don't go very far, you know? So, I've helped them set up a couple of accounts where they can phish, you know?"

Don pretended to know. "Identity theft?"

"Yep."

So Charlie was right.

"Why'd you decide to work with the FBI?" Robbie leaned in to whisper the question. "Do they have something on you, too?"

"No. Nothing like that. I have a son. I want him to grow up in a world where he can be happy and safe, not in the dangerous world the Turks are trying to build," Don said, taking a sip of his Dewar's. "That shit they're doing is crazy. How does that help anybody?"

Robbie looked at his beer. He leaned his arms on the table. Don sipped and let the boy think it through for himself for a few minutes, then offered to answer any questions he had. But before he could start, the pretty redhead was headed back their way, leading a white-shirted muscle boy with a tray. He put their plates in front of them and disappeared. She topped off their water, though it didn't need it, and grabbed ketchup, steak sauce, and sriracha from the booth next to them.

"I can bring back some more lemon for your swordfish if you like," she said to Robbie with a honeyed voice.

He'd already taken a bite, and swallowed hard. "No, this is just fine, thank you," he managed to say. He watched her leave again.

"You got a girlfriend?"

"Not really. I'm too busy."

"I guess that systems administrator work does keep you hopping, plus you got the Turks work, and your social media stuff."

"Yeah, and there's this other group that wants me to sign up with them. They're the real deal. Not like the Turks."

159

Robbie took another bite of the swordfish steak and downed a few fries drenched in ketchup. He pushed the broccoli to the side of his plate.

"You said I could ask you questions."

"Shoot."

"Why, as a white man, would you be okay with all the brown and black and yellow mongrels invading our shores?"

Don sighed.

They talked for an hour and a half about life in the United States, the countries Don had seen and fought in as a marine, the reason why terrorism, in any form, is cowardice. Don talked about his grandfather who had been an immigrant and learned English so he could help his parents navigate life in America. Don was no expert on the questions the boy asked about race, but he tried to remember the things he'd learned from Charlie and others he admired. He told Robbie the story about the young Muslim teenager who had saved Rudy's life. He also told him about his Little Brother, Derrick.

"I volunteer with Big Brothers. I spend time with him twice a week. His father isn't around, and his mother doesn't have a lot, but he wants to go to college and be a doctor. He loves math and science. He can't really talk about that in his neighborhood because the fellows would call him a sissy or a sellout."

"A lot of these niggers don't have fathers . . ."

Don slammed his hand on the table. "Don't use that word around me, Robbie."

The kid looked sullen and folded his arms. "All I'm saying is they're all on drugs or out making babies. All the Blacks want to do is smoke dope and party. They're bringing our society down."

Don folded his arms, too, and leaned back against the padded bench. "Is that what they say on those videos you look at? What about Asians, you hate them, too?"

"All the coloreds. All of them are changing America," Robbie said between clenched teeth.

Don looked at his watch. It was almost seven-thirty. "Look I have to wind things down. I'm meeting someone here at eight, but I want to talk to you some more about this. I think you're a smart kid."

"I'm a man," Robbie said, adjusting his shoulders.

"You're right. You're a young man, but I'm an older man and I think I know some things you don't. For instance, you need to watch some different videos."

Robbie rolled his eyes, but seemed more relaxed.

"Are you willing to have another conversation some time?"

Robbie nodded.

"Okay then, let's order a quick dessert. You aren't against desserts, are you?"

Robbie's smirk turned into a tight smile. "I'm fine with desserts. Do you think they have, like, a strawberry shortcake?"

"I'm positive they do," Don said, waving the redhead to the table.

Don paid for dinner with his Mr. Curtis credit card, left a nice tip, and then he and Robbie walked to the entrance of the restaurant. They shook hands with the promise to talk the next day. Don watched the kid twist his way through the Saturday night gamblers who were swarming the place. Don headed in the direction of the quarter slots. He knew they were Charlie's weakness.

Before he'd made it to the gambling floor, he felt a tap on his shoulder. He spun around and took a step back. A tall man with blue eyes was staring at him. Don's hand was already fingering the Ruger at his back.

"I know you," the man said.

"No you don't."

Neither of them was smiling. Don sensed this was not a friendly encounter about being mistaken for an acquaintance.

"What do you want with Robbie?" the man asked.

Don blinked. "Who are you, his father?"

The question caused the blue-eyed man to also blink. He shook his head. "No. No, I'm a friend."

"Well, I'm a friend, too," Don responded.

"Are you with the White Turks? I hear you guys have something coming up."

"I don't know what you're talking about." Don's hand tightened on the pistol grip.

The man gave Don a quizzical look, blinked again, then turned and quickly walked away.

Careful to make sure the man wasn't following him, Don worked his way across the casino, retraced his steps, and circled over to the rear slots. He spotted Charlie at a quarter machine. The seat next to her had a sweater draped over it. Don asked if he could sit and Charlie pantomimed her reluctance to let him do so.

"Are you good?" Charlie asked, hitting buttons.

"So-so. I just had dinner with Robbie. He's a mixed-up guy."

"Redeemable?" Charlie said over the noise of the machines.

"Maybe. He's smarter than I gave him credit for."

"Judy likes him."

"Who doesn't she like?"

Charlie turned her head toward Don. He was stuffing several twenties into the cash slot. The machine rewarded him with a display of his buying power and urged him to play the max bet. He did and the machine registered a ten-dollar win.

"Well, all right!" Don said.

"I like the beard. It grows fast."

"I'll be a wolfman by next week." Don kept his eye on the slot screen. "There were no surprises in the meeting with that Walt guy yesterday. He gave me cash. I was in and out in about fifteen minutes. Today, Agent K and I did a walkthrough of the parade job. He thinks it will be easy."

"Great," Charlie said. "Judy told me to tell you Rita and the kids are fine. Rudy thinks you're on a business trip, and he wants you to bring him a baseball cap." Charlie peeked at Don who kept his eyes straight ahead. "I'll see you later. James has invited me to ride with him to the parade job. We'll be out of sight, but nearby."

Charlie pressed the cash-out button. The machine simulated

the sound of falling coins, and she waited for the cash slip to appear.

"Wait a minute, Mack. A guy approached me tonight. He followed either me or Robbie. He asked who I was, and if I was with the Turks."

"What'd he look like?" Charlie said slowly, standing and putting the sweater across her shoulders.

"Lean, clean shaven, maybe mid-thirties. He had blue eyes. He came out of nowhere. I thought I was going to have to pull my weapon."

"Okay. I'll let James know."

Charlie made a show of looking at her ticket, then retreated down the aisle.

Don stayed at the quarter machine another fifteen minutes. He occasionally looked around for the blue-eyed man as the sixty dollars he had started with dwindled down to seven dollars and fifty cents. He punched the cash-out button and moved to the dollar slots. He sat at one machine for a moment then abruptly moved to sit on the other side of the aisle. Once he was sure he wasn't being followed, he left the casino only thirty dollars in the hole and counted himself lucky.

Robbie was already on the Turks' message board when Don fired up his laptop at eleven o'clock. He ate a bowl of cereal and watched the kid chat with a few other members about an Al Qaeda video. It apparently showed the beheading of a Christian missionary in Afghanistan. The members talked about revenge and used racial slurs, some that Don had heard before, and some not. A lot of the posts tonight were followed by *RAWA*, which Don had learned from Agent Garrow was a rallying call for a race war. He was about to sign off when another message popped onto the screen.

Posted by: SEEINGBLUE.
Hello. BIKERDUDE

BIKERDUDE Reply to: SEEINGBLUE.
How's it going tonight?

SEEINGBLUE Reply to: BIKERDUDE.
I thought you didn't eat red meat?

BIKERDUDE Reply to: SEEINGBLUE.
I don't. Only chicken or fish for me.

SEEINGBLUE Reply to: BIKERDUDE.
1 Timothy 4:3-5

SEEINGBLUE's post received ten likes.

Don had to look up the scripture reference: *Who forbid marriage and require abstinence from foods that God created to be received with thanksgiving by those who believe and know the truth. For everything created by God is good, and nothing is to be rejected if it is received with thanksgiving, for it is made holy by the word of God and prayer.*

Don didn't like what he was seeing. The guy seemed to be bullying the kid about his food preferences. He decided to get into the conversation.

SEMPERDON Reply to: SEEINGBLUE.
You don't have to eat red meat to be a Red-Blooded American.

BIKERDUDE Reply to: SEMPERDON.
LOL

Don's post received twenty-five quick likes. He suspected SEEINGBLUE was the blue-eyed man from the casino. He'd seen Don and Robbie leave the steakhouse. Maybe it was a warning to Robbie that he was being watched. The man ignored Don's post and continued his conversation with the kid.

SEEINGBLUE Reply to BIKERDUDE.
Looking forward to the Sunday Surprise you
mentioned. An eye for an eye. A tooth for a tooth.

BIKERDUDE Reply to SEEINGBLUE.
June is busting out all over.

Robbie's comment elicited a dozen likes and several
responses of RAWA. Don thought about an appropriate last
post for the night. Days before the so-called Sunday Surprise,
the FBI would be gathering up some of these crazies on charges
of conspiracy to commit murder, arson, a dozen hate crimes, and
second-degree murder in the death of Hassan Pashia. Agent
Garrow had clued Don in on another acronym used by some
of the Christian fundamentalist groups. Don decided to turn the
tables on this blue-eyed, Bible-quoting fanatic who was pressuring
Robbie and promoting violence.

SEMPERDON reply to: BIKERDUDE.
WWJD?

Chapter 23

Robbie had to work a half-day on Sunday. He didn't mind it. It was easier to get things done without the sales staff and bosses badgering him with their stupid requests. Some even called him to change the cartridges on the printer. He was tired of telling these snobs that the people in the mailroom took care of the printers.

Today he did regular maintenance on the system, cleaning out cookies, sweeping for viruses, and blocking sites that employees were not to use. On the first week of his new job, he had discovered the general sales manager was connecting to a porn site a few hours every day. When he'd told the network manager, he told Robbie to block the site from use. He was discouraged from following the guidelines in the employee handbook, which required a notification to the HR manager. Robbie later copied the guy's social security number along with his bank routing info.

After completing the work he was being paid for, he checked on his volunteer work. Volunteer might not be the right word for being an FBI informer. Agent Saleh recommended that Robbie use his work computer for this tracing rather than his own computer, but it really didn't matter. He had set up a half dozen VPNs and other anonymity tools to cover his tracks.

The trace on the Croft guy's computer had revealed some really interesting stuff. He was involved with political and social circles in Lansing, London, Germany, and Washington, DC. He sent regular payments to an overseas account at HSBC. It hadn't been difficult for Robbie to trace the withdrawals against the account to deposits to several members of the Stormfront leadership. But the most interesting information was that Croft knew Spader, his blue-eyed Stormfront contact. There were only a couple of email exchanges, sent last November after the US presidential election. Croft had sent a link to Spader connecting to a news report about a German right-wing populist group plotting the assassinations of Angela Merkel and Barack Obama. Spader had replied with a thumbs-up.

Robbie had kept the information about Croft and Spader's acquaintanceship to himself. He'd decided to keep a few more things secret as well. Like his new online romance with Kathy, whom he had connected with on a bike touring site, and the funds he'd diverted from Croft's HSBC account to one he'd established at a bank in Amsterdam. So far the funds had paid for a fake passport and a couple of gifts for Kathy. He hadn't actually met her in person yet, but she seemed to like the gifts.

Robbie felt things were looking up. He had a life now where he had choices. That's all he had ever wanted.

He shut down his desktop, stuffed his laptop and notebooks into his backpack, and took the stairs down to the street where he'd locked his bike to the rack at the corner. He squatted to insert the key in the lock and a shove knocked him down onto his face. Robbie struggled to turn over, but his backpack caught on the rack as someone kicked him in the ribs. On the third kick, he managed to grab the assailant's pants leg, then they were both on the ground grabbing and thrashing at each other.

Robbie didn't recognize the brown-skinned boy wailing on him, but he managed to get the better end of the deal because he had a few pounds on the boy, and his helmet protected his head. He head-butted the kid directly to the face, connecting with the boy's nose, and causing an immediate spurt of blood. The boy had been screaming and crying, and now he was bleeding and lying on his back. Robbie took advantage and pinned the kid to the sidewalk and whacked him over and over until two men passing by pulled him off the boy.

"He killed my father, he killed my father," the boy screamed, blood and snot dripping down his face.

"What's he talking about?" one of the men asked Robbie.

"Hell if I know," Robbie said, backing away. He grabbed his bike, rolling it in the opposite direction, and hopped on the seat. The boy was still screaming as he gained speed. He didn't look back.

Charlie was reading the Sunday papers when Judy called. Mandy was at work, and Hamm slept on the mat at the door. Somehow he knew it was almost time for Mandy's return and she would have treats for him when she arrived. Charlie was glad to speak to Judy because she'd been restless and anxious all day. Even a forty-minute workout in the basement gym hadn't eased her tension.

"Is this call business or pleasure?" Charlie asked.

"Business. I've spent the last hour on the phone. I called Rita to chat and to give her some encouragement. Don's absence is really starting to wear on her. She's thinking of staying with her parents until he comes home. It's getting too lonely for her at night."

"That's probably not a bad idea. It might be another five days before he's home."

"Has anyone spoken to him today? He must be nervous about tomorrow. I know I'm nervous, and I'm not going to be anywhere near the place," Judy said.

"To tell you the truth, I haven't been able to settle down at all today myself. It's only nerves. We're all on edge."

"I had another call, too," Judy said. "Robbie called, really upset. He had a fight on the street. A brawl apparently. Somebody attacked him. He was knocked down, and he and the guy were punching each other until two strangers saw the fight and came over to break it up. He said it was a young kid who came out of nowhere. The kid was yelling, "you killed my father!"

"Kamal Pashia," Charlie said.

"That's what I thought. You might want to call Kamal and see if he's all right. Robbie's a wreck. He started cursing and spewing that hate talk about minorities. I tried to settle him down and when I couldn't, I hung up on him."

"Okay. Thanks, Judy. I'll call the family now. I'll let you know what I hear."

The Pashia family insisted Charlie come to the house, hoping she could give Kamal some words of advice to comfort him. He'd come home bruised and battered. His nose had stopped bleeding, and the family doctor had packed it and bandaged him. When Charlie arrived, Mrs. Pashia was so upset she'd gone to bed. Amina brought her into the family room, along with Kamal's little sister, to meet with Charlie.

"In the last few days, Kamal has become sullen and angry. He doesn't come to dinner, and he won't tell me where he's going when he goes out," Mrs. Pashia said.

"We recently found a counselor for Kamal," Amina said. "Someone who could help him with his grief, but Um says today he ran out of the house, angry. He took my father's car."

Amina shook her head and continued. "When he came home, he wouldn't talk to me, but Um got him to speak. He told us about attacking that white boy. The one my father had helped."

"How did he know who the boy was? I didn't put that in my report," Charlie said.

"No. But you showed me his picture. We found an old yearbook with a photo of my father's class. The boy was in the photo, and his name was in the caption. I showed it to my mother and brother."

"But how did Kamal know where to find him? The young man was attacked at his job."

"I don't know," Amina answered. She looked at her mother.

"Did he tell you, Um?"

Mrs. Pashia's head dipped to her chest. "He would only say he tried to kill the man who killed his father," she said with almost inaudible sobs.

The youngest daughter moved to her mother's side.

"I know," Farah said. "He saw it on Facebook."

Charlie pulled up Robbie's Facebook page. James said he hardly used the platform, but he'd been active recently. There were posts of Robbie posing with a new bike helmet. His relationship status had changed, and he bragged of getting a raise at work. One post was an ugly meme about immigrants. The last post was probably what had set Kamal off today. "Gotta work today. Sunday's just another day when you're a man with a life full of choices," the post read. Attached was a smiling Robbie with a fresh haircut and a thumbs-up. He wore an expensive-looking watch on his wrist.

Charlie knocked at Kamal's bedroom door. She knocked a second time and announced herself before she heard the lock being released. Kamal's face was very bruised, and one eye was swollen. The bandage didn't fully cover his nose, which was darkened from the broken capillaries. He had stitches on his forehead.

"Kamal, your mother has given me permission to speak to you in your room."

Kamal turned and walked to his desk. He kept his back to Charlie.

"The boy you attacked is now working with federal law enforcement to bring all the men responsible for your father's death to justice."

"He's responsible, Ms. Mack. He's the one who killed Abi."

"We know he was in the mosque, but we also know another man planted the bomb that killed your father. These are despicable men who hate people who don't look like them, and blame others for their failures and situations."

"He bragged about killing my father, Ms. Mack. I can show you."

Kamal pulled up a website that linked to a message board. He scrolled through the archived posts from a month ago until he found the one he was looking for, dated six weeks ago.

Posted by: STORMTROOPER22
We killed another towel head. He had it coming.

Post after post, maybe thirty in all, from users with handles like Citadel, WhiteBrothers, Still the Confederacy, TakeBack-America, PatriotSC, and ProudRebel, replied to the message with the acronym: RAWA.

Kamal was right. The small picture next to the man who used the handle Stormtrooper22 was Robbie Barrett. Additional posts talked about using plastic explosives in the mosque. One post bragged that the FBI had raided his house, but they had to let him go. His posts were vile and filled with hate speech.

"You see, Ms. Mack. He is a killer, and I tried to kill him for my family. It is my right."

Charlie and Kamal spoke for almost an hour. She tried to help Kamal make a connection between the pain he was feeling and the tenets of martial arts. They talked about the technique of folding into a punch, absorbing it for a brief time, so that you could expel it from your body. She stood in the middle of his room and invited the boy to practice the technique—to strike, punch, and kick. Occasionally Kamal's blows connected, but Charlie remained in defensive mode. She blocked the kicks and sidestepped the punches.

Charlie walked out of Kamal's room, leaving him slumped on the floor, drained from the sparring, crying from his physical and emotional pain. He had promised to see the counselor his sister had found for him. He'd also agreed to be in her new Taekwondo class that began next month.

Mandy had changed into Sunday comfort clothes, and she and Hamm were on the back deck when Charlie pulled the Corvette into the driveway. Mandy noticed right away the bruise taking hold on Charlie's cheek, and the wrinkles in her slacks and shirt. Hamm had signaled her arrival and stopped barking only when Charlie climbed the deck stairs. She ruffled his ears, and he sat down in hopes of a snack. Charlie gave him a piece of cheese from Mandy's plate.

"You look like you could use some lemonade."

"Is that what you're having? Make mine with two fingers of vodka," Charlie said. "Then I'll answer all the questions I can see on your face."

The drink, the cheese and crackers, gazpacho, and dog rubs helped. The conversation helped even more. Later, Charlie and Mandy had an early dinner of chicken, and pasta in Alfredo sauce before heading upstairs. They showered together, and Mandy massaged the sore spots on Charlie's body. Charlie cried at the pain Kamal felt, his rage still stinging in the bruises on her forearms where she'd blocked his blows. They lay in bed a long time, talking some more about the day, and of a world so bitter that people hated others for just being different. Then they made love. The sounds of their passion mixed with Hamm's snores.

Chapter 24

The Memorial Day project was executed without any fatal hitches. At least, so far. Sadly, an elderly woman had been taken to the hospital after a heart attack, and a teenage boy suffered a cut leg when leaping over a fence during the stampede of terrorized parade-goers. An FBI agent, posing as a parade participant, was also injured when she sprained her wrist diving and rolling to the pavement after the third blast.

The agent had the presence of mind to smear the fake blood and damp dirt in her pockets onto her face and neck as she lay on the ground. No one had noticed that when she joined the parade two blocks before the planned blast, her pants were already torn, and she wore only one shoe. The EMTs who rushed to her side added more blood as they lifted her onto a gurney.

Several other deafeningly loud explosions sent flames twenty feet high. An agent near each explosion was tasked with herding parade viewers away from the blast by screaming, "It's a bomb. Get out of here!" then leading the running crowds away from the street and onto the sidewalks, to lots, and behind businesses on the east side of the Avenue.

Although agent K's explosives were strong enough to topple two trees and cause grass and dirt to be strewn into the air, the trajectory of debris went up, rather than out. That gave the agents-turned-actors cover to avoid the wreckage, and bite down on fake blood pellets, affix plastic scars to their limbs, and rip clothing.

The Inkster and Dearborn Heights police and fire departments, given only fifteen minutes' notice of the operation, were furious. As was the mayor of Inkster. Their complaints were being handled by the special agent in charge of the FBI's Detroit field office. James had just returned from the meeting with city officials where payments for damages, injuries, and hurt feelings were being negotiated.

"When we explained the full scope of the investigation, most of them understood the urgency of the operation, and the need for secrecy," James reported. "Captain Kerner was there and it helped that he was in the loop on the operation. But when I left he was still getting a lot of grief from his colleagues."

"I bet he was," Charlie said.

"How is the woman who had the heart attack?" Judy asked.

"She's in stable condition at Garden City Hospital and she's getting good care," Commander Coleman announced.

"I'm glad to hear that," Judy said.

Charlie had watched the event unfold from James's unmarked car parked on the west side of Michigan Avenue. Don, in case he was being followed, left the area as soon as the first explosion sounded. He was now in his apartment participating in the excited chatter on various hate-group sites.

"My guys saw a few people hovering and trying to get a look at the aftermath. We think they may have been Turks observers. But, I think we pulled off the charade," James said.

"The media is covering the incident as a terror attack," Coleman said. "Within an hour of the last explosion camera crews from all the local stations had set up satellite trucks at Inkster City Hall."

"Yes, we saw some of the broadcasts from here." Charlie pointed to the monitors in the DPD conference room. "What do we do now?"

"We wait to see what communication Don receives from the Turks. If they give him a 'go' on the church bombing for this coming weekend, we start the process of getting arrest warrants for as many of the Turks as we can identify. We'll subpoena their computers and do searches at their homes. We're already doing background checks on a dozen of them, and Robbie is flagging any relevant communications he sees. We can put the Turks out of operation."

"Is the kid working out?" Coleman asked.

"We think so. He's had a couple of meetings with Don. We're trying to keep him close, but not smother him. Don says his head is still full of the language and messaging of these hate groups, but he also likes the white-hat relationship he has with the Bureau."

"He called yesterday," Judy announced to the room. "He had a fight on the street with Hassan Pashia's son. Kamal was waiting outside Robbie's office building and attacked him when he came out."

'How did Barrett sound on the phone?" Coleman asked.

"Angry. Out of control. Like James said, he knows the language of these groups, and he used profanity and racial slurs I couldn't tolerate. I hope he finds a way to distance himself from these guys."

"I do too," James said. "If not, we'll swoop him up and he'll be locked up for a long time."

"What do we know about the man who's following Robbie? The one who confronted Don at the casino?" Charlie asked.

"We asked Robbie about that, and I was kind of pissed off he was keeping that info to himself. The guy calls himself Spader. Robbie says he's a recruiter for the Stormfront organization."

"Them again," Charlie said.

"We've found out that Walt Croft not only handles the financial work of the White Turks, but has also provided funds to Stormfront. He may even be the conduit for the group's North American contributions. Believe me, they have some very bad players and they have resources, personnel, and infrastructure far beyond the capabilities of the Turks."

"They sound scary," Judy said.

"They're lethal," James responded. "Stormfront never would have been fooled by our charade today."

"We don't even know that the Turks have been fooled," Charlie remarked.

"Well, that's right."

"And if the Turks don't take the bait?" Charlie asked.

James looked at Commander Coleman. "Well then the Commander and I will take the evidence we have, get warrants, and round up as many of these guys as we can. We can still shut down the Turks, but I'd rather have the opportunity to dismantle their back end, and take down a part of Stormfront at the same time. They're the big fish in this ever-growing stream of domestic terrorism."

Don gave the window shade signal. He needed to talk to James or Charlie. The chat board guys were gloating about loss of life in the parade. The media wouldn't confirm any fatalities, but were interviewing witnesses who claimed to have seen people who were maimed and bleeding, and bodies being taken away. Don wanted to know the truth.

Within five minutes he received a call. He didn't know the number.

"Hello?"

"Good Evening, Mr. Curtis."

"Who is this?"

"A friend. We're pleased with the results of your, uh . . ."

"Test?" Don asked.

The man on the other end of the call chuckled. "Yes. I guess that's exactly what it was. We've been monitoring the media coverage all day. Congratulations. You obviously know what you're doing, and we're ready for you to get started on the other job we talked about."

Don didn't recognize the voice. He was sure it wasn't Walt or Cortez, the Turks chapter president. It might be the money man at Croft's office.

"Have you settled on a location?" Don asked.

"Yes. Location number one. We want a big event that will

get the attention of the national media."

"Okay. The expenses I outlined are approved?"

"They are. Your funds are ready for you."

"Do I pick them up at the same place?"

"No. We'll have a courier deliver them to you this evening."

"You already know where I live?"

The man didn't respond. Don waited.

"We'll give the funds to Mr. Barrett, and you can arrange to meet him wherever you want."

"You think that's a good idea? I like the kid, but he's green. That kind of money is a big temptation."

"We trust Mr. Barrett. He'll call you when he has the funds."

"One more thing. I'll need a point person. Somebody I can call if I run into a problem. Please tell me that's *not* going to be the kid. I need someone who can make quick decisions," Don said.

"That'll be Mr. Croft. You have his number."

The caller disconnected. The Turks were clearly fans of Robbie. He'd told Don of his latest work, which involved writing software to capture the names, addresses, banking and credit card information from a half dozen travel businesses. The money stolen from innocent vacationers would provide an ongoing stream of funds for the group's organization. Robbie bragged his work had taken the Turks to a new level.

Although the knock at the door was expected, it startled Don and he popped up from his seat. He released his Ruger from its holster and opened the door. James and Charlie stood in the hall. Charlie held a large White Castle bag.

"Can we come in?" she asked. "Or are you going to shoot us?"

"Yeah. I mean, come on in. I'm just surprised to see you. I thought you would call. Aren't you worried the Turks might be watching me?"

"They *were* watching, but we haven't seen them in the last twenty-four hours," James said, pushing past Don. "We have a problem."

177

"I think we may have more than one," Don said, closing the door and holstering his gun. "What happened to your face, Mack?"

"Martial arts," Charlie lied.

"I thought the idea was to block the punches. You have a black belt. You must know how to do that."

"Long story. I'll tell you over these gas-inducing little beauties," Charlie said, dangling the bag.

They sat around the tiny table in the small kitchen. With one hand Don grabbed four burgers and opened the refrigerator. "You want a beer? Juice? Better make it juice, I guess."

"Robbie Barrett has turned on us," James announced.

"I wondered about that. I just got a call from some guy who says Robbie will have the funds for the church job. You think he's told them about me?"

"We don't think so. We're monitoring all his calls, emails, social media posts. All of it. It seems he still believes in the cause of the alt-right, and is planning a double cross."

"How do you figure that?" Charlie asked.

"Well, he likes the work he's doing for the FBI, and he likes Don. I know this because he's private messaging with a girl he's met in a chat room. Bragging about himself and the people he knows. He has several online aliases. Calls himself SPOKESMAN in this particular room, chatting about bikes and racing. We just found out about this. He's very talented in covering his trail and presenting different persona."

"I know. Kamal showed me some posts where he calls himself STORMTROOPER22. I'm surprised he doesn't know you're monitoring him," Charlie said.

"He knows. It's a game for him. He spots our trace and closes the door, or figures out a way to do a reverse trace. He's using all the tools at his disposal, but we're always a step ahead because, you know . . ."

"You're the FBI," Charlie competed the sentence.

"Judy didn't have any trouble finding Robbie through social media," Don said.

"Yeah, but those posts are a couple of years old when he was still just flirting with these fringe groups," James said. "He hasn't used Facebook much, but that's changed in the last few days."

Charlie recounted for Don the fight between Robbie and Kamal, Robbie's call to Judy, and Charlie's visit to the Pashia house.

"Kamal didn't have a weapon when he attacked Robbie. Just his fists and his rage."

"Apparently he still had plenty in reserve when you challenged him to spar, Mack."

"According to Judy, this fight with Kamal may have tipped Robbie's rage over the edge."

"I think that's very possible," James said. "Robbie just made a deposit of two grand in a bank account he thinks we don't know about. He's extremely active on the dark chats. He's BIKER-DUDE on the Turks membership boards, and SPOKESMAN on the biker websites, but we've discovered he uses another handle on the Stormfront sites."

"What's his handle there?" Charlie asked.

"GESTAPOGEEK."

"How do you want me to handle him when he calls?" Don asked.

"Meet with him. See if you can get his head back in the right game. Tell him you have a role for him in the church bombing operation. Tell him you want him on your team."

"And if that doesn't work?"

"We'll have to take him back into custody. We can't afford to have him blow your cover, and he may be on the verge of doing that. But as of this moment he still sees you as a friend."

Chapter 25

"Barrett." Don greeted the kid as he approached the truck. From across the road, he'd watched Robbie secure his bike to the rack near the bike trail. He'd honked the horn and waved him over. Robbie seemed confident. Don could tell by the set of his shoulders. He was wearing new bike shorts and a form-fitting jersey.

"Hey," he said as he began to remove his backpack. "I've got the package."

"No, not outside. Get in," Don ordered.

Robbie paused for a second, looked around, then ambled over to the passenger side of the truck.

"You're looking good, kid. New clothes and all, and now the Turks trust you to be the bagman."

"Bagman?"

"The guy who carries the valuables. In this case, the money. That's a big responsibility."

"Yeah, it is. I could have just taken the money and ridden my bike over the bridge to Canada," Robbie said with a slight smile.

Don didn't smile back. "Believe me, I know the temptation, but you don't ever want to do that. One way to get on the dead side of any deal is to mess with the money."

Robbie's eyes widened for a minute, and he removed his bike helmet to rub at his newly cut hair.

"Don't worry, kid. You might have a few mixed-up ideas, but I think you have good instincts about people. You can tell when somebody is a bullshitter. Like Frank Wyatt. He was looking out only for himself. I don't think you're like that. You have a mother and a little brother, right?"

Robbie didn't answer.

The Bureau was monitoring this conversation. Don's instructions from James were to get a sense of Robbie's state of mind. Push him, scare him, test his resolve to continue his agreement with the Bureau. They knew he was playing both sides, and perhaps ready to sell out the Bureau. If Don thought the boy had made a decision to side with the bad guys, he would give a signal and two cars of agents would sweep in to grab Robbie, his bike, and the money. Neither the Turks, Stormfront, nor his family would see him again for a long time.

"You're still good with things, right?" Don asked.

"Yeah," Robbie said unconvincingly.

Don made a decision to go off script. "Let me be real with you, Barrett. Let me speak to you man to man. Every man gets to a crossroads where their life presents them with two paths to take. One takes you in one direction; the other takes you in a totally different direction. Mine came when I left the Marines. I was about your age, and I was lost for a few years. Couldn't keep a job, I drank too much, and I didn't think I had much reason to get up in the morning. My family stuck by me, and eventually I got some help. It took two years until I finally got my job with the Detroit police. Not long after that I met the woman I later married. Your crossroads event is now. You listening?"

Robbie nodded.

"It's too bad you don't have the time I had to come to a decision. I'm sorry about that, but your time is now. You can follow these madmen who blow up churches to show their dissatisfaction with the way things are, or you can decide that the other path, even though it doesn't seem clear right now, is the smarter thing to do for you and your family."

Robbie *had* been listening. Intently. He'd placed his helmet on the floor of the truck, and his hands gripped his knees. "What do you think I should do?"

"I'm not going to give any more advice. Damn, I've talked more to you in the past week than I have to my wife. But I will make you an offer. If it's okay with Agent Saleh, you can work with me. I'll be going through the motions of preparing this church job for the Turks. I'm doing it to draw these guys out into the open so we can put them out of business. I don't want to live in a world where I just hate people and blow up things."

"I'd like to work with you," Robbie said.

"You have to be sure, Barrett. I'm going to be depending on you. Stay, and let's start planning. Or, get the hell out of my truck."

Don and Robbie were parked across the street from St. Anne's. The church's neo-Gothic architecture with double spires and red brick gleamed awesomeness in a way that caught the eye of even nonbelievers. It was one of the oldest churches in the city, and Robbie peered up through the windshield to see the full scope of the building. The historical significance of St. Anne's alone made it a worthy target, but the fact that a majority of its congregation were Spanish speakers made it even more relevant to the malicious goals of the Turks.

"Damn. That's a big place, and there are a lot of people around," Robbie said.

"That's going to help us to blend in as we check out the place. Let's get out and walk."

The St. Anne's complex took up a square block in south-west Detroit in an area some called Mexicantown. It faced a street named for the church, bounded on the north and south by Howard Street and Lafayette Avenue, and separated by hundreds of yards of industrial space to the east. It was adjacent to the US Customs Cargo Inspection facility, and just beyond that stood the Ambassador Bridge. The bridge's tower competed with St. Anne's two tower spires, which reached 180 feet into the sky.

They slowly walked along the side of the building, eyeing the windows and foundation vents. The red brick building was solid, and the grounds were maintained well enough that few places would provide cover for someone lurking in the shadows. As they rounded to the plaza, they stopped to read the sign indicating the church's historical designation and its association with Father Gabriel Richard who was enshrined there.

Three lancet windows, pointed arches, and wooden doors gave the building a welcoming look. The bricked courtyard included a few mature trees, several cement planters, and benches. The gabled façade of the central nave was separated from the west tower by a flying buttress. The circular window above the nave included a Star of David. The towers had two levels of windows and louvered bell openings below steeply pitched peaks topped with crosses, and the slate roof sloped into decorative ridges.

Don and Robbie continued around the building chatting nonchalantly and nodding to the one or two people they passed. A few of them, Don suspected, were tourists because they carried cameras and exclaimed their excitement about the building's beauty. The old nineteenth-century firehouse on the property was also a landmark. Don walked to the building, which still had its faded green double doors. From here, looking up Eighteenth Street, Don could see the corner of the old Michigan Central Station.

The mammoth train station was an iconic Detroit landmark. In its heyday, thousands of daily visitors, commuters, and workers had moved in and out of its doors. Now, after thirty years of neglect, the building and the grounds surrounding it had a dystopian feel. Still, the old girl jutted her concrete chin in defiance of those who'd abandoned her.

They rounded the corner walking past the rectory and the convent, and back to the car.

"It's a huge church," Don said. "I didn't remember how fortified it is. I'll need to go inside for a closer look at the interior."

"If you're not going to blow it up, why are you going to all this trouble?" Robbie asked.

"Don't you know people are following us?"

"What?" Robbie said, starting to look around.

"Hey, stop that, kid. Just look straight ahead," Don said. "We don't want them to know we're aware of their surveillance. We can't be sure who's working with the Turks. It might even be somebody associated with the church. You'd be surprised what people will do for money."

Don looked up at the building a final time before turning to the car. Robbie followed.

"We need to make this look good. Be seen all over this area, casing the church and the neighborhood."

"Oh, I get it. Otherwise, the Turks will be suspicious."

"Right. I'll come back later for the weekday mass. Then you and I should come back tomorrow. We can take a few pictures, have a cup of coffee. I have another guy who takes care of the explosives, but we need to be seen buying other materials. Between now and next Sunday I'll probably get a call asking for a status report. I'll work with James to come up with a plausible plan to draw them into the open. I think a lot of them will want to be around to see what happens on Sunday. Out of harm's way, but close enough to witness the explosions they think they're going to see."

"Got it."

"Here's what I need from you. Be on the listserv tonight. Talk up the Sunday Surprise without getting into any details. Don't mention the name of the church. At least not yet."

"What if someone calls me?"

"Who's been contacting you?"

"Depends. If it's to check on the phishing work, I usually hear from the chapter president. I heard from some other guy about picking up the money for you."

"Has Walt ever called you?"

"Uh no. Not directly."

"What does that mean?"

"Well, I found out the guy from Stormfront—his name is Spader—knows Croft. They've been in touch via email. Spader

184

calls me every once in a while."

"When are you supposed to speak with him again?"

"We don't have anything scheduled. I've applied for membership in Stormfront, and he says they're still working on my application."

"Hmm. Is that the dude I've seen you chatting with on the boards? The guy who calls himself SEEINGBLUE?"

"Yep."

"I don't like that dude, Barrett. He spouts all this Christian stuff but in a bullying way. He's trying to control you."

Robbie didn't respond right away. They sat in the truck staring at the side of St. Anne's. With the windows rolled down Don could hear the constant din from the cars and trucks traveling to and from Windsor, Ontario, on the Ambassador Bridge.

"Who *isn't* trying to control me," Robbie finally said.

Don barely heard the kid's response. He was focusing on the sound of traffic behind him. It was constant, so it just became white noise. He turned to look at the bridge. There were 60,000 crossings every day; 8,000 trucks going back and forth both day and night.

"What are you thinking about?" Robbie asked.

"Sorry, kid. My mind wandered for a moment. I was looking at the bridge."

"I've never been to Canada," Robbie said.

"You're kidding? I thought everybody who lives in Detroit has been to Canada at least once."

"Not me."

"Thirty years ago you could bike across the bridge. My father told me about it," Don said. "But times change. Let's go."

Chapter 26

Don had attended Catholic school all the way through high school. The Catholic church was strong then, and Hamtramck had some of the most stable parishes in the archdiocese. St. Anne's was the oldest Catholic church in Detroit, and the second-oldest continuously operating parish in the United States, so no matter what parish your family belonged to, every practicing Catholic had probably attended an event at the historic church.

It was hard not to be awed by the beauty of the building. As soon as you stepped into the nave your eyes were drawn upward to the eighty-five foot high, pale blue ceiling decorated with gold stars. The stained glass was breathtaking. Don sat in a pew about halfway between the sanctuary and the vestibule. He'd forgotten about the church's elevated pulpit and the spired pew ends. Polished, dark wood was everywhere Don looked— the confessionals, the beautiful altar rails, and the side altars. He glanced over his shoulder at the elegant organ on the second level, then back to the marble nave, which was clean and polished. The church wasn't rich, but someone was taking good care of it.

Although attendance at the Wednesday evening mass was decent, the pews were less than half filled. Don scanned the congregation of white, Black and Hispanic worshippers—most of them gray-haired, a few children, more women than men.

Earlier, he'd visited the church's food pantry, entering through the parking lot door, and standing in line with families and individuals who needed the help of the church to make ends meet. The volunteers distributed staples like toilet paper and soap, cereal, canned goods, and peanut butter. Don slipped out of line as he got to the front. He'd only wanted to see the interior of the building, and noted the extensive heating pipes crisscrossing the walls.

He shifted his attention to the rest of the church's vulnerabilities, including the many nooks and crannies that would not likely be examined on a daily basis. There were a few security cameras on the exterior of the building, and probably in the offices and sanctuary areas, but Don saw no cameras along the pillars in the nave.

He enjoyed the simple mass with a good message on life's seasons and how they reflect the seasons of the life of Jesus. Don knew the songs, although he hadn't sung them in years. Aware that he might be watched, at the end of the service he waited with others in a short line to use the restrooms.

He remained in his car well after the mass was over watching the people who lingered in the plaza. Little girls in colorful dresses chased after bubbles that one of the mothers blew into the wind. An elderly couple sat close, wearing matching knit caps, smiling and watching the children play. A man used his phone to take photos of the historical plaque. Next Sunday would be Pentecost. He wondered if the Turks even knew this.

A bomb placed in one of the planters, under the gladiola, would send visitors in all directions. Plastic explosive in the food pantry would blast a hole into the chapel if it were strong enough, and a blast from the organ area would send the upper floor toppling into the nave.

He watched the plaza area darken. Spotlights, probably on a timer, splashed the red brick. Something about the change of light made him think so strongly about Rita that he almost called home. But to do so might put her in danger. If he could speak with her, he'd want to know about Rudy's day, how he was getting along with his grandfather, and if Rita's school was gearing up for the summer break. He had never understood until now

187

how much the mundane patterns of family life sustained him.

As Don drove pass St. Anne's, he looked back. The view of the church towers captured in the spotlights, the soft illumination of the lanterns hanging at each door, the green trees and colorful blooms fading into shadows, and the thin lines of a pink sunset spreading behind the church gave him comfort.

He'd heard the phrase "our thoughts are prayers," and he felt guilt roiling in his chest like thick cement. Don knew God understood his detailed and intense thoughts of destruction of this house of worship were not those of a terrorist, but of a man of God who had lapsed in his duties to the church. A man who still had faith in the power of the cross. At least he hoped God understood.

Chapter 27

Despite James's report to the contrary, Don knew he was still under surveillance. He could sense it. So he insisted that he and Charlie maintain their covert meetings. He was parked in the lot of the MGM Grand staring at the entrance near valet parking. Remembering his run-in with the blue-eyed Spader inside the casino, he'd passed a note to Charlie as she sat at the quarter slots, telling her to wait a half hour then meet him outside. In the meantime, he bought two coneys from the food court and a giant soft drink. When he spotted Charlie coming out the exit, he pulled out the second bag and laid it on the seat.

"What's this?" she said stepping up into the truck.

"A coney and curly fries. I'll take the fries if you don't want them."

"Who said I don't want them?"

"Your face looks better," Don said. "I don't see that bruise over your cheek anymore."

"No. That was just a glancing blow, but I still have a couple of sore spots on my upper arms. That boy has a good kick."

"You wouldn't even believe how homesick I am. What have you heard about Rita and the kids?"

"Judy knew we were meeting tonight, so she spent extra time on the phone with Rita getting details."

Charlie spent ten minutes recounting the information she'd heard from Judy. Rudy's two grandfathers were in competition about who would pick Rudy up from school. It had always been Don's father's job, but now that Rita and Rudy were staying at her parents' house, Rudy's maternal grandfather thought it made more sense for him to take over that duty. Don asked questions and gave his personal opinion: His dad should continue to pick up Rudy so it wouldn't affect his routine, and Rita's dad needed to get over it. Charlie was done with her fries by the time she'd finished the report. "Oh, and Rita specifically said to give you her love. She said she would hunt you down if she hasn't heard from you by Sunday."

Don sat quietly for a moment staring out the windshield. Charlie bagged her trash and waited. "Did you buy me a soft drink?" she finally asked.

"No. Sorry. Do you want a swig of mine?"

Charlie made a face. "Uh no. I'll just chew a piece of gum. So how did it go the last few days? Are you still being followed?"

"Yeah. Someone's keeping an eye on me. I'd do the same if I'd just paid somebody twenty thousand dollars. They want to keep up with Barrett, too, I think. He has a lot of information about them now, and if he's anything like he is with me when he meets or talks to them, they must have a few doubts about him."

"How's he doing?"

"So far, steady. I'm talking to him like he's a grown man. He's curious, asks a lot of questions. There's a shitload of stuff he doesn't know about life, and there's a side of him that gets to you and makes you want to help him."

"That would be the side that Judy spotted right away. What kind of work is he doing for you?"

"Stringing along the Turks and the other loonies who want to see shit blown up. He's on the message boards. I told him to tease them. Don't give any details, but keep their anticipation up. He's doing a good job with that. Tomorrow, he and I are shopping for bomb components. I still have that list from Agent K. We'll make a day of it. Go to three or four different places. Leaving a trail if anyone wants to see one, and pretending I'm about to blow up one of the most important churches in the city."

"I've been thinking about that, Don. I know we both have fallen away from the church, but it's in our blood. It must be really hard to be thinking about all this insane stuff."

"I attended mass tonight, and as I knelt and made the sign of the cross, my twelve years with the nuns all came flooding back to me. Mack, when's the last time you been in that church? It's everything the Pope wants you to believe about the faith."

Don shook his head. "I just want to get this damn job over with."

"I know. We all do. I've got a bit of news. Frank Wyatt is making a deal with the FBI after all. He's confessed to being the bomb maker in the mosque explosion, and he'll say the chapter president is the one who ordered him to do it."

"That's something really useful to the prosecutor," Don said.

"James told me to tell you that they've been in touch with someone he trusts at St. Anne's to give them a heads-up that he may see a couple of strange men lurking about. He didn't give any details at all on the operation. He told the guy it was something the hate crimes task force has recommended doing at all of the key churches in the city."

"That's good. It will give me some cover. I've already been around the place three times in the last couple of days, and tomorrow morning Barrett and I will be taking pictures."

"That's all I have in terms of new information," Charlie said.

"Does James have anything more on this Croft guy, or the other guy, the recruiter?"

"He didn't say."

"I heard today from Barrett that the Stormfront recruiter and Croft are acquaintances. That might mean something to James's investigation."

"Okay. I'll pass that on. He may already know, if Robbie knows it."

"Also, I have an idea for how to get our hands on the top guys the day of the Sunday Surprise. It came to me when Barrett and I were checking out the church yesterday."

"Good. Let's hear it."

"I think it's a good plan," Charlie said to James through the car's speakerphone. "For these guys, the incident is all about the show. They want to see and hear the explosions and the resulting terror. I think Don's right. It won't be enough for them to watch on TV. They had one or two guys out for the parade bombing, but this time the whole rotten bunch of them will want to be front and center to see their production. And if we can have them in a fairly contained space it will make it easier to round up the lot of them."

"It could work." James's voice sounded through the car speakers.

"The Ambassador Bridge would give a spectacular view of the church being destroyed. It would also stop traffic on the bridge for a while."

"What's Don's idea to make them bite?"

"He wants to use Robbie to keep up the anticipation; then Don will call Croft to suggest the idea. He'd tell them when to be on the bridge to catch the fireworks, and when nothing happens, a roadblock can snag them coming off the bridge. They'd have nowhere to run."

"It sort of reminds me of our Belle Isle sting, remember?"

"How could I forget? Bullets were flying all over the place, and I was lucky I didn't get shot. By the way, Don's pretty sure he's being followed again. Do you have men on him?"

"No. But we do have eyes on Robbie so maybe it's my guys giving him the heebie-jeebies. Let me see what I have to do to get the Ambassador Bridge blocked off. You want me to get in touch with Don?"

"No," Charlie answered. "He and I are going off schedule to meet again tomorrow, and I can give him your instructions and any updates. He's getting kind of anxious, missing home, and this whole Catholic church thing is eating at him."

"It's only a few more days," James said. "Tell Don to hold on. His efforts have been invaluable to us. With Wyatt's deal, we're putting together a nice case of conspiracy and manslaughter. With the online snooping Robbie and my team are doing, we'll also have additional criminal charges."

There was silence from the speakerphone.

"Are you still there, James?"

"Yes, I'm here. I'll just be glad when we can lock these fuckers up, Charlie."

The kid's doing a good job of jerking these guys around.

Don was switching from one message board to another. Robbie had set up another alias for Don. As *BUICKLOVER* he was occasionally commenting on Robbie's posts and joining in the overall fervor being generated by rumors of something for the record books on Sunday. The phrase *Sunday Surprise* had taken on a life of its own, and Don had even seen it referenced a couple of times on Facebook.

Around midnight, Don spotted SEEINGBLUE liking and cheering the posts of other users. Then he posted a message to Robbie:

Posted by: SEEINGBLUE
BIKERDUDE. How's it going?

BIKERDUDE replying to SEEINGBLUE
Going well on my end.

SEEINGBLUE replying to BIKERDUDE
Need to talk to you offline. Will text you in five.

Don typed quickly into the chat room so Robbie would know he was still online, and had seen the last message from Spader.

Posted by: BUICKLOVER
Still awake here in the burbs. Anybody got a

recommend on a good movie?

The board lit up with the names of movies, most of which Don had already seen. *The Day of the Jackal, Death Wish, Gladiator, First Blood, Braveheart, The Delta Force, The Alamo.*

No matter how badass these guys believed they were, their bravado rarely came from real-life experience. It was inspired by popular culture. The books, movies, TV shows, comic books, and magazines in sync with their views, tastes, and levels of testosterone.

More movies popped up rapidly on Don's screen: *Rambo I, II,* and *III; Blown Away; Live Free or Die Hard.* Most had the same themes and always the same heroes. A white man spouting a nebulous set of values—independence, sacrifice, patriotism, tradition—and set on protecting the women, children and the American/Anglo-Saxon/Christian way from nonwhite bad guys. Or revenge for some perceived harm to those same values culminating in explosions, car chases, and gunfire. The end was always the same. The cinematic hero—Chuck Norris, Bruce Willis, Sylvester Stallone, John Wayne, Mel Gibson, Tommy Lee Jones—either walked away from harm in slow motion, flames and chaos all around him, or died with a hero's send-off.

SEEINGBLUE got into the conversation by suggesting *Black Sunday*, the film about a troubled former POW planning and executing an attack on the Super Bowl. *That asshole.* He hoped Robbie could stand up to this blue-eyed devil.

Chapter 28

"Does Don know? Is he treating the kid any differently?"

"Not as far as we can tell. They're meeting again today. Buying supplies. Barrett says he'll call in a full report when they're done," Spader said.

"He knows not to use his own phone?"

"I've given him three burner phones. He knows to use a different one every day. I was thinking of maybe moving him out of his mother's house."

"Won't that make the FBI suspicious?"

"Maybe so. But they were close to pulling him in the other day."

"I think we have to leave it like it is. We only have a couple more days. Let them think everything is okay. Let the Bureau and this Don guy keep doing the heavy lifting for us."

"Okay."

"Are the explosives ready?"

"They're assembled and in a safe place. We're just waiting to know where to place them."

"Good. Keep me abreast."

Spader's Jeep had become his makeshift office and hotel room. This job was more complex than he'd imagined, but he'd follow the Angel's wishes. The man was a good Christian, and he was exceptionally smart. Smarter than the FBI. He'd been a step ahead of them for months and always had contingencies.

When the police leak dried up, he already had a backup plan in place. He hadn't hit it off with the boy, so he'd put Spader in charge of handling Robbie's conversion. The man had a knack for making doors open to him. *I bet he could open the gates of Heaven themselves. Probably how he came to be known as the Angel.*

"Where you been?" Don asked. "You're late."

"Yeah, sorry. Something came up this morning," Robbie said, sitting on the bench behind Don so they were back-to-back on the plaza of St. Anne's.

"You can't be late on Sunday. They'll be watching."

"I know."

"You biked all the way?"

"Yeah. It was a good workout."

The sun reflecting on the plaza's red brick made the whole area glow. It had rained earlier, and the water drying in the cracks sparkled. A few tourists had already found their way to the church, and they moved around the courtyard taking photos of the building and posing for their own pictures. Don had a camera hanging around his neck and took a few quick snapshots himself. He pointed in the direction of the gargoyles on the roofline, and the shutter clicked rapidly. He aimed at the buttresses next, then the cement planters.

"Let's move to the side," Don said. "You take notes."

Robbie pulled out his phone and used a stylus. Don gave him numbers: "Fifteen feet between the planters. Mark them at twelve inches deep. The front roofline looks about fifty feet."

At the side, Don took pictures of the foundation and the door and entryway of the rectory. He aimed his camera at the roof again and fired off a few pics before replacing the lens with a panoramic one and taking some photos of the span of the Ambassador Bridge. Don headed back to the front, and Robbie dutifully followed. Don stood at the street wall to take a panoramic photo of the church's front façade. The tourists noticed him with his camera. As he moved toward the center of the plaza with Robbie on his heels, a young woman in the group—pretty, with blond bangs and a turquoise scarf flung around her neck—approached smiling.

"I was wondering if you could take a picture of me and my family," she said, holding out her small camera. "We're waiting to do a tour of the church."

"We'd be happy to, wouldn't we, Father Barrett?" Don said to Robbie, whose face froze in shock.

"Oh, are you a priest?" the girl asked with wide eyes and a more tentative smile. "You look so young."

Robbie couldn't speak. His face was flushed, and he shifted his helmet from one hand to the other. He glared at Don then turned and stomped to a bench and threw his helmet on the seat.

"He's still in training," Don said.

"Don't you ever do that again," Robbie hissed when Don returned to the benches. "You embarrassed me in front of that girl. This is serious business we're doing."

"I was just having a little fun, Barrett. Lighten up. I'd rather we look like a couple of happy tourists than two terrorists casing the joint. Come on. They're doing a tour this morning. We're going in."

Don followed the family into the church, and the young lady with the blond bangs held the door open for Robbie. Don put his hand on Robbie's arm so they could fall back from the group. The tourists *oohed* and *aawed* at the impressive view. Robbie stopped and, mouth open, looked up at the ceiling and its display of magnificent stained glass.

"Bet your church doesn't look like this one, does it, Barrett?"

"This really is something," Robbie finally answered.

Don led Robbie to the front, and they sat two pews before the transept, the area between the nave and the sanctuary. Don snapped a few photos of the elevated pulpit on the left of the church, the radiator in front of the altar rail, photos of the confessionals, and the open doors on either side of the sanctuary. One of them probably led to the sacristy where the priest and attendants prepared before the service. Don signaled to Robbie that they were leaving and stopped to take a photo of the organ on the second level over the vestibule.

The tour group was returning to the side aisles, and the guide was looking their way. "Let's head out," Don whispered. There were a few more people in front of the church. The temperatures were forecast to climb into the seventies today, and folks were taking advantage of the mild weather.

"Grab your bike. Let's put it in the truck. Then we'll get some Mexican food. I'm buying."

At Lowe's and Home Depot, they had bought some of the equipment they needed: pipe, ball bearings, duct tape, pipe ends, a few PVC parts, nails, and clamps. Next they had driven to a few hardware stores for other supplies, and now they were back in the truck.

"Are you only doing pipe bombs?" Robbie asked.

"No. A combination of IEDs and plastic. Some of the spaces inside will be easier to conceal plastic. Under the radiators, along the base of some of the columns. The pipes will go up in the organ balcony. Maybe a few taped to the underside of some of the pews. Outside will be all plastic. This is a strong building. But placed along the buttresses, an explosion should cause quite a bit of damage. We'll also place some in the lower hall where the food pantry is. That will take out the heating system and maybe do foundation damage."

Robbie listened intently and put a few notes in his phone. "Medium to heavy load on the plastic?"

"You've been watching those videos again, huh?"

"Yeah. I've seen a few, but now that there's a practical application, it's interesting to see how it would work. If it were real, I mean."

"We'll need to come back at night to make it look good. Put some of the pipe on the sides, on the roof, and in the planters. We'll probably have twelve, maybe fourteen dummy devices."

"When do we plant them?"

"Who's we?"

"You and me."

"This will be a three-man job, and it'll be me and two agents. If you want, you can meet me on Saturday for the interior work. That's when they do the cleaning, and I can slip in. It would be good to have an extra set of hands, and someone who can distract attention away from what I'm doing. Okay?"

"Okay, but how will you plant the exterior devices to make it look real to the Turks?"

"Use a crane with a bucket. Pretend to work on the outside lights or the trees and lob a couple of plastic loads with fake detonators onto the lower roof. We can be in and out in five minutes."

"Sounds good."

"What'll you do with the rest of your day?" Don asked.

"Oh. I don't know. Maybe take another bike ride. I took the day off from my job."

"Okay. Well, I'll see you on the boards tonight. Is this okay to drop you off?"

"Yep."

Don looked back at Robbie as he lifted his bike from the truck, and did a quick safety check. Tires, chain, pedals. He put on his helmet, nodded to Don, and swung onto the bike headed in the direction of Fort Street. Within seconds he was out of sight.

Spader waited for the call from Robbie. He sat in his Jeep five rows behind the truck and watched the back of this Rutkowski guy's head. He just seemed to be sitting there. Robbie had unloaded his bike and ridden off five minutes ago. His cell phone sprang to life. It was one of the burner phone numbers.

"Barrett," Spader said.

"Hey, Mr. Spader. I have a lot of information for you."

Spader flipped to a new page on his clipboard. "Okay,

kid. Let's have it."

Robbie talked fast about everything Don had said. He excitedly reported on the number of explosive devices, their placement inside and outside the church, the specific areas of the interior where Don had seen the most vulnerability, and his idea about posing as electrical workers with a bucket crane. When Don wasn't watching, he'd taken a couple of phone photos of their shopping cart with the tools and materials they'd purchased. He promised to send that photo, along with the ones he'd taken inside the church.

"That's very good work. Give me the timetable again."

"I tell you, Charlie, the guy has been following us since we left the church. We've shopped at five stores, and I've spotted the Jeep at each place. He's sitting behind me now just watching. I think I'm going back there to snatch him out of the vehicle."

"Don't do that, Don. Play it cool. We knew they were still keeping an eye on you and the boy. That's good. They see you going through the motions. That keeps them on the hook, and that's where we want them."

"Wasn't James checking on Spader? Have they found out anything about him?"

"I asked. He says the Bureau didn't have him in their database. The Jeep's license plate is registered to an LLC in Lansing. They've monitored the listserv you told them about and tried a reverse trace on his IP address, but he must be using a virtual network they can't track."

"I don't know what that means, Mack, but I guess it translates into they don't know shit about this guy. What if I can get a photograph of him? Don't they have some fancy technology to identify him from his picture?"

"It's called face recognition."

"Yeah. Well, I'm going to try to get a picture of the guy now. I have this spiffy camera with all these lenses, and I think one is a telephoto lens. Hold on, Mack. I'm going to try to get a shot of him now."

Using the FBI camera, Don switched out the panoramic lens he'd used at the church for one marked as a 600-millimeter lens. He turned in the truck cab and framed the blue-eyed devil in the viewfinder. He took several shots. They wouldn't be perfect because the photo was through the back glass of the truck and the windshield of the Jeep, but you could still see the man pretty clearly as he chatted on his phone.

"Got it, Mack. Look I'm supposed to meet with Agent K at the trailer. Why don't you meet me there? I'll call K and tell him you're coming. If this guy is following me, it might take me a few minutes to lose him, but I'll be there."

Chapter 29

The double-wide FBI trailer in the Donovan quarry had been transformed into a surveillance center and bomb-construction site. Charlie sat in a chair opposite the three technicians working under the supervision of Agent Peter Kapinski.

"As you can see, Ms. Mack, there's still a lot of work involved in making fake devices. The IEDs need to appear to be bombs and have the weight and sound of real explosives in case one of the Turks' observers gets close enough to look at the detail of the devices," Kapinski explained.

The plastic explosive, which would be placed in both external and internal areas, presented a more difficult problem. Technicians were mixing a clay-like substance to replicate the look and feel of C-4.

"I thought you used Semtex for the Memorial Day operation," Charlie said.

"Yes, but we were planting it outdoors, in tree boxes and such. Semtex has an orange or red color. To be placed around columns and foundations and pipes, we would use C-4 because it's white and blends in better."

Another technician moved from chair to chair around three desktop computers. She'd told Charlie she was monitoring a half dozen chat rooms, message boards, websites, and phones associated with the task force case. She was nimbly typing, printing, texting, and talking to another agent. She left her workstation for a minute to hand Charlie a printout. It was the verbatim conversation she'd had with Don an hour ago.

"It's from the bug in Don's mobile," Agent Garrow said in answer to Charlie's raised eyebrows. "He's right. We really don't know shit about this Spader guy. But when we get Don's photo that might really help."

Twenty minutes later, the radio in the room squawked with the message that Don had entered the Donovan quarry and was headed toward the trailer. Even with the warning, when Don burst into the room, every person looked up with alarm.

"Mack, glad you're here," he said, bypassing hellos. "It took me a half-hour to shake that asshole, but I left him somewhere on the freeway. The hard part was doing it without letting on I knew I was being followed," Don said, pleased with himself.

"Agent Garrow!" he called out. "What's shaking?"

She was on the phone and gave Don a thumbs-up. He dumped the camera on the desk next to her.

Agent K explained briefly to Don what they'd completed, and went back to work. Don joined Charlie in the rear of the trailer.

"You look tired," she said.

"It was another long day." Don looked at his watch. "I've been at it for ten hours. I spoke to James. He's going to call us back."

Agent Garrow headed their way, holding the Nikon. She was removing the back and held up the memory card.

"I'm checking it now. Should I pull off everything?"

"There are a lot of church shots, and the last three are of our guy. I guess it wouldn't hurt to have all the photos in case someone asks to see them."

"Got it," Garrow said, heading back to her side of the trailer. "Oh, Agent Saleh called. He said to let you know he's coming here."

"She's really good," Charlie said.

"That she is. She showed me how to use Facebook and set up my profile."

"Plan on using Facebook much after this case?"

"Who knows, Mack? I have forty-three followers, and I've already been invited to eight groups. I kind of like it."

"Maybe you should check in with Rita on that." Charlie smirked.

James arrived a half hour later carrying bags with a dozen Chinese food choices. All the work stopped for ten minutes as the agents, Charlie, and Don scooped shrimp fried rice, moo goo gai pan, mushu pork, egg foo yung, General Tso's chicken, and white rice onto their paper plates.

"Saleh, you're beginning to understand how I work best," Don said.

"Yep, I'm figuring out a few things about you." James winked at Charlie.

Garrow very quickly had printouts of the Spader photos. There were three of them, not very clear, but with enough quality to allow for matching. She placed them on the table in front of James, Charlie, and Don.

"Let's use this one," James, said pointing to the one where Spader was looking straight ahead.

Garrow scooped up the photo and left the others. They stared at the man.

"I don't like this guy," Don started. "I don't like the way he tries to manipulate Robbie online."

"He's obviously working for Croft," Charlie said.

"Maybe not. We found the two interactions with Croft that Robbie told us about, but we haven't found any other communication between them."

"Maybe it's phone calls."

"We're monitoring Croft's office calls, and mobile calls. It's possible Spader is using a burner phone," James said.

"It's very unusual when we can't identify a person through the normal channels. This Spader guy is an enigma. He could be with one of the agencies. Whoever he is, and whoever he's working with, he's done a good job of staying off the grid."

Charlie was on her way home. Although the quarry wasn't far from her east-side neighborhood, it would still be after ten before she got there. She was surprised when Judy called.

"You're working late tonight."

"I work late a lot of nights. Especially if it's online research," Judy said. "Charlie, I found something troubling about Gabriel Constantine."

Charlie downshifted into third gear and pulled into the right lane of East Jefferson Avenue. "What Judy?" Charlie said in a choked voice.

"He's not everything he appears to be. On the surface he's a philanthropist and communications advisor. He *has* worked in the Upper Peninsula for a long time. Before that he was in the military, working in surveillance. I can't find any evidence that he has children, or had a wife ..."

"Wait. I saw pictures of his children."

"You saw *somebody's* children. But not his."

Charlie's heart sank. She didn't want anything or anyone to hurt her mother. Her anguish quickly turned to anger. She gripped the wheel.

"Judy, I'll be home in a couple of minutes. I'm too pissed off to talk and drive at the same time."

Charlie and Mandy sat on the bed, the phone between them, while Judy reported the results of her research. Hamm, aware of the anger in their voices, had retreated to the doggie bed where he kept track of them with his eyes and ears.

Gabe Constantine had been a Reagan Republican in the late eighties and now was a major supporter of the new conservative Tea Party. He was fairly well known in conservative circles and was credited with helping the party raise more than $100 million, half of which had been spent trying to derail the

Obama campaign. Constantine was a longtime supporter of Libertarian groups, but he had also supported extremist conservative groups whose philosophies were steeped in racism, homophobia, Islamophobia, anti-Semitism, and misogyny.

"What's he want with my mother?" Charlie said between clenched teeth.

"I've been thinking about that," Judy said. "He came into your mother's life right about the time you had contact with James about the task force. I don't think that's a coincidence."

"So Gabriel has been using Ernestine as a source of information on the task force work?" Mandy asked. "That means he might be a leader of the Turks."

Charlie sat quietly on the bed, going back over the sequence of events. It all made sense. After the task force leak was closed, Ernestine had asked more and more questions about Charlie's work on the Pashia case and the rest of the investigation into these crimes. Egged on, no doubt, by the interest her new boyfriend showed in the cases. Charlie thought back on Commander Coleman's allegations that the leak might be the result of loose talk among family and friends. She sighed. Charlie tried to remember how much detail she'd shared with her mother. Had she told her that Don was working undercover? Had she mentioned the plan to use fake bombs to draw these bad men out?

"Shit!" Charlie said. "Shit. Shit. Shit!"

"You want me to get the information I have to James?" Judy asked. "There's a lot more, but I know the Bureau can get into places I can't."

"Yes. Please do that. Meanwhile, I'm going to try the impossible feat of kicking myself in the ass."

"Charlie, I'm really sorry. About Ernestine, I mean. That she'll be hurt."

"Yeah, me too, Judy. Goodnight."

Charlie leaned into Mandy. They sat like that a few minutes. Hamm got up and lay at their feet.

"What am I going to tell Mom?" Charlie said, wiping at her eyes.

"You'll think of just the right thing, but you don't have to do it now. You can wait until after Sunday."

"Mandy, I'm probably the source of the continued leak on the task force."

"Yep. You're going to have to forgive yourself for that."

"What a fucked-up situation."

Don was having a hard time sleeping so he navigated to the Turks listserv. There were a couple of guys chatting about weapons and ammunition, but no sight of Robbie or Spader. After fifteen minutes he logged into the private website of the Knights of the Citadel. Their chat room was active. There was a heated discussion about the dangers of Obama's economic policies and the tax increases that would follow. The language was vile and incendiary.

Don watched the back-and-forth for a while. He hoped the FBI was also tuned in to this site tonight because some of the members were making threats against the President and his economic advisors. One man whose handle was TeaPartyTony published the address of a Harvard economist who had helped shape Obama's economic stimulus package.

Let's kill this guy, someone posted. Followed by a flurry of "10-4" messages. Don scrolled through them and sat upright, as one post caught his eye. It used one of Robbie's handles. The one Kamal Pashia had showed Charlie.

Posted by: *STORMTROOPER22*
He should die. He's a traitor to the white race.

Don turned off his computer and returned to bed to look out the window. Out of habit he touched his revolver hanging on the bedpost. This case was feeding his depression, the kind he'd felt after his discharge, and he couldn't use his normal coping skills to move through it. No talking with Rita, or watching cartoons with Rudy. No bowling or working on his car. He thought about cleaning his gun, but he'd done that two nights before. He leaned against the headboard, grabbed the remote, and clicked through the channels.

Tomorrow would be another long day. After spending work hours in the trailer, Don would transport the dummy explosives away from the quarry—some back to his apartment, the others to be left at the church. James had arranged for the bucket crane, and Don, Charlie, and two agents would be dressed in city emergency vests when they planted the fake bombs on the lower rooflines at St. Anne's. It was an elaborate charade, and they hoped the Turks had someone observing. FBI agents would be in the area looking for those spying.

The fact that James couldn't immediately identify the blue-eyed man worried the Bureau, so starting tomorrow Charlie would shadow Don. She'd pick up a rental car, something compact and white, so she wouldn't attract the attention she'd get in the Corvette. Don already had a tracker on his truck, and Charlie would have a monitoring unit.

There were more than a hundred channels to choose from, and he was halfway through them when he stopped on a movie title he recognized. A guy using the handle *RedWhiteBlue4ever* on the Turks listserv would be glad to know Don had taken his recommendation. The film had come on forty minutes ago, but it didn't matter. He'd seen it before and the best part, when things started blowing up, was at the end. There were a lot of commercials, but the movie was pretty good. *Might as well get in the right mood.*

Chapter 30

"You'll just have to shake it off," Don said, loading a box of phony pipe bombs into the truck cab. "Like Coleman said, it could happen to any of us."

"Yeah, but I was so indignant when she suggested it could be me," Charlie said, shaking her head. "And it turns out it *was* me."

"There's nothing you can do about it now. Did you tell James?"

"Judy called him last night to report what she learned about Constantine. He's probably put two and two together."

"Where *is* Novak?"

"At the FBI Field office digging further into the life of Gabriel Constantine."

"I'm guessing you want to kill the guy, right?"

"What do you think? If he turns out to be one of the leaders of this mess, I might want to have five minutes alone with him before he's arrested."

"I'll hold your purse, Mack."

"You look terrible by the way," Charlie said squinting at Don. "Did you get any sleep last night?"

"Not much. I was feeling kind of blue, so I stayed up late watching a movie, and I had an extra beer I probably shouldn't have had."

Don retrieved the last box containing six square-shaped

packages, wrapped in the black material used in landscaping to slow the growth of weeds. Charlie carried a box with extra detonators and several cell phones.

"So that's your rental car."

"It should blend in nicely anywhere I have to park."

"That's the only good thing about it," Don said, raising an eyebrow at the little car. "Is your monitor working?"

"Yep. I see your blinking dot."

"Good. That'll allow you to hang way back in case anyone's spying."

"Okay, and when I get to your place, I'll just park across the street until you leave."

It was evening rush hour. Charlie stayed at a distance from Don's truck, keeping an eye out for the green Jeep and any other following vehicle. Charlie called Judy who excitedly reported on her work with the FBI.

"Charlie, you should see the equipment. They have access to databases around the world. You know how I have to pay for credit, military records, and education records? They can get that with a push of a button."

"Do you have any more on Constantine?"

"Oh, lots more. But I'll send it to you in an email. I've got to go. The agents received these new super-thin Apple laptops today, and I want to sit in on their training. Good luck tonight." Judy signed off before Charlie could ask more questions.

Don was in and out of his apartment in five minutes. Within ten they were headed to a parking lot near St. Anne's where they'd meet the two agents who would drive the cranes to the church plaza.

The cranes were smaller than Charlie had imagined. One was slightly larger, but neither much bigger than a full-size passenger van. The smaller vehicle had a telescoping arm attached to a one-man basket. The larger crane had a longer arm and a two-man basket. They rolled up the street mostly unnoticed by the cars and the few pedestrians they passed.

The vehicles moved easily up onto the church plaza. A couple sitting close by on a bench were the only people in view. They were watching the sunset. Charlie was dressed in her homeless clothes, carrying orange cones and wearing a hard hat and vest. She asked the couple in a low voice to vacate the plaza while they changed the spotlights.

"Oh, no problem," the man said. "We were just, uh, we're getting married here tomorrow and were taking in the beauty of the church at night." The couple moved away quickly without looking back. Charlie thought it might be because of the smell of her clothing.

The smaller crane moved directly under the light. The agent-slash-electrical technician emerged from the van carrying one of the cloth-covered plastic squares. He unlocked the basket and climbed in; then, using a remote, he lifted the basket into the air. Agent K suggested that if this were a real bomb attack, a small-load explosive in the light fixture would create terror as the shattered plastic and glass rained down on the plaza. The larger crane stopped close to the church's front wall. Don and the other agent lifted into the air. When they were perched higher than the small crane, the agent pretended to give directions to the other crane operator about which way to angle the light's beam while Don focused on the church's buttresses. Anybody watching the activity would see Don lob a small black object onto the roof.

They repeated the activity near the other light, and the cranes and personnel were moving away from the plaza within twenty minutes. No one from the church or the neighborhood had asked any questions. Back at the parking lot where they left the cranes, the agent in charge reported that a vehicle parked on a side street with two passengers had watched the light repair—through binoculars—with keen interest.

James called, requesting to meet with Don and Charlie, but not at the trailer. He suggested meeting at the FBI field office. After calling ahead to Mandy who said it was no problem to set two more plates, Charlie suggested her house. She knew, even when things were dangerous and intense, a little downtime could help everyone's sanity. She also believed a bit of dog petting and a home-cooked meal would lift Don's spirits.

Dinner was a hit. They agreed not to discuss the case while they ate the meat loaf, green beans, and garlic mashed potatoes Mandy had prepared. Hamm sat at Don's feet getting occasional ear rubs and bits of meatloaf, and James took off his suit jacket and loosened his tie. For an hour they were four Detroiters from different walks of life enjoying a meal.

After dinner Charlie cleared the table while James, Don, and Mandy chatted. Charlie loaded the dishwasher, then returned to the dining room with bowls, spoons, and a gallon each of rocky road and strawberry ice cream.

"You two really know how to pamper your guests," James said.

Don grunted his agreement and scooped huge amounts of both kinds of ice cream into his bowl.

"We should get down to work," James said. "I have a few things to report."

"Before we do, let me get something out on the table," Charlie said. "I apologize for my laxness in discussing the case outside the confines of the team. I've always talked to Mom about my work. But it was inappropriate to do so in this case. I was wrong."

There was a moment of silence. Then James spoke up.

"I feel some culpability, too. After I spoke to Judy last night, I tried to figure out how Constantine would have known you were connected to the task force's work."

"But I wasn't," Charlie said. "Not until the Pashia family called me."

James shook his head. "Nope. It was before that. *I* involved you when I called for advice on the makeup of the task force." James looked chagrined. "I discovered last night that my personal cell phone has a bug. I'm not sure when it happened. Maybe at the gym. Charlie, when I called you, I used my personal phone, and that's when the Turks got wind of your connection to me."

There was another pause, and then Mandy stood. "Okay. Now that the *mea culpas* are out of the way, I'll excuse myself so

212

you three can do your work."

"Wait," James said. "I'd like you to stay. I know you'll respect the confidentiality of our conversation, plus you're a good thinker." James put a notebook and phone in front of him.

"New phone," he said. "It's clean."

Mandy retook her seat. James cleared his throat before he spoke. "Thirty minutes after you left St. Anne's, two men scaled the walls of the church. They spent several minutes on the roof before they rappelled down. They then entered the church through the side door. They were inside fifteen minutes."

"Was it the Turks?" Don asked.

"Probably."

"That's what we expected, isn't it?" Charlie asked. "They wanted to confirm that the devices were planted. That's why we went through the trouble to make them look authentic."

"There's more. Whoever broke in tried to bypass the security system, but a silent alarm was sent directly to the city police. Because it was St. Anne's, Coleman was alerted and she drove over to check it out. The police found our phony bombs, but they also found real ones. The cops were about to do the whole red-alert, bomb squad thing, but Coleman called it off and called me. My guys are there now disarming the devices."

"Oh god. Real bombs?" Mandy blurted.

"We're dealing with some shrewd people. I've underestimated them," James said. "They've been on to us all along and, in some cases, a step ahead. They know technology, have surveillance experience, state-of-the-art equipment, and trained personnel. What I can't figure is if they have all these resources, why they'd need a bomb maker in the first place."

"Wait a minute," Don said. "The guys at the meeting I attended were no sophisticates. That Croft guy might have been cut from a different cloth, but the others were pure corduroy. No way they had guys who could scale a wall."

"Is it likely the Turks have paired up with Stormfront?" Charlie asked James. "We know they already have a connection through Croft."

"And Robbie," Don added.

"Right. That's the next thing to report. Robbie's turned. For good this time."

"Are you sure?" Charlie asked.

"Yes. We can't find him. He hasn't reported in to the handlers, and he's not at his home. And, yes, collaborating with Stormfront would explain the Turks' sudden competence."

"Do they know I'm a plant?" Don asked.

"They must. Either because Robbie has told them, or through their own surveillance. We got a hit on the photo you took of Spader. His real name is Thomas Fox. He's former DEA. Fired from the agency in '93," James said, reading from his phone. "He was spotted overseas in 2003, but he's been off the radar and out of our databases since then."

"Do we believe he's really a Stormfront recruiter, as Robbie said?" Don asked.

"Maybe. But he might be recruiting for other groups as well. There are a few guys who work across groups. Most of them have specialties, such as software programmers, weapons engineers, various kinds of trainers."

"So that brings us back to the question of why they needed to find a bomb maker," Charlie said.

"I'd guess it was the Turks who needed a bomber, but once this Spader guy got involved, with his connections to the larger network, the need was filled," Mandy said.

"Don, have you had any messages from them?" James asked.

Don shook his head. "They asked how the job went. I answered fine. Then the guy, I think it's the money guy in Croft's office, asked if everything was set for tomorrow. I told him we were a go. That was three hours ago. Nothing since then."

"What if they want to make a bigger point than any of us expected?" Charlie asked.

"Well, it's clear they were actually going to blow up the church," James said.

"But what if there's more?"

"What do you mean, Mack?"

"What if they want to show up the FBI?"

"They've been doing that all along anyway," James said.

"If that's the case, they know about everything," Charlie said. "Robbie. Don. The Memorial Day charade. The fake bombs."

". . . and the plans to nail them on Sunday," James said glumly.

"Right. So why keep Don on the hook?" Charlie said more than asked.

"Maybe just to make Don do all the legwork," Mandy offered.

"Mack, do you still have that whiteboard in your basement?" Don asked, rubbing Hamm's ears.

The whiteboard was mounted on an easel near Charlie's treadmill. Sometimes she worked through a case while she exercised. For tonight's brainstorm she moved the board to the bar side of the basement. Mandy sat on the couch with Hamm. Don and James grabbed bar stools while Charlie jotted questions, facts and other notes on Post-its. It helped to see all the questions at once. James filled in answers where he could.

At almost eleven o'clock, James made a call to his techs. "The fake and real bombs in and outside of the church have been removed and are on their way to the lab for fingerprint testing." James turned to the group. "These were big bombs, wired for remote detonation. Someone wanted to do a lot of damage."

"Damn," Don said.

"How do we know the bad guys aren't still monitoring your equipment?" Charlie asked.

James shook his head. "When I discovered the bug in my phone, we changed out all our communications equipment. Techs are sweeping our intranet network now for bugs, reinforcing our firewalls, and everyone's phone and laptop have been replaced."

"You can do it just like that?" Charlie snapped her fingers.

James raised his eyebrows.

"Yes, yes, I know," Charlie replied. "You're the FBI."

"There's one question that's not on the board," Mandy said. "What is Constantine's role in all this?"

"I forgot. Judy said she'd send me a file with the info," Charlie

215

said, grabbing her laptop. "Here it is."

James was still on the phone, but Don and Mandy watched Charlie read Judy's updated report with raised eyebrows, shaking head, and clenched fists.

Michael Gabriel Constantine was a former air force lieutenant colonel who resigned his commission after the Gulf War and started up a private security business. The company ran afoul of the CIA several times, and the Justice Department labeled them nothing more than mercenaries. The company was finally dissolved in 2000, but not before he made a shitload of money. He hadn't lived in the Upper Peninsula for the last twenty years. He had lived in Toronto and moved to the UP a few years ago where he had a private compound near the Menominee River.

"According to his tax returns," Charlie said, "he's worth $80 million. He's funded David Duke, The American Nazi Party, and he's a major sponsor of far-right media. He funds a dozen nationalist groups through a foundation he's set up and has supported right-wing candidates for local office in a half dozen states." She finally looked up. "This guy is an out-and-out racist."

"If you're going to catch these guys, you can't let them know you're on to them," Mandy said. "Don should be on the chat boards right now, mixing it up and joking. He's got to show up to plant the bombs inside the church tomorrow as planned."

"That's it!" Charlie said with alarm. "They want to show the world how they can make fools of the federal government. Don't you see? That's why they still have Don on the hook. They *want* him to show up to plant the fake bombs. There's a wedding tomorrow at St. Anne's—a young Latino couple. I talked to them for a moment tonight. There will probably be a hundred people there. The Turks and Stormfront, and god only knows who else, plan to bomb the church tomorrow, not Sunday. That's the surprise."

Chapter 31

Robbie looked out the window of the motel. Although the view was nothing to look at, he could keep an eye on his bicycle parked, and double locked, right outside his door. He'd finally made it to Canada. *Thanks, Mr. Don Rutkowski. I can take this off my bucket list.*

He'd had to pay a surcharge for a taxi ride across the bridge to Windsor, but it was the best way to travel without calling a lot of attention to himself. The Commuter Motel was fine for his needs. The room had two full-size beds and a small desk. After he arrived, he'd had a three-hour bike ride along the road where the motel was located. The road didn't have many hills, but it had some excellent curves. He found a pizza place, picked up bottled water and beer for the tiny refrigerator in the room, and got to bed early although he couldn't sleep.

He was feeling amped up. Normally when he felt this way, he'd take a long bike ride, but Spader had told him to stay close to the room today. He was the subject of an FBI man-hunt. They'd been to his house and the insurance company, and observers were parked near all the bike trails he normally used. Spader emphasized they couldn't protect him unless he stayed put.

They were also monitoring all his social media.

Robbie lay on the bed. The TV monitor was small, but he had it on mostly for company anyway. He'd walked out of his job, the Turks, and his family, and since then he'd spoken only to Spader. He looked at his new burner phone. He hadn't even said goodbye to his mother or brother. He thought about calling Kathy, but what had started off as an exciting online romance took a nosedive when she'd called him a racist. *Prissy, elitist bitch from Grosse Pointe.*

Robbie popped the cap on a beer and swigged down a third. He opened his new laptop and navigated to the Turks website where he logged into the back door as an administrator, using a portable Wi-Fi hotspot. The message boards were quieter than usual tonight. The chatter was mostly the same old stuff. People were reacting to news reports on immigrant crossings at the border, showing anger about attacks on the second amendment, and spewing threats and profanity directed at Obama. A couple of posts asked about the Sunday Surprise, with responses from one of the Turks leaders who was still in the dark. *Boy they'll really be surprised.*

It had finally been proven to Robbie what he'd suspected all along: Stormfront was light-years ahead of the bungling Turks. It took Spader and Croft to identify the FBI's infiltration of the Turks. Last night Robbie saw Don in the chat rooms trying to draw him into a conversation. But he didn't engage. Don was a traitor to his race.

Robbie hadn't realized how angry he was at Don, and all those federal traitors, until Spader showed him evidence that they didn't care a thing about him. Spader let him hear the taped conversations where FBI agents and Don talked about locking him up for the rest of his life. They'd also taken that Arab kid's side even after he attacked Robbie at work—but he'd take care of that kid himself. The final straw was when Spader showed Robbie photo after photo of Don with that Black woman. Spader said she was Don's boss.

Robbie looked at his desk where two IEDs were packed in his saddlebag. He'd receive the detonators from Spader tomorrow. He wasn't the only person bringing bombs; there were others. Spader had come up with the idea of moving up the timetable after learning there was a large wedding at the church on Saturday. While the FBI concentrated on how they would round up the Turks on Sunday, Stormfront would blow the hell out of that church, and all those illegals, the day before.

In six hours he'd return to Detroit on his bike in the deep cover of night. He'd scouted a spot to pull the bicycle off the bridge and onto the embankment well before he got to the customs checkpoints. At 4 a.m., he wouldn't be seen or heard.

Spader's plan was brilliant. But just in case, Robbie had stuffed a tin box with some cash, his new passport, and two thumb drives with all the account information he'd phished for the Turks and Stormfront in the last few months. He'd buried the box in the park he'd visited yesterday while on his bike ride. If shit hit the fan, he'd be coming back to Canada, sooner or later.

Chapter 32

Last night's discussion in Charlie's basement had gone far into the early morning, and an ambitious plan was set in motion. Even though the bureau had removed a dozen high-load explosive devices from the roof and interior of the church the day before, electronic surveillance determined that these paramilitary domestic terrorists were expected at the church again this morning. James speculated the Turks and Stormfront might bring additional explosive devices, but they certainly hoped to detonate the ones they'd already planted, and witness the ensuing chaos. The FBI, Detroit PD, and the Mack team were prepared to stop them, and Mandy volunteered to be part of the operation.

Charlie and Mandy arrived at St. Anne's at ten o'clock dressed as wedding guests. They'd received radio earbuds, which connected to the FBI command truck near the Ambassador Bridge, and Charlie had also been issued a bureau BlackBerry. They sat on one of the plaza benches and chatted, all the while keeping an eye on cars, pedestrians, and building rooftops.

Final preparations for the 11:30 nuptials were underway. What seemed to be a professional wedding planner team, plus a group of older Hispanic women, worked in tandem on exterior decorations. Following the ceremony, the bride and groom would exit the main door under a ten-by-twelve-foot canvas canopy draped in ribbon and flowers. A dark red carpet fringed in pink carnations had already been laid.

One side of the main door was open, and Charlie watched nine people, some already dressed in the burgundy and pink colors of the wedding party, others carrying garment bags, enter the church. No one looked suspicious, but it was impossible to tell who belonged and who didn't.

Charlie's BlackBerry vibrated with a message from Don, asking her to call him.

"Are you in place?" Don asked.

"We're in the plaza."

"The FBI's analysis of the bombs they retrieved last night suggests the triggers will be transmitters for either a car alarm or ignition starter, so whoever has the remotes won't be far away."

"How many people do we expect?"

"James says three, maybe four. Agent K says the church walls are so thick the radio signal for the interior bombs will need to be close. Probably not inside, but not much farther than where you are now."

"Are we sure they got all the live bombs from last night?"

"They did another sweep this morning. The church is safe," Don said with relief.

"Where are the Bureau agents?"

"Everywhere. They have people in a couple of nearby houses, and agents on the other side of the customs yard fence, and in the bell tower. I think they even have a drone."

"Okay."

"I'll be there in twenty minutes with the dummy devices. Judy's coming, too."

"Judy? No!"

"She wants to be involved, Mack. She's got to get her feet wet sometime. Plus, she's mad at these guys for turning the kid, taking a shot at her, and for what they did to Ernestine. Anyway, you can't talk her out of it. She's on her way now, and she's meeting me in the parking lot."

A few early wedding guests arrived and began filling the benches and milling around on the plaza. Two people joined

Charlie and Mandy on their respective benches so they moved to stand together beneath one of the lampposts. Although the sun was out, with temps in the 60s, wind gusts rippled the canopy and whipped at the hems of women's skirts. Don arrived with Judy, posing as florists. He pushed a metal cart with two shelves stuffed with blooms, while Judy pointed to areas to place the potted plants.

Charlie and Mandy tracked the flower cart's trek along the plaza. At one point someone on the wedding planner's team approached the two would-be florists, and Charlie noted how efficiently Judy handled the young woman's queries. Don made a show of putting two of the larger blooms in the center of the cement planters, and in the small beds between the three front entrances. A Turks' observer would see him going through the motions of placing bombs.

Don and Judy entered the church, each carrying a few plants. Don had a canvas bag draped over his shoulder. When they exited ten minutes later, Don wasn't carrying the bag. He glanced toward Mandy and Charlie, pointed to his earbud, then pushed the cart back to St. Anne's Street in the direction of the parking lot.

The wedding guests were arriving in steady streams now, and the wedding planner had arrived. She was a middle-aged white woman wearing a beige skirt suit, a floppy hat, and white gloves. She opened both doors of the main entrance and beckoned family and friends to enter the church. She stood at the entrance smiling, nodding as invitations were presented and guests were ushered through the door. The young Latino standing next to her, wearing a dark suit and tie, held an electronic tablet. He checked names against the invitation list as each person stepped through the threshold.

"I bet he's an agent," Mandy said.

"You're probably right."

There were two long lines of guests now, and Charlie and Mandy split up. Mandy walked to the back of the plaza, moving back and forth along the perimeter. As she walked, she spotted a woman and a man wearing the small pineapple lapel pin identifying them as part of the operations team.

Charlie kept her eye on the crowd, scrutinizing each person in line. No one stood out so far, but many more people were arriving. The crowd seemed in a pleasant mood, ready to witness the joyful union of the two people Charlie had spoken to briefly. They'd never recognize her as the man who had asked them to leave the plaza last night.

Charlie moved deeper into the church courtyard to scrutinize the guests in the back of the line. Many of them took note of her stares. Some smiled; others raised eyebrows. She was too focused to be concerned with their reactions. Abruptly, Mandy's voice rang in her ear.

"There's a guy on a bicycle who just stopped at the flower boxes. He's headed to the west door."

Charlie couldn't see the west side of the plaza from her position, and she brusquely broke through the two lines of people to get a look at the entrance closest to St. Anne Street. She spotted the bike leaning against the raised flower planters and headed toward it. Out of the corner of her eye she caught a glimpse of a man stooping near the base of the green and gold sign marking the church's historical designation.

Charlie was more focused on the bike, which she circled. It was a well-maintained hybrid with brown saddlebags attached to a rear mount. The saddlebags bulged with something large. When she glanced back at the marker sign, the man was gone.

"I have an unattended bicycle on the plaza," Charlie said, trotting toward the sign. "And a guy dropped a bike helmet near the front walkway. I think he turned your way, Don."

"A bike?" Don asked, then shouted out orders in urgent staccato. "Charlie, get out of there. Now. It's a bomb. I see Robbie. He's walking away. James, do you hear? We got a bomb on the plaza, and Robbie planted it. I'm watching him now, and he just turned onto Lafayette Street. He's shaved his head, but it's him. I'm giving chase on foot."

"Bomb!" Charlie shouted running and waving her arms at the wedding guests. "We have a bomb."

Most of the people in the line watched, unmoving and confused, as Charlie ran first to the rear of the plaza to flag down Mandy, and then, screaming, charged toward the lines.

"Evacuate the plaza and the church," James's voice sounded in everyone's earbuds.

The other agents in and around the plaza went into action, running toward the crowd. The agent at the door of the church ran inside.

"There's a bomb. Everybody has to get out of here," Charlie screamed, pushing the family in front of her with both arms.

Either the sight of four men and two women running through the crowd, waving and pushing, or finally the recognition of the word *bomb* sent the crowd of nearly a hundred people moving all at once. Charlie and another agent tried to stop the crowd from running toward the bike, but the crowd's retreat was disorganized. Mandy yanked the wedding canopy poles out of their stands, and the canopy crashed to the ground, forming a barrier. The tangle of aluminum, fabric, and flowers sent guests fleeing in the opposite direction.

"Robbie's getting away," Charlie heard in her earbud. "He had another bike stashed, and he's pedaling up Lafayette Street. I'm getting the truck to go after him."

"Don. I'll meet you at Lafayette and Eighteenth."

Charlie took off at a full run, looking back at Mandy who was still herding guests away from the front of the church. Three agents flanked the bicycle. Charlie sped through the alley between the church and St. Anne's school—past the chapel, the loading area, and the rear of the convent—and darted across the lot where the brick nineteenth-century firehouse stood. As she closed the distance to the intersection, Don's truck rounded the corner from West Lafayette onto Eighteenth Street. Charlie adjusted her direction to intersect the truck's path. She saw Don swivel his head her way but he didn't stop.

"Don, wait," Charlie hollered waving her arms futilely as the truck tore up the street in pursuit of Robbie.

For a second, as the truck raced by, Charlie had locked eyes with a wide-eyed Judy in the passenger seat. Charlie readjusted her angle to head toward the Corvette. She hit the key fob before she got to the vehicle and snatched open the door. As she slid into the seat, she heard an explosion.

He'd already removed the lock from his new bike when he heard Don lumbering up the street at a fast pace. *He moves pretty good for an old man.* There was no time for Robbie to store the lock, so he dropped it and pulled the bike away from the shrub and the chain link fence where he'd stashed it twenty-four hours before. He pedaled hard for forty yards before looking back. Don had already turned and was running back toward the church.

Robbie had a good pace going on the new bike. He noticed his pants leg flapping and slowed. It took no more than ten seconds to clip his pants cuff and he was on his way again.

When he heard the explosion, he turned to look again toward St. Anne's expecting to see a massive cloud of dark smoke. What he saw instead was a truck—Don's truck. It was still four blocks away but it was barreling toward him. Robbie pedaled harder.

Up ahead he could see the broken shell of the old train station looming like the backdrop of a doomsday movie. If he could get there, he could hide among the rubble and overgrown lots surrounding the ghost building.

He pedaled like his life depended on it. With only an eye wiggle in both directions, he glided the curve onto Bagley Avenue at twenty miles per hour, and then onto Sixteenth Street where, with every bit of energy he could muster, he raced toward the train yard.

Don saw Robbie turn onto Bagley Avenue, but he had to screech to a halt when he ignored the red light and almost hit two passenger cars. The drivers slammed on their brakes and horns and might have stopped for an altercation if Don hadn't rammed the truck in reverse and maneuvered around the furious drivers. Judy was too scared to talk. She just tried to keep her eye on where she'd seen Robbie veer off the road.

"Did he turn here?" Don asked.

"No. There, there," Judy said pointing up Sixteenth Street. "I saw him turn in there."

Don drove quickly in the direction of the train station with its dozens of windows lined in rows and columns over the eighteen-floor main building and two office towers. When Don veered the truck onto the narrow and damaged Newark Road, they were moving parallel to the train yard and a brick storage shed with undergrowth that was shoulder high. Don stopped.

"He could be anywhere in here," Don said. "The rail yard, under the train overpass on Vernor Highway, in one of these buildings, or in an abandoned vehicle. All these streets loop back to Bagley, too, so keep your eyes peeled, Novak."

Don crept the truck forward. "I think he was wearing a green jacket or bike shirt," he said.

At Seventeenth Street Don turned back toward Bagley Avenue, searching for any signs of a biker. Then he looped back toward the rail yard and continued to the overpass where they stared into the darkness of the tunnel.

"He could have gone in there," Judy said.

"He could be anywhere."

"I think we should double back," Judy said. "He has to be exhausted. He was pumping that bike at full speed ever since he saw you following."

"Okay. I hope you're right. If we don't find him, he could be gone for good."

"Don, I heard an explosion back there. I'm worried about Charlie."

"Okay, call her. My earbuds aren't working, so we might be out of range of the command truck."

"She didn't pick up," Judy said putting the phone in her lap.

"Mack's okay, Novak. Keep your eyes open."

"What's that?" Judy said pointing ahead toward the brick wall.

The fifteen-foot-high wall was really a storage tunnel with a series of openings covered by rusting metal doors. Along the wall was a dense growth of weed trees and tall grass.

"I thought I saw a glint of light. Back up."

Don put the truck in reverse, and within a few yards they both saw the reflection of sunlight on metal.

"Don, there's a bike behind that bush."

They left the truck doors open as they ran to the wall. The bike was well covered, and Don had to step behind the bush to grip the handlebars. He backed the bike into the open.

"It's a brand-new bike," Judy said.

"Yeah," Don said, looking around. "He must have gone over this wall. Look at all the missing bricks here. It would be easy to climb up."

Don ran back to the truck, shut the passenger door, and jumped behind the wheel. He drove it up on the curb and into the tall grass, parking the truck as close to the wall as he could.

"I'm going after him. You stay here."

"Call James and get some help," Judy pleaded.

Don was already in motion. He'd removed his jacket, and wedging his boot onto the tire, he lifted himself onto the hood of the truck. He had to lean a bit to get a hand grip, but when he stepped onto the cab roof he could see over the wall. It was, indeed, a tunnel-like storage building.

"Go ahead and call James. I'm going after the kid," Don said.

Judy retrieved her phone. As she did, she watched a vehicle round the corner and slowly move toward her. As the Jeep crept by the driver looked at her. He had the most beautiful blue eyes she'd ever seen.

The explosion came from the front of the church, and the first thing Charlie thought about was Mandy. So instead of following Don's truck, Charlie turned toward the church plaza. Howard Street was primarily a pedestrian walkway, but Charlie eased the Vette onto the short curb and moved onto the plaza. An FBI agent, dressed in bomb squad gear, moved to block her path, but waved her on when Charlie pointed to the pineapple. She passed the bike which was now lying on its side, the saddlebags removed.

"What was the explosion?"

"We found an IED in a bike helmet. A small load. We blew it up over there," the agent said, pointing in the direction of the US Customs yard. "It was amateur work."

"What about the bike saddlebags?"

"Large load. Mucho dangerous. Whisked away already."

Charlie moved forward, easing the tires over the metal poles and twisted flowers that had been part of the wedding canopy when she spotted Mandy still at the rear of the Plaza. She was part of a human chain of agents holding back a crowd of onlookers.

Mandy's safe.

Charlie gunned the Corvette to Eighteenth Street, and turned on the tracker for Don's truck. The red point wasn't moving, but it was straight ahead and beeping loud and clear.

The blue-eyed man stopped the Jeep and walked back to the truck. Judy frantically punched James's number into her phone. It was ringing when the man snatched it from her hand and put it to his ear.

"Hello," James said. "Judy?"

"No, it's not Judy," Spader said, turning off the phone. He dropped it the ground and smashed it with his boot, then pulled out the SIM card and bent it with his teeth.

"You Judy?"

Judy didn't answer. She looked at the keys dangling in the ignition.

"No, no, no. I better take those," Spader said. "Where did Don Rutkowski go?"

Judy clenched her teeth and folded her arms.

"Don't make me hurt you, Judy."

When the shot sounded, they both jumped.

"I guess that's Don there," Spader said, jumping onto the hood of the truck and then, with a quick glance at Judy, effortlessly hoisting himself up onto the wall. Judy jumped out of the truck and ran toward Seventeenth Street. She was on Bagley, running in the direction of the church, when Charlie's Corvette turned the corner. She waved until Charlie saw her, then darted to the car.

"Don's in trouble," Judy shouted.

Charlie's phone rang. "You answer it, Judy," Charlie said, controlling the wheel on the damaged road running parallel to the train station yard.

"Hello?"

"It's James. Your phone disconnected, Judy. You're with Charlie?"

"Yes. We're near the train station on Newark Road. Don's gone after Robbie, and that guy with the blue eyes . . ."

"Spader?"

"Yes. Him. He went after Don."

"Put Charlie on the line."

"I can hear you, James."

"Wait for backup."

"I'm not going to do that."

Charlie pulled in next to the truck. She removed her suit jacket and grabbed sneakers from the trunk. She'd run in boots back at the church, but there were yards of train tracks on the other side of the wall, and Charlie wanted good footing.

229

"Stay in my car, Judy. If you see Spader come back over that wall, get the hell out of here."

Judy couldn't even respond before Charlie stepped onto the bumper of the truck, up to the hood, and on top of the cab. She didn't look back before pulling herself onto the wall and then out of sight.

Chapter 33

The 200 yards between the wall and the rear of the train station was crisscrossed by a half dozen railroad tracks. Don had played football in high school. Then, moving up and down a field that size had been effortless, but that was a long time ago and the sight of Robbie's slight body so far ahead of him made him sigh. *If I can get close enough, I'll just shoot him.*

The disuse of the yard had allowed the weeds, errant grass, and bushes to have free rein. Here and there short trees with squat trunks had gained a foothold.

Don discovered quickly that the only way to move without injury was to watch his every step. He'd already shocked his knees with the drop from the wall and had almost twisted his ankle treading on loose gravel that gave way to a hole in the asphalt underneath.

Robbie was moving at an angle that would take him east of the old station, and Don adjusted his path of pursuit, using the trees to give him a bit of cover in case the kid looked back. As he moved closer, he noticed that Robbie wore a small backpack, and he was having as much trouble as Don making the hike on the scraggly ground. Don unholstered his Ruger, holding it in two hands. When Robbie got to a clearing, he turned and spotted Don. Don fired in his direction and missed. Darting from door to door at the rear of the vacant building, Robbie found an opening and slipped into a crevice.

Shit. Don picked up his pace. Sweat dripped around his ears and neck, and gnats and early mosquitoes swirled around his face every time he stepped on vegetation. When he cleared the rail yard, he paused to gasp for breath and stare at the space where he'd seen Robbie disappear. He moved cautiously toward the opening. James had said Robbie owned a couple of long guns, and maybe the kid had a firearm in that backpack.

Don peeked around the portal with a quick dart of his head, the brass door was long gone to the scavengers and vandals who had picked away at the metals that once adorned the station. Don stepped inside and winced as his nose was assaulted by the smells of dampness and desecration. Areas of the floor were covered in six inches of water, and much of the broken marble surface was covered in mounds of debris—fallen molding, concrete blocks, torn mattresses, glass, and twisted steel pieces. Rotting columns were on either side of the open middle. The walls were blanketed in graffiti.

Robbie was either running or hiding. The kid didn't want a fight so he was probably searching for a way out of the building. Don stopped to listen. He knew there were people and animals who had made this empty building their home, but he heard a noise that sounded like someone sloshing on the flooded floor. He moved toward it.

Spader was fit and had no problem navigating the wall's ascent and the drop to the rail yard. He stopped to take in his surroundings. It reminded him of places in Europe he'd seen. Areas of former commerce and vitality scarred by war and blight. Eighty yards ahead he saw Rutkowski moving over the tracks. There were no signs of Robbie. Spader tucked his gun at his waist and put his phone in his back pocket. He'd trained for this kind of pursuit, sometimes across miles of desert, other times over the roads and destroyed homes of bombed villages. *Time to move.*

It took him less than five minutes to get to the door he'd

seen Don enter. He retrieved his gun and stepped inside. It was quiet, wet, dank. He shivered, and his nose twitched with the mix of mildew, urine, and cold air. It was almost seventy degrees outside, but in the dark bowels of this old ruin with its marble walls, columns, and floors, it felt like forty degrees. There were holes in the floor where old benches and seats were once anchored. Metal girders protruding from the walls and ceiling had likely held clocks, train schedules, and signs. Foul water pooled in the middle of the room.

A pigeon flew overhead and angled into the next room, with Spader following its path. This would not be a good place to fire a gun. Bullets would ricochet dangerously and loudly. The next room looked like the last except splotches of daylight illuminated the peaks of the back wall and ceiling. Spader stopped and spun around. He saw a rat scurry into a hole near the broken base-board. Several birds perched in the ceiling corners. Spader tilted his head, thinking he heard voices. Then he heard them again, not words but urgent tones coming from an archway to his right. He moved swiftly across the marble floor, his steps splashing water.

This room's only source of light spilled in from the larger room beyond the archway, and it took a moment for his eyes to adjust to the dimness. The voices were louder as he moved forward, not yelling but speaking with an angry staccato. Spader paused when he made out Robbie's lean form huddled behind some large square object. He held a backpack in front of him. Rutkowski stood twelve feet away, his arm extended.

"Don't come near me. I have a bomb," Robbie said.

"Give it up, kid. It's all over," Don replied. "Whatever you have in there, you need a way to trigger the blast. And if you move, I'll kill you."

"*I* have the remote," Spader said loudly.

Both Robbie and Don jumped at the sound behind them. Don spun his gun in the direction of the voice. Spader had dipped behind a column, his gun trained on an exposed Don.

"Who is it?" Don asked, squinting.

"Drop the gun. Now."

"Who are you?" Don asked, dejectedly dropping the Ruger with a loud clang.

"Haven't you figured that out by now?" Spader asked derisively. "You and your FBI friends have been bungling amateurs."

"SeeingBlue," Don stated.

Spader's laugh was mocking. "You can get up now, Robbie. Come over here."

Robbie rose from his hiding place, bumping an old heating vent protruding from the floor. Robbie's squeal of pain distracted Spader, and he stepped away from the column. Without hesitation, Don charged the man, knocking him off balance. Don grabbed at Spader's gun, and they wrestled with the firearm for a moment until Spader gave Don a headbutt. Don fell back, holding his bleeding nose.

"You won't have another chance to do that," Spader said, breathing hard, raising his arm.

"Don't move and drop your gun!" Charlie shouted.

Spader made a half turn to look behind him.

"I mean it. Don't move!" Charlie yelled.

Spader's gunshot was aimed at Don, who was charging again, but the bullet rang off the wall just a second after Charlie's shot echoed in a deafening sound. Spader sank to the ground, and Don fell on top of him.

Don had a self-diagnosed broken nose and his shirt was covered in blood. His ego had taken more punishment than his body. Spader still had a pulse as Don and Charlie dragged him through three rooms to the train station's rear pavilion. Robbie was nowhere to be found. Outside, Don and Charlie leaned against a cracking concrete berm.

It was less than fifteen minutes before a wave of FBI agents and Detroit Police poured over the back wall. A few more entered the rail yard from the front of the station, including James and Mandy.

"Where's Judy?" Charlie asked.

"She's safe. Still sitting in your car and protecting it," Mandy said with a tight smile. "Are you okay?"

"I shot somebody," Charlie said, trying to shake off the guilt building in her chest. "It's becoming a bad habit." She looked up at Mandy ruefully.

"I'm okay, too," Don said. "In case anyone cares. Mack shot that asshole to save my life."

James and Mandy nodded.

"Did you find Robbie?" Don asked.

"No. He's not in the train station. We've searched every inch of the ground floor, and he didn't have time to access the upper floors."

"He said he had a bomb in his backpack."

"He might have. He left a very rudimentary IED in his bike helmet. It was crude, but still dangerous. We detonated it safely," James said. "We're looking at security footage in the area now to see if we can track Robbie."

"Did the bicycle have explosives?" Don asked.

"Yes. Very powerful devices."

"What about the Turks?" Charlie asked.

"We rounded up a bunch of them at home. A car full of guys was also parked near the bridge ready to see the explosions. Croft was in that car. My guess is the crossover members between the Turks and Stormfront knew what was happening today. Most of the Turks were still waiting on the Sunday Surprise. We caught a few more guys in black cars with active bombs. We were on them before they could move, but there were a few casualties," James said in the FBI language that meant people were dead.

"Is the church safe now?"

"We're sweeping inside and out again, but we think it's safe. We scrambled all the radio signals as soon as we arrived this morning. That's why none of the other devices were detonated."

A medical tech walked over and insisted on examining Don's nose. He protested loudly, but finally let the pony-tailed young woman lead him over to her ambulance. Charlie watched as another EMT crew lifted Spader's covered body into an ambulance.

"He was a bad man, Charlie," James said.

Mandy joined Charlie on the berm and took her hand.

"What about Constantine?" Charlie asked.

"Oh yes. We have him, too," James said. "He was leaving his apartment building with a suitcase when two agents took him into custody. He was known to this paramilitary group he led as the Angel. You know, Gabriel, the archangel."

"I need to talk to Mom," Charlie said.

Chapter 34

Don went home to Rita and the kids with his nose packed and a white bandage over his face. James loaned him a clean shirt and personally drove him to Hamtramck. James promised a visit to the Mack team on Monday.

Charlie, Mandy and Judy gathered in the lobby of Ernestine's building. Judy insisted on being there for the awkward conversation with Charlie's mother. The staff at the front desk were all too willing to tell Charlie about their role in the arrest of Mr. Gabriel Constantine on the fourth floor. One of them had signaled the FBI agent when Constantine exited the elevators. That agent had joined two others in confronting Constantine in the parking lot. According to Gloria, Constantine struggled a bit before they shoved him into a dark sedan.

"I never liked that man, Miss Charlene," Gloria said. "He always seemed off to me, you know?"

Ernestine opened the door with what Charlie recognized as a very embarrassed smile. Charlie moved forward and kissed her mother's cheek.

"Come on in, you all," Ernestine said, moving away from the door and receiving hugs from Mandy and Judy. Ernestine gave Judy a wink.

Mandy headed to the kitchen to make a pot of coffee, and Judy pulled out goodies purchased from Mexican Village, including chicken enchiladas, salsa and chips, and beef burritos.

There was also plenty of beans and rice. The women ate and chatted for almost an hour before Ernestine herself brought up Constantine.

"Judy called me this afternoon to tell me about Gabriel. She was very, very kind."

"What?" Charlie said, glaring at Judy. "I was going to . . ."

"Do you know how hard it is to talk to your mother about a no-good man?" Judy asked. "No. Ernestine needed a friend, someone with a little more emotional distance, to tell her this crazy news."

"Judy's right, Charlene. I don't want to give you another reason to be disappointed for me. Judy and I trashed Gabriel. Called him names, and . . ."

"And I put a Polish hex on him," Judy said, pleased with herself. "Good riddance."

The Mack team was somber Monday morning. Tamela didn't know quite what to say when Don arrived with the wide bandage across his nose. Instead of entering the office like a marauder, he quietly opened the door, nodded to Tamela, and moved to his desk. Judy had arrived an hour before, walking stiffly, saying her bruised leg was still bothering her.

Charlie didn't have any physical ailments, but her first call of the day had been to her therapist. She needed to discuss her sadness. The last time she'd shot and killed a man—during their Auto Show case—she was in therapy for six months.

Charlie, Don, and Judy stayed at their desks quietly with a minimum of conversation, doing paperwork, catching up on missed calls, and eating the lunches they'd each brought in.

James arrived at 1:30 with a tray of cookies. Tamela made a pot of coffee, and they gathered around the conference table.

"How's the nose, Don?" James asked.

"Sore as hell. But Avalon Bakery cookies make it feel better. Did Charlie tell you I love these?"

"She didn't have to tell me. Next time I'll bring you Lebanese pastry, too." When his smile faded, Charlie knew James was ready to talk business. "We found out where Robbie went on Saturday. He went to the Pashias' house with the bomb in his backpack."

"Oh no," Charlie said, horrified.

"It's okay. No one was harmed. He tried to trigger the device, which, thankfully, didn't work."

"What happened?" Judy asked.

"When he escaped the train station, he flagged a cab on Vernor Hwy. that took him to a bike shop near Farmington Hills. He bought a new bike, in cash, and rode to the Pashias' home. He put his backpack on the porch, called Kamal Pashia's number, and told him to come out of the house to fight," James said. "He'd been at their home before, you know."

"For the study groups," Charlie said.

"Right. Kamal opened the door, and Robbie used a phone to try to detonate the bomb. When it didn't work, Kamal caught up with Robbie and kicked his ass."

"Again," Judy said.

"Mrs. Pashia called me, and we got over there to disarm the bomb, but Robbie got away. He took off on the bike and so far we haven't been able to find him."

"What a waste. He's a smart kid," Judy said.

"He really is," Don said, sadly.

"We'll get him. We have to get him. We don't need anybody with his hacker skills working against us."

"What happens next with the task force?" Charlie asked.

"Commander Coleman is moving into the lead. She'll keep it going. We'll have seats, and so will DHS. There's no shortage of cases to investigate. This is only the beginning of these groups. Croft has direct ties to state legislators. Constantine has had a US Congressman at his compound for a hunting and fishing vacation. When we examined Spader's home in East Lansing, we found bank statements with deposits to accounts all across the US, Europe, and South America. He also had records on another five groups in Michigan. Some were paramilitary organizations, like Constantine's people. Unfortunately, these men—and more and more women—are more often than not just plain folks. Office workers, teachers, babysitters, dog-walkers, retirees, employees at Walmart. What they have in common is their feeling of disenfranchisement and anger. They're gun owners, and they're mostly white. They're gearing up for a race war, a class war."

"What about the Muslim groups—Al Qaeda, Hezbollah, those guys?" Don asked, trying not to crinkle his nose as he chomped on another cookie.

"They're dangerous and extremist. Without a doubt," James said. "We're keeping an eye on them. I'm talking about these homegrown terrorist groups that are growing in number and power. Their actions keep escalating. The Turks were a small, badly organized, amateur group. We may have stopped them, but they're just the tip of an iceberg. Stormfront is the rest of the iceberg, underground and hard to break up."

Robbie was fed up with his motel room. It was small, and he'd been holed up for two and a half days. His room was a mess. He hadn't allowed the old lady who had knocked on the door for the past two mornings to clean the room. She had given him a trash bag, and it was filled with pizza boxes, cans, and wrappers of the fast food he'd been eating.

He'd decided to bring his new bike into the room, and it made it difficult to get in and out of the bathroom, but it was safer to have it out of sight of anybody looking for a biker. Not that it really mattered. He knew lots of people were looking for him, but he felt safe here. Early that morning he'd taken the chance to ride to the park where he'd buried the small box filled with cash, thumb drives, two new passports, a debit card and a new driver's license. He looked pretty good in the ID photos. One of his names was Christopher Brodie. The other was Robert Huffy.

He'd booked a flight to Toronto using the name Huffy. From Toronto he was flying as Brodie to Amsterdam. He'd thought about taking his bike but that required a packing box or a hard bicycle case, and he didn't want to take the chance of visiting a bike store. So the bike would stay here in the room. Maybe the cleaning lady would be happy to get it.

Using a Wi-Fi hotspot, he'd scrolled through the message boards since Saturday night. The Turks website was down, but there was chatter about arrests made over the weekend, and the death of one of the Stormfront members.

The shootout at the train station had scared him shitless, and he had had to think quick to get out of there. He was pissed that his bomb hadn't exploded to kill that Arab kid, but at least he'd been able to escape from that situation. He counted himself lucky.

He still hadn't said good-bye to his mother or brother. He would mail a postcard tomorrow from the airport. Maybe later he'd send them some money. He had almost $10,000 in his bank account, half of it from some of the losers who worked at the insurance company. *Thank you, suckers.*

If America didn't want him anymore, it was their loss. He'd hook up with Stormfront in Europe and set himself up as a valuable member of their team—a team that understood that the white man topped the food chain. The FBI had lost its way. That's what the book he was reading said. It had protected America's way of life under J. Edgar Hoover, but now the Bureau was full of lackeys for Obama and the other elites.

Some of the Turks had talked about taking back America. Maybe he'd come back someday to help, but for now he was turning his back on Detroit, on Michigan, and on the USA. In the meantime he'd go someplace where a white man could still get respect.

Chapter 35

"I'm glad it's over, hon." Mandy looked into Charlie's eyes. "It's really good to have you home at night."

"James says it's not over."

"I hope he's wrong," Mandy said. "I want to believe in the hope Obama promised us. C'mon outside with me. I mean, us," she said holding the door for Hamm.

It was easy to believe in hope on this first day of June. They used the grill for the first time since last fall to make veggie burgers and sweet potatoes, and watched new blooms push up in the flower bed around their new fence. Hamm was splayed out on the deck, enjoying the sun that wouldn't set until almost nine.

Charlie's phone buzzed with a message.

"I have an appointment for therapy on Wednesday morning," she reported to Mandy.

"Good. It'll help you. Hey, why don't we take a drive? See the sunset over the water?"

"Belle Isle?"

"Yep. Let's take my car so Hamm can come."

The view of Downtown Detroit's sunset from Belle Isle was always spectacular. The sky behind the Renaissance Center blended oranges, purples, and streaks of red that stretched past the distant Ambassador Bridge. Charlie and Mandy joined scores of other cheerful people enjoying nature's light show. Some brought chairs, but Charlie and Mandy sat on the thick grass, stroking Hamm who lay between them.

"You know what I'm thinking about?" Charlie asked.

"St. Anne's?"

"Yep. It's a gorgeous church. Hard not to think of it when you see the bridge."

She squinted and traced her finger along the bridge's trek across the Detroit River to Canada. "I have an idea. Why don't we do a road trip this spring? Get out of town for a little while. I'd like to spend some time outdoors, and clear my head of these people who hate. You know, we haven't had a real vacation since we bought the house. Maybe we can go to the U.P. We could rent a house, and hike, and see the waterfalls."

"That sounds wonderful, and Hamm would really like it too, wouldn't you, boy?"

Hamm rose to agree and placed his big paws on Mandy's lap. "Maybe we can ask Ernestine to come along. We could all benefit from a bit of head clearing."

Charlie reached for Mandy's hand. "Don't ever leave me. I don't know what I'd do without you."

About the Author

A Detroit native, Cheryl A. Head now lives on Capitol Hill in Washington, DC. She is a two-time Lambda Literary Award finalist and winner of the Golden Crown Literary Society Ann Bannon Award. In 2019 Head was inducted into the Saints & Sinners LGBT Literary Festival Hall of Fame. She currently serves as a national board member for Bouchercon.

Bywater
BOOKS

At Bywater, we love good books by and about women, just like you do. And we're committed to bringing the best of contemporary lesbian literature to an expanding community of readers. Our editorial team is dedicated to finding and developing outstanding writers who create books you won't want to put down.

For more information about Bywater Books, our authors, and our titles, please visit our website.

www.bywaterbooks.com

Mystery
Head
2021

1685900

CPSIA information can be obtained
at www.ICGtesting.com
Printed in the USA
JSHW030935020721
16463JS00001B/2